338.83 P534t   FV
PHALON
THE TAKEOVER BARONS OF WALL
STREET
                              13.95

St. Louis Community College

Library

5801 Wilson Avenue
St. Louis, Missouri 63110

The Takeover Barons of Wall Street

The Takeover Barons of Wall Street

Inside the Billion-Dollar Merger Game

by
Richard Phalon

G. P. PUTNAM'S SONS
NEW YORK

A portion of Chapter 1 appeared originally in *Playboy* magazine.

Library of Congress Cataloging in Publication Data

Phalon, Richard.
  The takeover barons of Wall Street.

  1. Consolidation and merger of corporations—United
States. I. Title.
HD2785.P48 1981   338.8'3'0973   81-10561
ISBN 0-399-12661-9   AACR2

PRINTED IN THE UNITED STATES OF AMERICA

Second Impression

For Miriam Harvey Phalon

Contents

Author's Note

Most of the quotations attributed to individuals in this book are taken from pre-trial depositions, trial testimony, personal interviews or all three. Secondary sources are credited in the text. I am grateful to my colleagues on *Business Week, Forbes, Fortune,* the *New York Times,* and the *Wall Street Journal,* among other publications. No one could have written a book like this without the help of their work. I am also grateful to all—some named in the text, some by their request unnamed—who took generous chunks of time out of busy lives to contribute to my education. I owe thanks to N. L. Hoepli, editor of the Foreign Policy Association, for help on the intricacies of foreign takeovers; to Linda Gasparello for her sensitive, intelligent, and unfailingly good-humored interviewing skills; and to my editors at *Forbes*—Malcolm S. Forbes and James W. Michaels—for time and space to work in. I also owe a thank you for the industry of my mother, Mrs. Richard F. Phalon, who typed most of the manuscript with an occasional assist from my sisters, Marie and Anne. Opinion expressed in the book is my own, and so is the responsibility for any errors.

The Takeover Barons of Wall Street

1

The Midnight Raid

Richard G. Rosenthal—"Rosey" to his friends—was un-
characteristically edgy as he sat at his desk overlooking the
cavernous trading room of Salomon Brothers, an investment banking firm, on this blustery Monday afternoon in
mid-January. The weekend had been a wipeout. A blizzard,
one of the heaviest in years, had blanketed the eastern
seaboard. Rosenthal had not been able to log his customary
twin-engine flying time, a pursuit that helps him achieve
"total detachment" from the pressure-cooker world he
inhabits as one of Wall Street's most skilled traders in
merger and acquisition situations. The job requires almost
instant buy or sell decisions on deals that often involve
tens of thousands of shares and millions of dollars.

Much of Rosenthal's weekend, in fact, had been chewed
up by a series of seemingly endless phone calls aimed at

ironing out some very heated last-minute disagreements over key strategic elements in a deal he and other merger and acquisition experts at Salomon Brothers had been hatching for the better part of five hectic weeks. The client was one of the firm's major corporate accounts. There was big money involved—perhaps as much as $350 million—in a carefully plotted blitz that might prove prelude to a 100-percent takeover of another company. The first step was designed to net the client at least 20 percent of the target company's stock by no later than midnight on this snowy Monday, now less than nine hours away.

The tactical clock had been running for hours. Rosenthal was convinced the coup would work, but his timetable had been upset by the eleventh-hour wrangling over detail and a long cautionary skull session orchestrated by the dozen or so lawyers who by now were swarming all over the forty-first floor of Salomon's headquarters in downtown Manhattan.

In terms of the manpower, money, and strategy, it was the most unusual deal Rosenthal had seen in the twenty years since he had quit Erasmus High School in Brooklyn and landed his first job on the Street as a clerk with the now-defunct brokerage firm of Ira Haupt & Co. Incredibly fast on the uptake, Rosenthal was trading over-the-counter stocks with the best of them while still in his teens and was made a general partner at Salomon in 1969 at the unheard-of age of twenty-seven. His realm is the higher calculus of what he calls "market judgment, psychology—and how people feel about a stock." Rosenthal talks with big institutional investors—insurance companies, banks, pension funds, mutual funds—all the time. Hence, part of his assignment on this deal was to pinpoint the identity of institutional investors with big holdings in the target company and work out a price that would make the institutions eager to sell what amounted to the single biggest block of stock in the target. The client would clearly have to pay above the market. The key question was how high it would have to go to shake the stock loose without getting caught in a bidding match. The first price had to be right, a tricky business to figure. The incentives were there, from Rosenthal's point of view. As one of Salomon's senior partners, he stood to share handsomely in the $350,000 fee his firm would earn if the blitz worked.

A lot of things could go wrong, and Rosenthal carefully worked his way through the checklist as the clock moved toward 2:45 P.M. The institutions were going to be solicited after the 4:00 P.M. close of the market. They had to be sworn to absolute secrecy as to the identity of the target. Any tipping of the client's hand might give the intended victim time enough to run to the courts for a stop order that could stymie the deal. The lawyers had leaned heavily on the need for secrecy in the "dos and don'ts" outlines they had put together for Rosenthal and the eight other high-level executives who would be working the phones. Portfolio managers talk to one another all the time. Was it really possible to approach thirty or so institutions without some word of the offer getting out to the grapevine? Would the price hold?

Rosenthal was sufficiently worried about the two-tier $40- to $45-a-share offering price he had settled on to have tried it on for size that morning with Dan Lufkin—a founder of what had once been one of the hottest research "boutiques" on Wall Street, Donaldson, Lufkin and Jenrette, and spokesman for a group that owned about 94,000 shares of the target. Lufkin was not interested in the $40 "favored nation" offer that would guarantee his group more money if the Salomon client made a higher bid for the target company's stock over the next year and a half. The $45 alternative, on the other hand, reflected a $12-a-share premium over the then-going market. It looked so good that Lufkin, without any prompting, offered to pass it on to a long-time friend who headed a major investment company. Rosenthal took that as a useful sign that a sufficient number of institutional investors would follow suit and yield the Salomon client the minimum 20 percent of the target it was seeking. No minimum, no deal—and no fee for Salomon or for F. Eberstadt & Co., another old-line investment banking firm that had been brought into the situation. "To cut through all the esoteric," said Rosenthal, "the fundamental question posed to me" was whether the client could acquire a minority interest in the target. "After examining the stockholders list," he continued, "my answer was yes."

Rosenthal's answer was based on research which showed that institutions held the balance of power in the target company's stock. The First National Bank of Boston alone, for example, controlled almost 780,000 shares; the I.D.S. group of mutual funds in Minneapolis some 450,000 shares; and the T. Rowe Price group of mutual funds more than 1.2 million shares. Given the fiduciary nature of their responsibility to the trusts, pension funds, and other clients whose money they managed, the institutions would be hard put to turn down an offer that gave them a chance to get out of the stock at a good profit.

Though it would be several hours before the machinery really started to roll, Rosenthal had already made a couple of calls around the Street to establish that people with the power to make quick decisions on the offer would be around after 4:00 P.M. Several of the other solicitors had done the same and now, at 2:45, Rosenthal was on the line to an old friend in San Francisco, Jack H. Leylegian II, senior trust investment officer for the Bank of America.

"Hi, Babes," said Rosenthal with the breezy air he reserves for such big clients as the Bank of America. He and Leylegian had been doing business for the better part of a decade. This call was a follow-up on the one Rosenthal had made to Leylegian three days earlier. At that time, Rosenthal had cryptically asked if the bank would be able to respond quickly to a two-tier offer to buy one of its portfolio stocks at a premium. The name of the stock was not mentioned and neither was the size of the premium. Leylegian's interest was sufficiently piqued, though, for him to ask Rosenthal if there was a takeover involved. "There were a number of takeovers taking place," recalled Leylegian, "and if it was a takeover, the mood of the market was such there were large premiums being paid." When Rosenthal told him it wasn't a takeover situation, Leylegian shrugged in sudden disinterest. "I didn't know what the name of the stock was, if we actually held it or not, or if the deal would come off," he said.

Now came this second call from Rosenthal, who was once again asking Leylegian if he would be willing to sell the still-unidentified stock at a premium. Leylegian was a little miffed. It was 11:45 A.M. in San Francisco; he had a lunch date on his calendar and was pressed for time.

"We will have to stop playing games," Leylegian told Rosenthal. "I don't know if I own the stock and I have a client to meet in fifteen minutes."

Rosenthal asked Leylegian if he would be back in his office around 1:00 P.M.—4:00 P.M. and the close of the market in New York. Leylegian said that in "all probability" he wouldn't, and put the ball right back in Rosenthal's court.

The Bank of America executive recalled telling Rosenthal that "if he wanted to let me know, based on a long steady relationship with him, what the name of the stock was, I would be happy to tell him if we owned it; and if we did own it, whether we had any power to do anything with it. So between he and I and the lamppost," says Leylegian, "he told me the name of the stock was Becton, Dickinson."

Leylegian responded with a groan. "Dick, we don't own the stock; we sold it all several months ago, but I will check to make sure." Leylegian walked down the hall to one of his portfolio managers, asked him to find out whether the Bank of America had indeed unloaded all its Becton, Dickinson stock, and hurried off to lunch.

Leylegian was vaguely aware that the Bank of America had sold a lot of the East Rutherford, New Jersey, medical supply manufacturer's stock in the $28–$29-a-share range and now here it was, suddenly being bid for at what promised to be a fat premium. Leylegian was also acutely aware that his old friend had laid a heavy burden of secrecy on him. The risk, he knew, was that "if someone is contemplating a large transaction and it is going to be done at a premium, if a person was not particularly scrupulous, he might at eleven forty-five in the morning buy that stock either for himself personally, or his client." Back in New York, a disappointed Rosenthal dropped the phone back in its cradle. He would have to do better with the next institution on his list, Bankers Trust Company.

Less than a dozen miles west of Rosenthal—across the frozen Hudson and the tundra of the New Jersey meadowlands—Marvin L. Krasnansky had been on the phone to California, too. Then head of corporate communications for Becton, Dickinson, the fifty-one-year-old Krasnansky is extremely well connected on Wall Street. Before joining Becton in 1974, he had been a copy editor on the *Wall Street Journal* and done public relations for both the New York Stock Exchange and the brokerage firm of Paine, Webber, Jackson & Curtis. Krasnansky is gregarious, with an easy sense of humor, and one of the things he likes about his job is keeping in touch with securities analysts who specialize in drug industry stocks.

Now, late in the afternoon of this Monday in mid-January, Krasnansky was troubled. He'd just finished talking with Mary Ann Beck, a bright, personable analyst employed by Norton Simon. Simon's image as one of California's most opportunistic industrialists had with age diffused into the softer personality of Norton Simon, art collector and benefactor. But there was a sizable investment portfolio to manage, including a batch of Becton, Dickinson convertible debentures.

That was all part of Beck's responsibility. She checked in with Krasnansky on a fairly regular basis, mainly with questions about how B,D was doing, but this time she had a story of her own to tell. Norton Simon had been in New York over the weekend, she said, and had heard that someone was "almost momentarily" going to make a bid for

[19]

B,D stock at $48 to $50 a share. Was it so? What did Marvin know about it?

It was the first Krasnansky had heard of that particular rumor. There had been others like it before, but lately the rumor mills had quieted down. There was no way he could assess the validity of the rumor, said Krasnansky. The two chatted for a few minutes more and then rang off. Krasnansky briefly weighed the idea of checking out what he'd just heard with other friends in the Street, but decided that doing so might just add substance to the sort of gossamer that was always floating around.

Takeover rumors about B,D had been rife nine months or so earlier, when the lid blew off a row that had been building for a long time between management and Fairleigh S. Dickinson, Jr., son of a founder of B,D and its long-time chief executive. The introspective, unpredictable Dickinson had stepped upstairs as chairman in 1973 after a quarter century at the helm, and turned over the day-to-day running of the company to two highly professional managers, Wesley J. Howe and Marvin A. Asnes.

Dickinson, however, could never quite let go. The generous sweep of such family philanthropies as Fairleigh Dickinson University was not enough to keep "Dick" busy. A major stockholding in Air New England, a regional carrier with pronounced growing pains, helped somewhat, but Fairleigh Dickinson always had time for a sympathetic chat with old-line B,D employees. Many of them, predictably enough, had serious reservations about where the new management was headed. Dickinson himself was worried that the company, in a renewed drive for profits, was beginning to lose its touch with people. It was a classic generation gap in search of an accident. The collision came when Dickinson—with the help of critical studies he'd asked Salomon Brothers and Eberstadt to do—torpedoed a major acquisition move that Howe and Asnes had put together in January 1977. Efforts to patch up the relationship failed, and four months later, Dickinson was deposed as chairman. Word began to drift back to Howe and Asnes that the founder's son had asked Salomon to engineer a possible third-party takeover of B,D, using the 5 percent of the company he and his family owned as a fulcrum.

All that was in the background as Marvin Krasnansky chewed over the substance of his conversation with Mary Ann Beck. Like any good securities analyst, she was always chary of revealing her own sources of information. Over the years, though, Krasnansky had developed a "fairly good suspicion" that a lot of what Beck knew came from Salomon Brothers.

H. Robert Sharbaugh, the then chairman of the Sun Company, first heard Becton, Dickinson mentioned as a possible acquisition at a meeting of the big oil producer's senior managers at remote and exclusive Hilton Head Island, South Carolina. It was top-level stuff, a four- or five-day session designed to give "the group of ten" senior vice-presidents and executive vice-presidents who run Sun a chance to brainstorm such long-range topics as corporate development away from the workaday intrusions of headquarters at Radnor, Pennsylvania.

One of the major items on the agenda was Sun's need to diversify out of its petroleum base, preferably by a series of major acquisitions. The subject was high on Sharbaugh's personal agenda, too. A giant of a man built along the slab-like lines of an all-pro tackle, Sharbaugh had joined Sun in 1946 while still a student at Carnegie Tech. He'd taken over the presidency in 1970 at age forty-one with a mandate to decentralize a company that had become increasingly muscle-bound at the top. He split Sun into fourteen units, and thrust as much autonomy on the divisions as they could absorb. There had been some modest-sized acquisitions as Sharbaugh moved on to become chairman and CEO in 1974—$2-million to $5-million forays into such non-energy ventures as trucking, convenience foods, and hydraulic systems, but nothing really big. Sun's assets amounted to more than $5 billion. The company was loaded with cash and the great fear was that if Sun did not start moving in a big way into new fields now, it might be trapped in a dwindling-resource business almost certain to be reshaped by major technological changes fifteen or twenty years down the road.

Thus, acquisition was very much on Sharbaugh's mind as he was having cocktails before dinner with some of his fellow executives at Hilton Head. "It was Sunday, the fourth of December, about six o'clock in the evening," recalled Sharbaugh with the engineer's precision that punctuates much of his speech. Ted Burtis, Sun's chief operating officer and a fellow Carnegie Tech alumnus, drew Sharbaugh aside and told him that Horace Kephart "would like ten or fifteen minutes with us." Kephart, senior vice-president for finance and investments, had been working on a recapitalization project for Sun with two Salomon Brothers partners for almost three months. One of the Salomon partners had suggested that Becton, Dickinson might fit Sun's diversification blueprint. Sharbaugh later recalled Kephart as saying "there was a possibility that at least one of the directors of the company was desirous of selling his shares. He mentioned his name—Mr. Dickinson."

There was one problem, however. The Salomon partners had warned Kephart that three other companies were also interested in making a bid for B,D. If Sun was going to move, it had better move fast. A series of crash meetings began almost immediately. How did B,D stack up with the competition in the health-care industry? What was the company's potential impact on Sun's earnings? How much would it cost to be acquired? What was the best way to go about doing so? By this blustery Monday morning—January 16, 1978—Sun's financial people, headed by Kephart; a Salomon Brothers team that included Richard Rosenthal; and an outside legal team advised by takeover specialist Martin Lipton of Wachtell, Lipton, Rosen & Katz had worked out a detailed step-by-step scenario.

Sun would try to pick up anywhere from a minimum of 20 percent to a maximum of 34 percent of B,D through a secret approach to Fairleigh Dickinson and a few other large individual holders. That first step would be followed almost immediately by the simultaneous and equally secret sweep of no more than thirty big institutional holders. The initial objective was not a complete takeover. Sun was reaching for less than half of the stock, but wanted enough leverage to gain the board representation it would take to find out from the inside how the company really worked. If B,D looked as good close up as it did on paper, there might be a second-stage takeover of 100 percent of the company.

Sun in any event would accept nothing less than 20 percent. Anything below that figure would not permit it to include a pro-rata share of B,D's profits in its own earnings.

[23]

Sharbaugh was willing to go as high as $50 a share for the stock if he had to negotiate. Sun's executive committee had approved a maximum outlay of $350 million, but Sharbaugh thought the optimum combination would be 34 percent of B,D for about $297 million. The 34 percent would give Sun "negative control." Careful study of the bylaws had shown that B,D would not be able to take countermeasures—merge with another big company or entertain a competing bid that might force Sun to up its ante—without a two-thirds vote of its outstanding stock. The best strategy was to shut off those possibilities by becoming a bone in B,D's throat.

Sharbaugh and everyone else on the Sun side was sure that the reaction would be hostile. There had been a flat-out declaration of independence after American Home Products—with a nudge from Salomon Brothers and the by-then-deposed Fairleigh Dickinson—made a pass at B,D. The bid had been rejected out of hand by the health-care company's board, and Marvin Krasnansky made sure a formal resolution stating that B,D intended to remain free got wide distribution. B,D had also taken the precaution of retaining the other big name in the takeover bar—Joseph Flom, of Skadden, Arps, Slate, Meagher & Flom.

The wily, resourceful Flom has been in the takeover game since the mid-fifties—he practically invented it. His good friend Martin Lipton had told Sun real bullets would be flying if Flom started shooting. Horace Kephart had made the same point. He had told both Sharbaugh and the Sun board that "the purchase would most likely result in some legal actions to thwart the acquisition and that would be bad publicity."

The absolute certainty that Howe and Asnes would fight

underscored the need for total secrecy. Sun could not run the risk of getting caught in mid-stream—i.e., in a position where a B,D injunctive action might prevent it from getting control of stock for which it had already laid out large sums of money.

The ingenious response to that peril was the machinery Robert Sharbaugh hoped to set in motion after the market close. Sun would bypass any heavy open-market purchases that would have been betrayed by telltale trading volume on the New York Stock Exchange tape. And Sun would skirt the ambush of a formal tender offer to shareholders that would require advance notice to the Securities and Exchange Commission. Sun would get to where it wanted to go by using Richard Rosenthal and the other telephone solicitors as a kind of cut-out to gather yes or no responses from the institutions after the close. As soon as it was established that 20 percent or more of B,D's outstanding stock was ripe for the plucking, Horace Kephart, operating from his command post in Salomon's trading room, would close the deal separately with each of the institutions. There was to be no commitment—and no mention of Sun's name—until the 20 percent minimum was reached.

The scheme looked airtight, but it was freighted with enough unknowns for Kephart to have christened the new Sun subsidiary that had been created to acquire B,D stock with the cryptic abbreviation L.H.I.W.—"Let's Hope It Works." The new creation was off to a flying start, though, as Robert Sharbaugh learned when he arrived this Monday morning at Sun's modernistic offices in Radnor, a half-hour drive from downtown Philadelphia. Kephart was already on his way to Salomon in New York with a group of five or six other Sun people. Fairleigh Dickinson, his daughter,

Ann Dickinson Turner, and one of Dickinson's oldest business associates had all been approached over the weekend. It looked as though their combined holdings of 1.1 million shares were already in the bag.

A good omen, but Sharbaugh, like almost everyone else on his team, was worried that word might somehow leak. The price on B,D might run away from the market and knock the carefully plotted scenario into a cocked hat. Sharbaugh stolidly worked his way through his calendar for the day—a visitor from outside the company first thing in the morning; a luncheon meeting with a representative from a university that provided Sun with some of its best engineering talent. Sharbaugh had been scheduled to attend a meeting of the Bryn Mawr hospital board in the late afternoon and abruptly decided not to go. Ted Burtis shared his uneasiness. He kept coming by Sharbaugh's office, chatting for a few minutes and then leaving. There was some talk about Burtis' having given Kephart approval to go along with Richard Rosenthal's insistence to shoot for a minimum of 20 percent rather than the 25 percent that Sun had decided on over the weekend. Rosenthal insisted the "psychology" was such that the institutions would rush to fill the smaller quota. The train was leaving the station: time to get aboard. As Sharbaugh recalled, he and Burtis "went over the numbers a couple of times, calculating average cost to Sun if some shares were bought at one price or another," and trying to figure out what kind of ceiling they would give Kephart if it turned out that he had to negotiate with the institutions. They talked about ways of trying to help B,D's management save face, but most of all the two Sun executives worried about whether the blitz "was still to move that night." The decision was

Sharbaugh's responsibility alone, and it would be hours before he'd have enough information to act on. The waiting wasn't easy.

The flip side to the controlled tension at Radnor was "controlled mayhem" in New York. That, at least, is how Horace Kephart described the atmosphere on the forty-first floor at Salomon Brothers. The final preparations for the raid took place against the customary tumult of Salomon's trading floor—a Babel of traders and their clerks conducting two or three phone conversations at once: "Hold him at a quarter!" "Fifty thousand at an eighth, an eighth!" "Sixty-three to sixty-five and a half!"

Even Richard Rosenthal felt his own natural habitat had been turned into "a zoo." There was a lawyer for each of the phone solicitors and that meant eighteen people right off, most of them running in and out of what seemed to be one continuous meeting—a meeting that began around noon and didn't end until almost the close of the market. "At that point there must have been a dozen attorneys all over the place," Rosenthal recalled. "I don't mean to make an overstatement, but there were a lot of attorneys."

All the lawyers were fascinated with the technical virtuosity of the plan of attack. Charles M. Nathan, for example, a partner in Cleary, Gottlieb, Steen & Hamilton, is no novice to the takeover game. Over the last seven years or so, he has worked on at least thirty mergers. Yet even he admitted to having been curious about how the approach was going to work, and was eager to get it on the rails. "I had never before seen a transaction quite like this," said Nathan.

Part of the virtuosity lay in the single-mindedness of the

approach to the institutions. Much of the early part of the day was consumed by a study of the list of institutions Richard Rosenthal had drawn up. Rosenthal and the eight other solicitors parceled out among themselves the institutions they knew best. Rosenthal drew the Bank of America, for example, because of his long acquaintance with Jack Leylegian. James ("Pike") Sullivan, an Eberstadt partner who'd been brought in to help on the telephone campaign, had a good working relationship with James F. Jollay, first vice-president in charge of investments for the First Wisconsin Trust. Morris Offit, a Salomon partner with good connections in Baltimore, was given the T. Rowe Price mutual fund group to call. Joseph Lombard, head of Salomon's Boston office, was patched into the meetings in New York by a conference call. Lombard was told to take on the First National Bank of Boston and two major mutual fund groups where he was a familiar figure—the Massachusetts Investors Growth Stock Fund and State Street Research & Management Corporation.

That done, the lawyers picked their way through the decalogue of dos and don'ts the callers were to follow. "The mandatory selling points" included a warning to the institutions about the need for "absolute confidentiality" and emphasis on the fact that "your principal will not finally commit to purchase until a block meeting its minimum requirements is assembled." The "don'ts" included a warning that the price ought not to be characterized as a "take it or leave it" proposition. "Be appropriately responsive to negotiating initiative by institution," the solicitors were told. The time constraints put on the institutions to get back with a yes or no answer should not be any shorter "than is customary for institutional block purchases."

The caveats were laid down to keep the deal from running afoul of the securities laws—a potential slip that might add weight to the reaction sure to come from B,D's fearsome litigators. Each of the solicitors at Salomon Brothers had a script in front of him and a lawyer beside him as he made his pitch.

When the blitz began at 4:00 P.M., none of the institutions was given much time for reflection. During the planning, Richard Rosenthal had told the lawyers he thought any professional worth his salt should be able to make a decision on a block trade in "five or ten minutes." "A half hour would be generous," he had said. The bandwagon psychology again. Thus, when Pike Sullivan called his good friend Jim Jollay at First Wisconsin at 4:05 P.M., he went quickly through the canned spiel (". . . an undisclosed party had an interest in taking a substantial minority interest in B,D . . ."), and then told him he needed an answer "in a half hour." Jollay said that would be okay. He talked the proposition over with the chairman and president of the bank, ran it by a hastily summoned meeting of his research director and portfolio managers, and was back to Sullivan by 5:00 P.M., New York time. First Wisconsin would be more than happy to sell 96,625 shares held in forty-two different discretionary accounts at $45 a share.

The effort gathered momentum. At 4:02 P.M. Rosenthal was on the line, outlining the proposition for William Dudley, a senior vice-president of the I.D.S. mutual fund group in Minneapolis. He told Dudley the deal "had to be done that day." Dudley, like Jollay, had already done some homework, thanks to a couple of guesses he'd made on the basis of the will-you-be-around-after-four-o'clock call Rosenthal had made earlier in the day. When the deal went live on the second phone call, Dudley checked out the price charts on B,D, liked what he saw, was told by Rosenthal there had been a "heavy response," and by 5:15 P.M. had agreed to sell 450,000 shares.

Some institutions, though, felt they were being stampeded. Both Dennis Evans of the First National Bank of Minneapolis and James Clark of the North Carolina Bank, in fact, thought they were looking at the opening moves of a surprise tender offer being made to all B,D shareholders. They did not bite, apparently because they thought they were being pressured into selling at a price that might sweeten later on. David H. Carnahan, head of the personal trust and investment group at the United States Trust Company, was also wary. Robert Zeller, then chairman of the executive committee at Eberstadt and a long-time friend of Fairleigh Dickinson, had come on strong with the U.S. Trust executive. Zeller had opened the conversation by introducing himself as a "personal friend" of U.S. Trust's chairman and telling Carnahan that Eberstadt considered the bank a "long and valued customer." At the same time, he held the banker's feet to the fire. Zeller, according to Carnahan, said he would "appreciate hearing from us within thirty minutes." "The offer was filling up fast," Zeller continued, "and there was no assurance that it would still be open" by the time Carnahan got back to him.

John S. Crowl, a senior portfolio manager at Bankers Trust, also felt very much under the gun. It was a "novel

situation," he said. Rosenthal had called Crowl at 4:10
P.M., explained the package, and told Crowl he had "until
midnight" to respond. In the end, both banks backed away
from the deal, mainly on the grounds that they didn't have
enough time or information to weigh its full implications.
Rosenthal announced that he was particularly "vexed" at
Bankers Trust. He felt his call earlier in the day had given
Crowl more than ample notice that the bank's portfolio
managers had to be in a position to move swiftly.

All of Rosenthal's missionary work was rewarded,
however, when he finally got a return call from a jubilant
Jack Leylegian. The computers showed the Bank of
America had not sold out all of its B,D stock after all.
Leylegian again quizzed Rosenthal closely on whether the
deal was a takeover. Assured that it wasn't—a sign he was
getting all the premium there was in the stock—Leylegian
committed the bank to a delivery of 143,000 shares the
next day.

The bandwagon was really rolling—rolling so fast that
Horace Kephart was hard put to keep up with the totals
pouring in on him at his command post just off the
Salomon trading floor. By 4:45 P.M. he had enough
information to call Ted Burtis at Radnor with the good
news that Sun had commitments on 3.1 million shares. By
5:35 P.M. the tally was 4,226,000 shares—a magic mark,
some 22 percent of B,D's outstanding stock. A time for the
big decision, via conference call between Burtis and
Kephart, the latter flanked by Rosenthal and James H.
Fogelson, the deputy for Sun's lawyer Martin Lipton.
Sharbaugh recalled "getting in the middle of" the call and
being given a rundown on the institutions who had already
agreed to deliver. He was told there was a good chance that

most of those not yet heard from would be in the affirmative, too.

Sharbaugh gave Kephart the word everyone had been hoping to hear all day: Go! Feeling very relieved, the methodical Sharbaugh made the ten-minute drive to home and dinner, while Kephart started bringing in the sheaves. "Hello," was his introduction. "I'm Horace Kephart, president of L.H.I.W., a subsidiary of the Sun Company, and I understand you're interested in selling . . ." Jack Leylegian remembered the call sounding as "if this guy was reading from something," and indeed the guy was. Horace Kephart was reading from what was in effect an official victory script. Sun had contracted to buy 34 percent of B,D in its brilliantly planned $297-million blitz of six individuals and thirty-three institutions. The sweep of the institutions took no more than an hour from start to finish and appeared to have been accomplished in total secrecy. What's more, only one of the institutions had attempted to bargain the $45 price higher, and Kephart had simply refused to do business with it. There were a lot of details still hanging fire: couriers had to be dispatched all over the country to pick up the stock, preferably before Wesley Howe and the rest of B,D's management realized what was happening. And the New York Stock Exchange had to be told just enough to persuade it to keep B,D stock from trading tomorrow, but not enough to reveal Sun's identity. Tuesday, however, was another day. An expansive Richard Rosenthal got a group of eight or so of his colleagues together and took everybody uptown for dinner at "21."

2

Office Politics and the Honorary Chairman

The celebration at "21" seemed to mark the end of B,D as a truly independent, self-directed organism. With 34 percent of the company in its pocket, Sun could block every effort of Wesley Howe and Marvin Asnes to shake off the influence of their new and biggest individual stock-holder. Without Sun's approval, they could not seriously dilute the big oil producer's holdings by issuing more shares; they could not try an end run by merging with another major company; they could not even call off the annual meeting scheduled for next month, at which Sun could almost certainly defeat any management proposals it cared to contest. Despite the defiance they had hurled at the menace of takeover, Howe and Asnes had been sapped; sapped, ironically enough, by the man to whom they owed their jobs, the figure who for thirty years had personified B,D—Fairleigh Stanton Dickinson, Jr.

Richard Rosenthal had said it all months before when he learned how deep the rift between the tall, introverted Dickinson and his handpicked successors ran. "When management is split, you have a better opportunity of having a merger take place than you do when management is uniform. The only important thing about Mr. Dickinson to me," the Salomon Brothers partner continued, "was the fact that there was a schism in management that could lead to a transaction."

Certainly there was nothing in Fairleigh Dickinson's background that would suggest the maverick. He was brought up in Rutherford, New Jersey, one of a string of blue-collar towns nestled on the heights above the Jersey meadowlands less than a dozen miles south and west of the George Washington Bridge leading to Manhattan. Though Dickinson has long since moved to the somewhat tonier reaches of Ridgewood, an upper-middle-class suburb a few miles away, his roots are still in Rutherford. His office is in the family home there—on a broad, tree-lined street not far from the public library he and his mother helped to expand with a gift of $1.3 million dollars; not far from the university named after his father; and not far from the red brick four-faced clock tower that has marked the presence of the Becton, Dickinson Company in neighboring East Rutherford for almost three quarters of a century.

The elder Fairleigh Dickinson, a stationery salesman— pads, pencils, notebooks, and ledgers—founded the company in 1897 with a fellow North Carolinian, Maxwell W. Becton. Becton had been a sales rep and partner in Randall

& Becton, a Boston-based purveyor of clinical thermometers and surgical supplies.

The salesmen's paths crossed frequently enough on the road for them to become good friends and ultimately partners in the enterprise they started on one floor in a pinched six-story cast-iron loft building on Vesey Street in downtown Manhattan. The rent was $45 a month, but diversifying from thermometers into hypodermic needles and syringes gave the partners a nicely balanced product line that spelled early and consistent success. The move to New Jersey was the end of a search for more manufacturing space. Becton was Mr. Outside, the easygoing, persuasive salesman; Dickinson was Mr. Inside, a tough-minded administrator with a gift for dealing with balky machinery.

Young Fairleigh started working summers for B,D in 1932, when he was thirteen. One of the things about that depression year Dickinson remembers is how his father and Max Becton came to the rescue of East Rutherford. "The town was in bad shape and B,D saved it from going into bankruptcy by paying the company's next quarter's real estate taxes in advance. That isn't anything anybody has to know about," he adds modestly. Fairleigh Dickinson's sense of *noblesse oblige* started early and runs deep. For a man of Dickinson's time and station, it was all hornbook sociology—local grammar schools, prep school at the New York Military Academy in Cornwall, New York, and then on to Williams College. Dickinson was Phi Beta Kappa and graduated cum laude, with a degree in political science. Dickinson is an avid yachtsman. With war just over the horizon in 1941, he joined the Coast Guard; he was discharged as a Lieutenant Commander after five years' service, three of them on sea duty in the North Atlantic and South Pacific.

After the war, Dickinson didn't have to look far for a job. There was a vice-presidency open for him at B,D. When his father died two years later, the twenty-nine-year-old Fairleigh Dickinson, Jr., became president and chief executive officer. Henry Becton, son of co-founder Maxwell Becton, had also come back to East Rutherford after a couple of years in the Air Force. The founders' sons had grown up together, and there were direct family ties, too. Henry Becton's sister Susan was married to a first cousin of Fairleigh Dickinson's. Both men were major stockholders in a company that was still very much privately owned; both men were active in the management of a bank that controlled a number of family trusts; and both men reinforced the family presence in charities their fathers had supported for years.

Fairleigh Dickinson talks a lot about his father. One of the things he remembers is how his father and Max Becton used to sit at rolltop desks "out in the open, where everybody could see them." He also remembers Armistice Day and the tradition at the plant to observe a minute's silence at 11:00 A.M., marking the end of World War I— the eleventh hour of the eleventh day of the eleventh month. "All that old belt machinery would shut down," recalled Dickinson, "and there would be my father on the telephone, talking to Cincinnati as if he could reach it by shouting through the window. I decided," added Dickinson with a smile, "that I would be different from my father. There'd be no shouting on the telephone at eleven o'clock on Armistice Day." It is hard to imagine Fairleigh Dickinson, Jr., shouting at any time. He is a big man—better than six feet two, jowly now and running a bit thick around the middle—but courtly to the point of diffidence, as if all the overt aggression had been bred out of him.

The transition to the second generation was not an easy one. Maxwell Becton, though seriously ill, was still a power to be reckoned with, and there were plenty of people in management who found it difficult to get around their memories of Fairleigh Dickinson, Jr., and Henry Becton as kids in short pants. On the whole, Dickinson thought "that things had worked out fortunately, but by chance, when my father and Mr. Becton were ill and there had been no designed order or plan for succession in the company."

Dickinson himself had no worries about succession. He was a good deal more interested in running things than was the mild-mannered Henry Becton, who was content to stay in the background, filling in over the years in such fringe positions as chairman of the executive committee and vice-chairman of the board. Dickinson was willing to delegate, but no one ever forgot that he was president *and* chief executive officer. That was especially true of John W. Simmons, who had been Dickinson's roommate at Williams and had also served in the wartime Coast Guard. Dickinson had brought Williams into the company in 1946 and subsequently appointed him executive vice-president and chief operating officer, with major responsibility for the day-to-day running of the concern.

It was a job that Simmons held for more than a quarter-century. In any other company, he might reasonably have expected to move up to the presidency at some point during that long time span. Not at B,D. Simmons was to remain executive vice-president until the day he resigned to take over as president and chief executive officer of Morton-Norwich Products, Inc. Leaving the details to somebody else gave Dickinson the time he needed to shoulder all of the public responsibilities that went with being head of Becton, Dickinson. There were the schools, of course—chairman of Fairleigh Dickinson University and membership on the boards of Bennington College, St. Peter's College in Jersey City, Bard College, the New York Military Academy, Montclair Academy, and the Kent School. There were two hospital boards; Girl Scout and Boy Scout Councils and the United Fund; the Urban League and the March of Dimes; the New Jersey Television Broadcasting Corporation and the New Jersey Symphony; the Prudential Insurance Company Board, the New Jersey Meadowlands Regional Planning Board, the Advisory Council of the National 4-H Foundation, and a tour as a Republican State Senator from Bergen County from 1968 to 1971.

Fairleigh Dickinson was in demand partly because of the family benefactions. They were invariably generous. One long-time friend, for example, recalls hitting Dickinson up on one occasion for a donation to the Girl Scouts and being startled when he later got an elated call from someone on the Scouts' Bergen County Council who said, "Hey, thanks for that check for twelve thousand dollars." As a heavy contributor to the Republican party, a well-known businessman, and a "Mr. Clean" in a local organization often rocked by scandal, Dickinson was a shoo-in when he ran for the Senate. Like most freshman senators, he tended to go along with the leadership, and newsmen at the State House found him diligent on such matters of major interest to his constituents as a Meadowlands regulatory commission. Nobody in the pressrooms, on the other hand, thought of Fairleigh Dickinson as one of the Senate's movers and shakers. He often seemed intimidated by the rough and tumble of a legislature that has never been mistaken for the Queen of Parliaments.

"There are good people in Trenton and I enjoyed politics," Dickinson said, and then went on to explain why he served only one term: "It's just so hard getting anything done." Even now people in Bergen County still address him as "Senator"—his father carried the honorific title of "Colonel"—and Dickinson seems pleased with the attention. He is by no means a backslapping glad-hander, though; he tells jokes with the air of a man who has worked hard at studying the delivery and often appears to be ill at ease in any company outside his own family. Almost everyone who has had more than brief contact with him thinks of him as a loner. "I like him," says one man who has known Dickinson for the better part of two decades. "He is a nice person, but you always have the feeling when you're with him that one of you—either you or he—is uncomfortable."

Dickinson's own office calendar, in fact, shows a great many laconic "lunch alone" entries for places as plastic and anonymous as a Holiday Inn not far from his Rutherford office. Like many shy people, Dickinson tends to hide squid-like behind clouds of vague polysyllabics. Talking about foreign takeovers of U.S. companies, for example, he at one point said, "I consider it contrary to the balanced best interest of this country for ownership of corporations or any part thereof to substantially transfer offshore. I realize that anybody is entitled to do that which he

[39]

pleases," continued Dickinson, "but at least I personally have no desire to favor such a prospect."

However murky the dialogue, there was no mistaking Dickinson's deep emotional attachment to B,D as an extension of himself and his family. "You have to understand, this involves my whole life and indeed two generations of my family, maybe three," he said. From this remove, it is difficult to tell how much of the credit for B,D's growth between 1946 and 1972 should go to a chief executive who admittedly had a lot of other irons in the fire. The numbers, superficially regarded, are not bad. B,D was grossing about $10 million when Dickinson took over. Sixteen years later, it was grossing what he calls "give or take" $300 million. One of Dickinson's smartest moves was in taking the company public. During the great bull market years from 1962 to 1970, the second generation of Bectons and Dickinsons (and other insiders) capitalized on the efforts of the first generation by selling around two million shares of their stock at prices ranging from $25 to $62 a share. The proceeds totaled about $90 million.

Going public made Fairleigh Dickinson Big Rich. The cash flow from his B,D holdings has helped to finance a couple of outside flings that haven't worked out too well— a major stake in Air New England and a hotel in St. Croix—but with an income that probably runs to several million dollars a year, Dickinson needs all the tax shelter he can get. The lifestyle, though, is casual Old Money. The homes in Ridgewood, Martha's Vineyard, and St. Croix are comfortable, but not ostentatious. "Dick is a very unassuming guy about material things," says one friend. "He drove that old car forever and that's all he had—that and the Jeep. He's never dressed particularly well and you don't see a lot of servants around the house. There's a guy who comes and cuts his grass and there's a cleaning lady," continues the friend, "but lots of people have a lot more than that in Ridgewood."

There was one luxury that came out of the great bull market years. Fairleigh Dickinson and his investment bankers were quick to squeeze maximum advantage out of the fact that B,D was a hot stock. Much of the company's growth between 1964 and '71 came from a series of twenty-two acquisitions made with the strongest currency the company could offer, its own common stock. Acquisition wasn't a particularly new tack for B,D. The founders had built the company by buying their way into surgical instruments, Ace bandages, and bulb syringes. There had been some turkeys along the way—a medical bag line that had to be dropped, for instance—and the second generation made its share of mistakes, too. There were several ill-advised sorties into such lines as Sportade, a Gatorade-like soft drink, and other items alien to the B,D basic product mix. Liquidating those problems and tightening up internal controls generally became the responsibility of Wesley Howe, who was moved up from executive vice-president to president in 1973. That was a big move for both Fairleigh Dickinson and Howe, for it marked the emergence of an heir apparent. Dickinson became chairman and a year later ceded the chief executive's title to Howe as well.

By the end of '72, Dickinson was ready to formalize what had been becoming increasingly clear for some time. He had virtually nothing to do with B,D's day-to-day operations. As he now saw things, "I had been responsible for the vicinity of thirty years. It was time to have orderly change and this should be a case of new heads, new hands gradually taking control." For the first time in seventy-seven years, B,D did not have a member of the founding family at the helm. There was no doubt, though, that there had been a laying on of hands. Cautious and reserved—qualities that dovetailed nicely with his under-graduate and graduate engineering degrees from Stevens Institute of Technology—Wesley Howe had spent virtually all his working life at B,D. He'd joined the company in 1949 when he was twenty-eight, and by the early sixties had moved through the engineering, manufacturing engineering, and research development departments into general management. Almost all of Wesley Howe's close friends are from inside the company. There was relief that Dickinson had chosen an old hand rather than going outside in what seemed a long overdue effort to institutionalize B,D's power structure.

It quickly became apparent, however, that there were some ambiguities in the grant of power. Dickinson expected to be an "active participant" in "general policy overall decisions," with "substantial responsibility" in such areas as mergers and acquisitions, and the hiring and firing of top executives. There was no "formal" description of the responsibility in either the B,D charter or bylaws, of course, but Fairleigh Dickinson said it was "understood, and indeed quite desirable, that there be mutual consideration of problems of that magnitude." There were times when mutual consideration seemed to be a one-way street. Given a mandate to ride herd on some of the acquisitions that hadn't quite worked out, Howe replaced the head of a major division. A director who had been a major stockholder in the division before B,D acquired it complained directly to his old friend, Fairleigh Dickinson. Howe's order was countermanded. There were a number of other irritants like that, irritants that made it difficult for Howe and his executive vice-president, Marvin Asnes, to get the job done; irritants that would soon split the company and its board of directors into warring camps.

One major bone of contention was a deal Dickinson himself had negotiated for the acquisition of the modest-sized Mountain Paper Products Corporation. Both Howe and Asnes had serious reservations about buying the company. So did a number of directors, including W. Paul Stillman, a doughty, outspoken octogenarian known to generations of newspaper feature writers as "Mr. New Jersey" for the wide range of his business and civic pursuits. Stillman had been chairman and CEO of the First National State Bancorporation, one of New Jersey's biggest bank holding companies, since 1931, and for much of that time also nimbly served as chairman of the Mutual Benefit Life Insurance Company as well. Fairleigh Dickinson had tapped him for the B,D board in the late sixties. The banker spoke from a promontory of more than sixty-five years in business, and when he said flatly that "Mountain Paper Products did not appear to be a very desirable situation," most of his fellow directors listened.

One who did not was Fairleigh Dickinson. He persisted in pushing for the acquisition though it was clear, as Stillman said, that "most of his associates would rather B,D not go through with it." William F. Tompkins, an old friend of Dickinson's and a former U.S. Attorney, was despatched on a flying trip to England, where the B,D chairman was visiting Fairleigh Dickinson University's Wroxton Abbey campus. Tompkins' mission to resolve "any further split" on the board came a cropper when

[43]

Dickinson refused to budge. The chairman insisted on putting the acquisition to a vote. It was shot down eight to seven. Howe and Asnes diplomatically went along with Dickinson, despite the doubts they had voiced. It was a safe enough thing to do. Dickinson clearly didn't have the votes to push the deal through, even though Paul Stillman (like a number of other directors) also supported the chairman on the theory that for "the board to deny him his desire on this particular thing would not be good for the company." Fairleigh Dickinson, however, responded quickly to what he interpreted as a stiffening attitude to his jurisdictional prerogatives. It was shortly after the Mountain Paper flareup that Eberstadt partner Robert Zeller, with the B,D chairman's blessing, began scouting Eastman Kodak and other potential buyers as a new home for the Dickinson block of stock.

Fairleigh Dickinson didn't think it necessary to let Howe, Asnes, or any of his fellow directors know that Zeller was out testing the market. Dickinson did begin to communicate his growing dissatisfaction with the performance of his two top managers, though. Asnes, in particular, seemed to be getting under the chairman's skin. It wasn't anything in particular. Certainly Asnes' credentials were solid enough. He was graduated from M.I.T. in 1949, went on to the Harvard Graduate School of Business, and joined B,D in 1964 when it acquired the Clay Adams Company. As an executive vice-president of the clinical laboratory equipment producer, Asnes went on the B,D board as part of the merger agreement. An important shareholder in B,D in his own right as a result of the merger, Asnes is quick, articulate, intense. Even at rest he is continually in motion. When Asnes sits behind his desk, his right leg is continuously in motion, as if he is operating some kind of cosmic sewing machine. He has a sharp tongue and a lively sense of humor. "When you are in the soup, you are already cooked," says what purports to be an old Chinese proverb on the scroll in his office.

Late in 1976, it did indeed begin to look as if Asnes was for the kettle. Dickinson had been complaining to Paul Stillman that Asnes "wasn't running the company in the way it should be, and really should be asked to leave it." Stillman recalled hearing Dickinson "maybe once or twice more on the subject," and telling him: "if you think he should leave, you are the chairman of the board and the biggest stockholder, why don't you fire him?"

"Maybe I will," the chairman replied.

Dickinson evidently tried the subject for size with other directors as well, because William F. Tompkins recalled hearing after a meeting of B,D's audit committee at the Pennington Club in Newark that Dickinson "intended to speak to Mr. Asnes."

Fairleigh Dickinson described his objections to the executive vice-president he had anointed only months before as "intangible in one way and quite real in another." He said he had come to the "personal or I guess subjective conclusion that Mr. Asnes was extremely impersonal concerning people and that his entire point of view was inconsistent with the complete continuity of the traditions of B,D as a company."

Those traditions, as Fairleigh Dickinson saw them, were "broadly humanistic. Nobody can run a business as though it were a kindergarten," the B,D chairman added, "nor can it be run like an army. At B,D there was intense emphasis on my father's part and, I think, particularly on my part, on the entire humanistic tradition; the emphasis on values of the academic, almost, that we were in a very complicated and technical field. We had a customer who almost by definition [was] ultimately ill," Dickinson continued, "and this provided strong, to me, overwhelming reason for the company to be an open place and for the company to have ultimately a broad consideration of humanistic matters."

Ask Dickinson to refine that statement and what comes through is an almost metaphysical sense of the patrician—a deep sense of regret that B,D has burst the mold of the family business and been institutionalized to the point where the rolltop desk has vanished and the machinery belts no longer shudder to a halt on the eleventh hour of the eleventh day of the eleventh month. "Maybe it's a question of scale," said Dickinson. "I realize I'm talking as if I still own twenty percent of the stock, but you have to take the long view to get the company out to the year 2000. I'm afraid the technocrats are concentrating on short-term profits."

The unanchored, impressionistic quality of the chairman's thought process was apparently one of the reasons why the impatient Asnes subsequently told a friend, with evident bewilderment, that he "had never once, in ten years, had a meaningful business discussion with Dick." On this day in mid-November 1976, however, Fairleigh Dickinson's drift was unmistakable. Dickinson called Asnes into his office just before a board meeting was scheduled to start and told the executive "I didn't think he should be in his then job." Dickinson recalled the encounter lasting "perhaps thirty seconds," or maybe as long as "two or three minutes." He said he did not tell Asnes to leave the company or that he was fired. The exchange, said Dickinson, "left nothing definitively answered and was kind of unsatisfactory."

Dickinson remembered the board meeting that followed as being freighted with "obvious and somewhat unusual tension." Paul Stillman also recalled that the room did not have a relaxed atmosphere. The directors had been waiting for Dickinson and Asnes to appear. When they came in, said Stillman, "Mr. Dickinson proceeded to stand up and make his pitch to get rid of Mr. Asnes. It was obvious that he had no support whatever for it and Mr. Asnes proceeded to go ahead with his business." The issue never got to a vote, and Dickinson later denied ever trying to lift Asnes' scalp. It was Stillman's opinion that Dickinson had no power under the B,D bylaws "to unilaterally fire an officer," and he had warned the chairman that "if you are going to get rid of Asnes, you better make sure you have the votes on the board."

"I have them" was the reply, according to Stillman.

The attack on Asnes shocked Stillman, Tompkins, and several other outside directors into a series of meetings with Fairleigh Dickinson and Wesley Howe aimed at bringing peace to the fifth floor. It required no genius to diagnose what the problem was. As "Tommy" Tompkins put it, Dickinson "felt he should participate in management decisions; Howe and Asnes felt he shouldn't. That was the bottom line."

In the ensuing six weeks the outside directors, led by Stillman, tried the social lubricant of inviting the antagonists to five dinners—two at "21," two at the exclusive Links Club, and one in a private dining room at Windows on the World. The dinners left the irrepressible Stillman

out-of-pocket to the tune of $1,060.63. The progress made
can be summed up in his reason for taking the group to the
top of the World Trade Center for the last peacemaking
dinner he threw. It was Stillman's hope that a change of
venue from the east side of Manhattan to the exhilarating
heights of Windows on the World would give Howe and
Asnes on one side and Dickinson on the other "a different
view of things."

Stillman, trying to piece together a compromise, argued
that "life is not a bed of roses. I told them many times," he
said, "that any business has its problems, and personalities
that don't mesh." His basic message—that reasonable men
can always work things out—fell on rocky ground. When
you got Howe, Asnes, and Dickinson together, he found,
"it was not what you would call a pleasant sociable
evening."

Dickinson's now-familiar complaint was that Howe and
Asnes "were not doing the job for the company as he
envisaged the job and there should be some changes
made." The chairman never said in so many words that the
two should be fired, but it was an easy inference to make.
Stillman found the chairman hard to pin down on
specifics. At one meeting, for example, which started in
Stillman's New York apartment and continued at Links,
the banker remembered Dickinson as talking for an hour in
"this rather lengthy monologue" and leaving him with "no
idea of what he said."

Howe and Asnes, on the other hand, were very precise
in their objections. A three-page handwritten agenda that
Howe drew up for discussion with Stillman notes that
Dickinson had subjected the company to "public scandal"
by trying to unseat Asnes. He had been "less than candid

on so many occasions" that Howe thought him incapable of change. "As an operating matter," wrote Howe, "a chairman actively working behind management can't be tolerated. It is currently all over the company," he continued, "and I'm sure it's leaking outside." Howe's solution was a "face saver" under which Dickinson would resign for "personal reasons" in favor of Henry Becton. "The board simply has to take some action," said Howe.

Stillman agreed that something had to be done, but discovered he was dealing with terribly adamant material. "Nobody gives," he complained. Stillman described one meeting, for instance, where Dickinson did seem "somewhat more accommodating than usual" and announced himself as "rather happy to go along and try to patch this thing up." Asnes brightened at the suggestion, but "Howe didn't say much—he looked at his vest, mostly. There was very little discussion; there was mostly looks." After the meeting at Windows on the World, even that indefatigable check-grabber threw in the sponge. "There was nothing I could do, or any of the rest of us," said Stillman.

He and the other outside directors didn't know that they were innocent bystanders in a game of three-dimensional chess. With nothing concrete likely to come out of the peace talks, each of the two sides was busy trying to assemble an acquisition that would neutralize the opposition. Eberstadt's tireless Robert Zeller, having failed to interest Eastman Kodak and a number of other companies in buying B,D, was now launched into what looked like promising conversations with Avon Products Company. It was all preliminary stuff. There was always the possibility, though, that the leverage of the Dickinson stock could swing the acquisition of B,D in a deal guaranteeing

Fairleigh Dickinson the unchallenged position of, say, vice-chairman, in a much larger company—a much larger company in which Howe and Asnes would have a lot less say.

On their side, Howe and Asnes had picked up the threads of a merger conversation that had been dropped a couple of years earlier. The subject was National Medical Care, a Boston-based concern that operates more than a hundred outpatient dialysis centers for people suffering from chronic kidney failure. It was a high-growth situation, thanks partly to a tidal flow of Medicare funds into the company. Between 1971 and 1975, earnings had expanded by more than 400 percent. The group of physicians who controlled NMC felt the track record entitled them to a sizable premium. Howe and Asnes had taken a close look at the company in 1974, but decided the 100 percent over the market price of National Medical Care's stock they were being asked to pay was just too high.

Now, however, in the fall of '76, with Fairleigh Dickinson snapping at their heels, the perspective had changed. And National Medical Care, itself threatened with a hostile takeover, suddenly seemed anxious to throw in its lot with B,D. By January, B,D's internal studies of what Howe described as "a very significant and high-growth segment of the health-care industry" had gone far enough for a series of face-to-face meetings with NMC's principals.

Howe and Asnes returned from one such meeting and dutifully reported to both Dickinson and Henry Becton a "probability of a mutual interest" that should be further explored. By January 26, the deal had jelled to the point where Marvin Krasnansky was able to put out a press release proclaiming that NMC and B,D had agreed in principle to a merger. Subject to further negotiation, B,D would exchange about 4.3 million shares of its stock, worth $142.3 million, for NMC—a premium of 63.4 percent over the market. As part of the deal, NMC would get one seat on the B,D board.

The proposed consolidation would enhance B,D's earning power. It would also dilute Dickinson's position in the company, and add yet another friendly face to the list of directors Howe and Asnes could count on in a pinch. The NMC proposal was a serious threat to the sub-rosa merger talks Robert Zeller was conducting with Avon products on behalf of Fairleigh Dickinson. The B,D chairman, in fact, learned of the NMC deal only a few days before he himself was scheduled to sit down to lunch with the president of Avon in a tête-à-tête that might once again assure his ascendancy over a management he now saw as hopelessly derelict. Dickinson was convinced that the NMC proposal clinched the case against Howe and Asnes. He saw the terms as "highly disadvantageous," engineered to place a "substantial block of stock in the hands of shareholders friendly to management." Dickinson kept that thought to himself for a while, however, and played his customary close-to-the-vest game.

Howe had put Dickinson in the picture on what the chairman called a "discreet basis." He had been told a "biggie" acquisition was being discussed, but was not given the name of the company and there is no indication that he asked for the name. As Dickinson understood the term, "biggie" described what he took to be "a largish-small transaction."

Howe again talked to Dickinson eight days later, the

evening before the press release went out, and told him what was coming. Looking into the gun barrel of a deal involving an exchange of almost as much B,D stock as he owned, Dickinson suddenly decided the proposition was "very large." Ever courteous, Dickinson had congratulated Howe on negotiating the deal and, according to Marvin Asnes, "stood silent" when the agreement was laid out in detail at an organization meeting of the B,D board. Some directors were upset that they hadn't been consulted on the merger at a regular board meeting held just a week before the agreement was announced. "We were not told a thing," complained Tommy Tompkins. "I felt the management owed us a duty of telling us about it." Howe explained that there had been a sizable run-up in NMC stock while the deal was developing and insisted that the prudent thing was to keep it as quiet as possible.

The agreement in principle was not a binding contract. The final handshake was contingent on whatever came out of the additional spadework being done by both B,D and its investments bankers, Paine, Webber, Jackson & Curtis, on such questions as potential antitrust problems, the potential impact on B,D's relationship with the medical community, and the prospect of regulatory changes that might affect NMC profits.

The internal study would take some time to finish, but by early February a "concern decidedly developed" in Dickinson's mind that the timetable was "indeed compressed in light of what I now knew to be a larger acquisition." Unknown to Howe or anyone else at B,D, announcement of the NMC acquisition had put the kibosh on Dickinson's own merger talks with Avon Products. If they were to be resuscitated, the NMC deal had to be killed. In a memo to Howe and the B,D board, the chairman announced that he was "preparing a series of questions . . . about the merits of the merger."

The questions were to have a certain professional spin on them. Dickinson had taken his worries to his old friend William Salomon, the senior partner at Salomon Brothers. Without consulting Howe or his fellow directors, Dickinson commissioned Salomon to do a study of the NMC proposal and draw up a list of queries that B,D directors should raise before okaying the merger. The chairman then proceeded to load the other barrel. Again without consulting B,D or his fellow directors, Dickinson asked Robert Zeller to have Eberstadt do a study of the merger too. The investment bankers were kept in the dark. Neither Salomon nor Zeller had been told they were plowing the same furrow and it would be several months before either of them would be told that each had been asked, *in camera*, to check out merger possibilities for Fairleigh Dickinson.

As "a friend of the firm," Dickinson carried a lot of weight at Salomon. The team set up to vet the NMC deal was headed by Kenneth Lipper, a young Salomon Brothers partner and Harvard Law School grad whose brother, Jerome, was Dickinson's personal lawyer. Kenneth Lipper and Dickinson had known each other socially since the early '70s and had lunch or drinks together a couple of times while work on the NMC study went forward. The report, for the most part, drew on published sources— newspaper clippings, annual reports, and the like for its conclusions. It was dated February 14—Valentine's Day— and headed "Issues for Consideration Concerning the Proposed Acquisition of National Medical Care." The opening was sure to catch the eye of any director worried about the potential liability of stockholder suits over the merger. The report, the lead sentence said, "raises fundamental questions which must be considered in detail prior to any discussion on the merits of the acquisition."

Among the questions were such posers as:

- Would hostile publicity about the way NMC was drawing patients from municipal hospitals in New York City into its own treatment centers damage B,D's reputation with other hospitals that were among its major customers?

- What was behind the resignation of Arthur Andersen & Co., the accounting firm, as NMC's auditors after a difference of opinion over how the stock options granted the doctor-managers who ran the NMC out-patient center should be treated?

- Would the mounting costs of dialysis provoke the government into regulating fees?

The final draft was written by Kenneth Lipper, approved by William Salomon, and then despatched to Fairleigh Dickinson. A copy of the report with its covering letter was circulated for comment among other Salomon partners. One of them scrawled an appreciation on the Xerox copy. "Ken Lipper, great work if you want to kill the deal—which, I assume, is the whole idea," the note said.

Dickinson bucked his copy of the report on to Howe with a note of his own: "Complete answers to these questions are essential to an objective and reasoned

[54]

consideration of the merger proposal. May I stress the importance of providing answers sufficiently prior to scheduled consideration of the proposal, so as to afford members of the board ample time to give this very important matter most careful study and consideration." It was signed "Dick."

Marvin Asnes went through the roof. He considered the Salomon report "capricious," and argued that the company's own research, reinforced by Paine Webber's legwork, "explored in much greater depth than Salomon all of the issues—and then some." He and Howe moved swiftly to contain the impact of the report by calling a special executive committee meeting to make sure that all of Dickinson's questions "were included within our own normal investigation." The chairman went off for a couple of weeks to St. Croix while Howe's people frantically pulled together information for another executive meeting scheduled for March 3. To Paul Stillman, it was already clear that the merger was "going to run into a lot of rough water."

He could not have been more prescient. The March 3 meeting was rough and murderously short. Howe launched into his response to the Salomon interrogatories and had barely gathered headway when Dickinson announced himself as "unalterably opposed" to the deal. "He really gave us to believe he wasn't interested in the answers to the questions," recalled Howe, "so the meeting was terminated." The issue was not put to the B,D directors for a vote, and the very next day Marvin Krasnansky put out a release indicating that the deal was off.

Dickinson was quick to press his advantage. By late March, there was a meeting at Salomon Brothers. As

Dickinson put it, "The clear purpose of the meeting was to find out what the reaction of the financial community would be if there were management changes at Becton, Dickinson."

Apparently sure that his blocking of the NMC deal had solidified the board behind him, Dickinson could once again seriously contemplate the prospect of removing not only Asnes, but Howe as well. The particular question in front of the Salomon Brothers meeting, said Dickinson, concerned Howe and Asnes all right, but there was the "long range or not so long range consideration of the absence of myself, and an overall consideration of just what sort of effect this would have on the stockholders, and indeed the personnel of the Becton, Dickinson Company."

Dickinson dropped the gauntlet at yet another B,D executive committee meeting a few days later. Both Howe and Asnes flatly asked the chairman what he didn't like about the way they were running the company. That question, the chairman said, had "come up an awful lot" and he dismissed it as "rhetorical." The meeting was being held in Paul Stillman's office. As Stillman recalled, "It was once again one of those situations where you cut the air with the knife; very unfriendly." The banker resolved whatever ambiguities there were by putting the question to both sides.

"I remember saying to Mr. Howe and Mr. Asnes, 'What you are saying is, you want this man out, is that right?' And they said yes. And I said to Mr. Dickinson, 'What you are saying is you want these fellows out.' And he said yes.

"And obviously there was nothing more to do," continued Stillman, "so we broke the meeting up. A difficult meeting and a pathetic meeting." A meeting that painted everyone into a corner. Howe and Asnes talked it over and painfully reached what the executive vice-president called the "only viable alternative"—Fairleigh Dickinson had to go. Once the decision was made, Asnes was not one to lose any sleep over it. "The question," he said, "was how to do it."

Howe had thought he and Asnes could count on nine board votes, but the fallout from the NMC debacle left no room for complacency. Howe and Asnes polled the directors they thought they had in their corner and tapped a friendly intermediary—Paul Miller of First Boston Company—to sound out Paul Stillman. Stillman, in turn, still searching for a compromise, met with Asnes. The banker said Fairleigh Dickinson might find it possible to cooperate with Asnes as president, but that his good friend Howe would have to be sacrificed. "I told him I would not consider such a venal, disloyal act," recalled Asnes.

The notice of a special meeting at which Howe and Asnes hoped to strip Dickinson of his chair went out on April 18, two days before the directors were scheduled to convene. The purpose of the meeting was vaguely defined as one more effort to resolve what everyone by now knew as "management differences." It was all so low-key and disarming that Fairleigh Dickinson's friends seem to have caught something in the wind. Dickinson's lawyer, Jerome Lipper, called Dr. Charles E. Edwards, a board member and head of B,D's research department in an attempt to sniff out what was going on. Some saw Edwards, who was widely regarded as a swing vote on the board, as a possible contender for the presidency if Howe were fired. Howe thought he knew how Edwards felt in general, but did not know how he was going to vote.

[57]

Some of the outside directors complained that the meeting came at a bad time. William Tompkins was tied up on a major law case that for the moment required all his attention, and Paul Stillman was in Florida. Stillman assumed the meeting was important—"the thing was boiling so rapidly you would have to assume that something was coming to a head." Stillman had been told a company plane would be despatched to pick him up, but decided to stay right where he was. "I just wasn't going to break up my holiday for Becton, Dickinson," he said.

Fairleigh Dickinson did not go to the B,D board meeting either. He chartered a plane and by 9:45 that morning was off to Washington, D.C., and a gathering of the Building Committee of the National Cathedral, still another institution to which the Dickinson family has contributed handsomely. Dickinson flew home by way of Baltimore, where he lunched with his old friend and fellow major stockholder and director, J. H. Fitzgerald Dunning.

One of the things the two old friends talked about was the meeting then going on in East Rutherford. Howe by then had called the B,D board to order and read a carefully prepared statement stressing how badly the company had been hurt by the management split. Inside, the impact on the "morale and operating efficiency of senior management . . . had been devastating." Outside, the price of B,D stock had suffered because of "rumors circulating in the Street." Efforts to repair the breach were "hopeless." "The chairman has stated—and I think he would now confirm— that the chemistry is wrong." Then came the vote. There were nine ayes, one no, and one abstention on a resolution that kicked Fairleigh upstairs as "honorary" chairman and installed Henry Becton, the other founder's son, in his place as chairman. The lone "no" came from Henry Becton. He could not bring himself to vote against a Dickinson—a Dickinson who, some inferred, had along with his own faction boycotted the meeting in the hope of preventing a quorum. As it turned out, management would have had enough backing to carry the day even if Dickinson and the outside directors had elected to fight the resolution. And now Henry Becton was deputized to call with the bad news.

Dickinson's first reaction was amazement. "Nothing like that had ever happened to me, nor did I ever envision it happening," he recalled. "Secondly, right or wrong," he continued, "I was angry. Next, thinking more deliberately about it, I thought this is darn serious, and that I'd better get terribly good advice, because this was, I guess, as bad a crisis as I knew." A few of Dickinson's friends—William Tompkins and Jerome Lipper—rallied round the next day at a gloomy lunch given by fellow director David Kane. Kane recalled the lunch as "generally a wake. It was more or less a meeting to commiserate with Dickinson on the shabby way he had been treated by the people he had put in office," added Kane. "Everybody was still in shock," and no one more so than Fairleigh Stanton Dickinson, Jr.

Dickinson's shattered emotional state was clear to everyone in the group that gathered at Salomon Brothers after the lunch. All of the investment banking firm's top people were there—William Salomon; senior partner John Gutfreund; Kenneth Lipper; and Richard Rosenthal. Eberstadt had at least one person on hand, and Martin Lipton had been asked to attend as Salomon Brothers' outside consultant on merger law and strategy.

Dickinson opened the meeting by detailing his plight

and laying out his objective—to wrest control of B,D from Howe and Asnes and change the composition of the company's board. Dickinson thought there might be two ways to do that—litigation, or a proxy fight. Martin Lipton and the rest of the group worked out the probabilities. Surprised at the comparatively modest amount of stock Dickinson controlled, Lipton ruled out a proxy fight as an extremely expensive undertaking. He also saw no "basis for a meaningful litigation that would result in the accomplishment of Dickinson's objectives."

Lipton urged Dickinson to try to work something out with management. "Why don't you just cool everything and see how you feel a few weeks from now, rather than reacting so shortly after the event," he suggested. There was no missing the honorary chairman's deep sense of identification with B,D and his family's good name. "He was very concerned," said Kenneth Lipper, "that the company was identified by the name, its origins and stewardship, up until that point, with his family. He was very concerned that [management] could injure the name of the company as well as his own reputation." Dickinson was furious that he had "in effect created these people and put them in their positions, and they were excessively greedy and pushed him out without merit," the investment banker continued.

To Martin Lipton, Dickinson at the time appeared to be "a man who had suffered greatly," and who was not "emotionally capable of running a company or being a significant factor in the management of a company." The Salomon Brothers and Eberstadt people concurred in that judgment. There was another thing almost everyone, including Dickinson, agreed on: One way to maximize the leverage of the Dickinson stock would be to seek a merger or business configuration that would result in a change of management.

Eberstadt's Robert Zeller, of course, had been pursuing that prospect for the better part of a year and a half, and now Fairleigh Dickinson decided to bring Salomon Brothers into the quest, too. Zeller had no trouble agreeing to throw in with Salomon. "Fifty percent of something," he pragmatically told Salomon Brothers' John Gutfreund, "is better than a hundred percent of nothing." The bankers' first move was an attempt to breathe new life into the talks with Avon that had been sidetracked by the National Medical Care imbroglio.

Word that the Dickinson stock was being shopped got back to Howe and Asnes very quickly this time. Hazard Gillespie, a former U.S. Attorney who from time to time did some work for B,D, also represented the investment banking firm of Morgan, Stanley & Company. Morgan Stanley, in turn, represented Avon Products. Avon wanted a favorable reaction from B,D's management and no part of an unfriendly deal.

In the next couple of weeks or so, Zeller and Lipper approached Bristol-Myers and Pepsico with no success. And not long after that, Dickinson himself sounded out American Home Products Corporation. Word of that move got back to Howe and Asnes in the form of a direct approach from William Laporte, chairman of the Manhattan-based pharmaceuticals producer. Dickinson had suggested to Laporte that a combination of the two companies would require a change in top management at B,D. Anxiety rolled over B,D like gunsmoke. Dickinson was still a director, but his removal as chairman had shattered a cozy paternalistic cocoon and left B,D employees vulnerable to every kind of rumor. There was a great deal of worry, for example, that with Dickinson out, production—and jobs—at the East Rutherford plant would be cut back sharply.

Old loyalties were frayed to the breaking point. Henry Supplee, long B,D's general counsel, was one of those caught in the middle. As general counsel, Supplee was management's in-house lawyer. Asnes complained that every time he wanted to talk to Supplee about something confidential, the message would immediately get "back to others, including Mr. Dickinson." In the end, Supplee was forced to resign.

On his side, Dickinson had unearthed an employee who insisted that Wesley Howe was to blame for a serious outbreak of mercury poisoning at one of B,D's plants in Puerto Rico. Dickinson saw that the story was circulated among the outside directors, even though Paul Stillman dismissed it as "company gossip, for the most part, of a dissatisfied individual."

The atmosphere was so polarized that Dickinson's movements during working hours were under almost constant surveillance by an underground volunteer network headed by Howe's secretary, Mrs. Dorothy Matonti.

Outspoken in her own loyalties, petite, carefully turned out Dottie Matonti had started at B,D in 1949 as a factory worker, thinking she would stay no more than three months. Thanks to her quick intelligence, Mrs. Matonti was soon moved into the office, where the first person she worked for was Wesley Howe. She moved up through the ranks with Howe, and now, as his $19,800-a-year executive secretary, saw in the struggle with Fairleigh Dickinson "a plot possibly to destroy or damage management, the company that I love and worked so hard for."

Dottie Matonti was plugged into an intelligence network that included Fairleigh Dickinson's driver, the secretary to his executive assistant, and other secretaries in the hierarchy. The network was helped by the configuration of B,D's executive suite. Howe and Dickinson shared a common office wall. Dottie Matonti sat at a desk about three feet from the door of Wesley Howe's office—a position from which she had no difficulty making notes on what Adele Piela, Dickinson's long-time executive assistant, said over the phone in her customary "very clear, loud, penetrating, shrill voice." Soon, Howe was getting a steady flow of memos that wound up under lock and key in the credenza in his office—the so-called "Spy File." Howe didn't encourage Dottie Matonti's intelligence gathering, but he didn't discourage it, either. Much of what his secretary was picking up gave him useful assessments on the disposition of the enemy forces.

At one point, for example, Matonti reported that "Adele has been working desperately for a week or more in trying to get a group together for a meeting at Salomon Brothers. I believe she has not been able to get everyone she has been after. At this point, I know of FSD, CCE [Edwards], Bill Salomon and, I think, Jerry Lipper. . . ."

At another point Matonti reported on a phone conversation between Dickinson and his executive assistant. "Bob McCable of Lehman Brothers called," the Matonti memo said. "He had a more specific request from Colgate-Palmolive to take up with FSD re merger. The request comes from top management of Colgate. . . ."

As the odds-on prospect that the chairman's peripatetic

investment bankers would come up with a workable deal grew, Dickinson appeared to be bent on a flat-out rule-or-ruin strategy. There were at least two offers to buy out Howe with a million-dollar settlement. His replacement would be the formerly *non grata* person of Marvin Asnes. Dickinson would come back as chairman, and he and Asnes would share in the picking of a new board. If there was no compromise, Asnes would find himself facing the anvil and hammer of a takeover.

Howe and Asnes weren't intimidated. The stalemate settled into a war of attrition. Paul Stillman and the other three outside directors resigned en masse in the hope that the demonstration might somehow provoke intervention by the Securities and Exchange Commission. It didn't. There was no real movement until lightning struck in the form of the Sun Company.

It was a bad time for Fairleigh Dickinson. Even Kenneth Lipper was complaining about his mercurial personality. Lipper described the honorary chairman as such an unpredictable person that he could not be sure whether Dickinson really wanted to sell his stock "on the basis of price or anything else."

Dickinson was under severe stress. By mid-December it was clear that Sun was seriously interested in B,D, and Kenneth Lipper had set December 21 as the date for a dinner meeting at his Park Avenue apartment between Dickinson and the Sun people. That was a day after Henry Becton told Dickinson that management had dropped him as a nominee for director at the upcoming annual meeting. By two P.M. on the 21st, Dickinson had been admitted to Columbia Presbyterian Hospital in New York City. He was home for Christmas Eve, and rushed back to the hospital on Christmas Day for a stay that lasted five weeks. He was apparently being treated for some sort of difficulty with his central nervous system. Dickinson recalls being "under heavy sedation" from Christmas Day until January 10. By January 14, though, he felt well enough to listen to Zeller and Ken Lipper detail the Sun offer. Dickinson remembers being "quite tense" in his hospital room on that snowy Saturday in mid-January when he made the fateful decision to sell out.

3

The Runaway Acquisitive Itch

Sun's acquisitive itch is in a long and hallowed tradition. The nation's industrial landscape has been reshaped by a series of major merger waves. Consolidations were a dime a dozen during the Great Bull Market of the twenties, for example, and their speculative quality was nicely summed up in one of the semi-ironic wheezes of the day: "We'll merge Worthington Pump with International Nickel and call it Pump 'n Nickel." The big acquisition binge of the sixties, fueled by indulgent accounting practices and rising stock prices, generated a certain amount of cynicism on the Street, too. Conglomerates, in search of the supposed "synergism" to be found in a blend of unrelated businesses (the old "two plus two equals five" syndrome), were buying up everything in sight with bundles of highly inflated stock and debentures known variously as "Chinese trading stamps" and "Castro Convertibles."

[66]

In the mid-seventies, the takeover game began to take on new and significant aspects. There were fewer deals for stock, and many more for cash or some two-step combination of the two. Many of them were very big indeed—Shell Oil's $3.6 billion buyout of Belridge Oil; Kraft, Inc.'s $2.4 billion purchase of Dart Industries; Fluor Corporation's $2.7 billion bid for St. Joe Minerals Corporation; RCA's $1.35 billion acquisition of C.I.T.; and Exxon's $1.17 billion purchase of Reliance Electric. Those deals, huge as they were, turned out to be mere curtain raisers for the record-breaking $8-billion plus poker game in which Du Pont Co., Seagram Co. and Mobil Corporation bid one another up in the struggle for control of Conoco, Inc. The way the game is going, bids of $100 million or less have become penny ante stuff. And it's not just the money. As the blue-chip cast of those names suggests, the quality of the players has changed markedly. The character of The Game has changed markedly, too. There are many more hostile deals—or at least deals that start out that way. As recently as five years ago, the unfriendly takeover was perceived as pretty much infra dig—all right for on-the-make conglomerators, maybe, but not a done thing for such outfits as the Sun Company and others in the Olympian reaches of the top 500 corporations. As attorney Joseph Flom put it, "The game gets more respectable every day."

The level of play has taken on Darwinian proportions. Rather than run the risk of being acquired themselves, many corporations have gone out on defensive buying sprees of their own. Still others have escaped predators by merging into friendly hands. For example, William H.

Spoor, president of the Pillsbury Company, has told friends he snapped up the Green Giant Company as a kind of insurance policy against raids on his own company. "We were on every hit list in town," he said. C.I.T., loaded with cash from the sale of a couple of major subsidiaries, also sensed some movement in the underbrush. Unhappy with the prospect of being forced to grapple with some unknown, it scrapped a defensive takeover program of its own and fell gratefully into the warm embrace of RCA.

Another new ingredient in the mix is the high frequency of competing bids. Once a target company turns down an offer, there's blood in the water and the sharks begin to gather. The high stakes auction for Conoco, for example, the nation's ninth largest oil company and its second largest coal producer, started with a seemingly improbable bid from Dome Petroleum, Ltd. Dome wanted only 20 percent of Conoco and offered $65 a share at a time when the stock was selling for just under $50 a share. Conoco's assets were valued at around $138 a share, and the company's directors turned down the offer almost as a matter of course. No one was more surprised than Conoco's board when the Dome bid drew more than half the company's outstanding shares. Dome subsequently swapped the stock, plus $245 million in cash, for its real and somewhat more limited target—Conoco's majority interest in a Canadian concern, Hudson's Bay Oil & Gas Co. The unexpected success of the Dome strike demonstrated that Conoco and its rich reserves could be had. Du Pont, Seagram and Mobil were more than happy to make the effort at escalating prices of better than $85 a share that proved to be a bonanza to Conoco shareholders. Or take the case of ERC Corporation, a $1.4 billion insurance holding company. The first pass was made by another major factor in the insurance trade, Connecticut General, at $80 a share. When ERC rejected that offer, Connecticut General raised the bid to $90. A competing bid by the Charter Company was withdrawn, but with pressure for some kind of deal building from within (four major stockholders wanted out at a profit), ERC finally ran up the white flag. The price of its surrender? A plump $97 a share—a total of $540 million. ERC's sole owner and proprietor is now Getty Oil Company, a major integrated producer that has been diversifying into financial services and was a surprise entry in the fight.

Then there was also the epic five-week-long bidding battle between McDermott and Wheelabrator-Frye for control of one of the oldest names in rail cars, Pullman. McDermott, the New Orleans–based offshore-platform producer, which had earlier won a hot two-way fight with United Technologies for control of Babcock & Wilcox, opened the chase for Pullman with an unlikely low bid of $28 a share. Wheelabrator, in hot pursuit of a company three times its size, raised the ante to $43 a share, topped McDermott's counteroffer of $43.50 a share with a bid of $52.50 a share and won out in the end despite an even higher offer from McDermott at a cost of almost $600 million. Wheelabrator, which produces energy and environmental systems, is a good example of how manic the level of play has become. It had earlier set its cap for Huyck Corporation, a Wake Forest, North Carolina, maker of felts and fabrics, only to have a $127 million offer topped by the American subsidiary of BTR, a British holding company. Huyck, in turn, had put itself on the block in the hope of escaping the clutches of Victor Posner, the Miami-based entrepreneur widely regarded as one of The Game's most contentious practitioners.

Competition, in fact, has become the name of The Game. Behind every offer and counteroffer there is a set of strategists much like those who engineered the midnight raid on B,D—lawyers like Martin Lipton, traders like Richard Rosenthal, deal-makers like Kenneth Lipper. There are probably no more than a hundred such specialists in the Street. Though often on different sides of a deal, many of them are good friends. Martin Lipton and Joseph Flom, for example, though pitted against one another in many situations besides the Sun–B,D battle, usually lunch together at least once a week. When the RCA–C.I.T. deal broke down in the early stages of negotiations, the two investment bankers involved—Nicholas Brady of Dillon, Read & Company and Felix Rohatyn of Lazard Frères— met by chance at a dinner party and helped get the proposal back on the track.

The social lubricants help to take some of the stress out of what is basically a young man's game. Stephen Friedman, for example, Goldman, Sachs & Company's top acquisition man, is in his early forties. Robert F. Greenhill, co-manager of Morgan Stanley & Company's investment banking division, is in his mid-forties. Friedman is a former national AAU wrestling champion; his counterpart at Morgan Stanley crewed at Yale and his idea of a vacation runs to month-long canoe trips north of the Arctic Circle.

There is a lot of machismo in the game. The objective is to panic the opposition into selling at the lowest possible price. The defense calls for delay and counterattack—all aimed at beating off the raider, or at least exacting a higher price. "You have to keep escalating the pressure," said Felix Rohatyn. "The pressure is unbelievable," said Steve Friedman. "It's like being a platoon leader on a beachhead." "It's just like being in combat," said Richard Cheney, a vice-chairman of Hill & Knowlton, who coined the term "Saturday Night Special" to describe the quick weekend strike once favored by takeover strategists.

With mind sets like that, it's no surprise that the buzzwords of the war room have infiltrated the argot of The Game. Target companies are often given code names to preserve secrecy; many executives keep under lock and key the "black book" that details the defensive strategies they are to follow in the case of an attack; a "white knight" is a friendly second bidder brought into play, while "shark repellent"—bylaws that make it harder to get control of a board and require "supermajority" shareholder approval of mergers—has become a standard ploy to discourage aggression.

Aggression these days more and more takes the form of a tender offer—a bid made over the heads of often-protesting management directly to shareholders. There are two advantages to that strategy. Tender offers are quicker and cheaper to mount than outright proxy fights. As Joseph Flom notes, "You don't have to go through a slugging match to find out where you are. You pretty much know how you're doing within a matter of days." From the technicians' side, big fees such as the $350,000 Salomon Brothers stood to pick up on the B,D deal add spice to the appeal of the game. The premiums the merger and acquisition professionals build into tender offers—sometimes as much as 100 percent over market—have proved irresistible to shareholders, too. Becton, Dickinson, for example, hadn't traded as high as $45 a share in six years. It was much the same with the $65 a share in cash and preferred stock RCA paid for C.I.T. The finance company hadn't sold anywhere near that price for more than a decade. Small wonder that any company hit by a tender offer, according to Martin Lipton, has no better than a 15 percent to 20 percent chance of escape.

To the extent it helps investors cash in on their holdings, The Game creates wealth—a worthy capitalistic end. The high attrition rate among target companies, though, raises some tough socio-economic questions. The concentration of ownership in American business is seemingly already very high. Federal Trade Commission estimates, for instance, indicate that the nation's two hundred biggest manufacturing concerns have increased their slice of U.S. industry from 45 percent at the end of World War II to better than 60 percent today. And it's no longer a case of smaller companies—suppliers, for example—disappearing into the maw of a behemoth. The behemoths are going, too. Over the last twenty-five years, more than 125 of Fortune's top 500 corporations have been merged out of existence.

Does that mean takeovers are sounding the death knell of competition? Not really. Too much significance can be read into the FTC figures. Much of the increased concentration the government agency reports has come in older, capital-intensive industries such as steel and autos—proof enough that size isn't everything. It certainly hasn't protected U.S. Steel and General Motors from the competitive onslaught of such highly efficient producers as the Japanese. And in high-technology products, such as computers and word processors, where brains are as important an asset as capital, even mighty IBM is being given a run for its money by such fast-growing competitors as Amdahl Corporation and the Harris Group. Corporate power in the United States is considerably more diffuse than the FTC numbers suggest. There are, for example, more than a thousand public companies with annual sales of over $350 million, and the rate of growth among companies with sales of less than $50 million is little short of phenomenal.

Much of that growth, inevitably, has come from acquisition. Becton, Dickinson's own history is a good example of the pattern. Few companies have remained independent over the long haul. They have either acquired, or been acquired. As William T. Comfort, chairman of Citicorp Venture Capital, one of the nation's most aggressive small business investment companies, puts it: "Most companies are agglomerations of other companies. As long as you have marketplaces like ours that allow the continual creation of smaller companies," Comfort told *Forbes*, "periodic sellouts of small companies to big companies are just natural evolution." In that respect, American business has always been predatory. The new takeover techniques have unquestionably made business even more so. The unhappy side effects can be seen in distorted capital flows and big-ticket acquisitions that just don't work. That doesn't mean that takeovers as such are bad. They have simply accelerated a trend toward conglomerate diversification—the result of an increasingly complex economy that

[73]

leaps traditional industry boundaries and has made much antitrust law a burdensome anachronism.

There are securities laws, of course, and they have been gradually tightened as the stakes and tempo of The Game escalated. Prior to 1968 and enactment of the Williams Act—named after its sponsor, New Jersey Senator Harrison Williams—the "Saturday Night Special" ruled supreme. Public relations man Richard Cheney, in a dazzling epiphany, invented the term to describe the surprise raid made on one of his clients by that famed old producer of revolvers, Colt Manufacturing Company. Many such raids were sprung over weekends, when management would be hard put to rally its forces—dragging rattled lawyers back from vacations on the Costa Brava, searching the slopes for executive vice-presidents off on skiing trips. Many tender offers, in fact, and for much the same reasons, are still timed to burst on late Thursday or Friday afternoon after the close of the market.

In its heyday, the Saturday Night Special was a truly formidable weapon. All the momentum was with the bidder, who did not even have to disclose who he was, let alone reveal where the money for the offer was coming from or what he intended to do with the target if he got control. The offer was almost invariably on a first come, first served basis, with no right of withdrawal, good for a limited time only. The first news the target management got of the strike was often contained in advertisements in the *New York Times* and the *Wall Street Journal* announcing the bid. The ensuing stampede to the cash-in window gave stockholders little room (or information) on which to make investment decisions, and management almost no

[74]

chance to get its side of the story across. The Williams Act attempted to redress the balance by pinning some common-sense disclosure requirements on the bidder. Thus, under Section 14(d) of the Act, when the bidder opens a tender, he has to file with both the Securities & Exchange Commission and the target a statement on such details as the terms of the offer, his background, the source of his cash, and his plans for the company—merger or liquidation, for example—if there is a takeover. Section 13(d) demands the same information within ten days from anyone who acquires more than 5 percent of a company. The law mandates a minimum offering period of twenty business days and gives people who tender their stock fifteen days to change their minds. The law also requires pro-rata acceptance if the bid is for a limited number of shares rather than for all of the outstanding stock. The objective was not to outlaw takeovers, but to make the rules of combat a little more civilized and to give the SEC a chance to become a somewhat more effective referee. The potential economic impact of tender offers was tucked into the ambit of the Hart-Scott-Rodino Act, which requires the bidder to file a notice with both the antitrust division of the Justice Department and the Federal Trade Commission. The law gives the government fifteen days to dig into the competitive aspects of a takeover, with the option of a ten-day extension if more time is needed to develop a preliminary case. The bidder can go ahead with the tender during that period, but cannot formally acquire the shares until the regulatory clock runs out.

Charges of fraud or some other illegal outrage aimed at bringing the SEC into action are among the standard defenses against takeover. So are allegations that the antitrust laws would be breached by a combination of the two companies. The first objective of the defense is to buy time—time to unearth a more friendly, higher-bidding white knight; time to scrape together enough information for what might prove to be a knockout blow in the courts. Time is such a vital commodity in The Game that thirty-six states have adopted laws requiring bidders to give their targets more notice—in most cases, substantially more notice—than the Williams Act demands. The state laws, though, are under heavy constitutional attack as a burden on interstate commerce and, like most constraints on The Game, have done little to deter the takeover engineers. As attorney Martin Lipton notes, "Takeovers and successful defenses of takeover raids are accomplished by those who have the courage to innovate and be aggressive."

No one, however aggressive or innovative, operates in a vacuum. The climate has never been better for takeovers. The stock market just hasn't been reflecting the rising curve of industry profits. B,D is a good example of that lag. At its 1970 bull market high of 62 the company was earning $1.08 a share. By the time it had caught Sun's fancy, B,D was selling at 33, while profits had more than doubled to $2.45 a share. Thanks to the long bear market of the seventies, stocks had become a bargain. Many companies were trading at prices well below replacement value, a plight that left them extremely vulnerable to well-heeled corporate bargain-hunters.

The Woolworth Company of five-and-dime fame is one example of the acquisition values that have been popping up on the merger and acquisition computer runs. The chain is much more than a jumble of low-end department stores. Its Kinney Shoe outlets are a money machine that ring up more than one-third of the company's profits. Woolworth's international division (Canada, West Germany, Mexico, and Spain) does extremely well, too. Taking all its assets together, including a lot of prime real estate that has been on the books for years at low, low depression prices, Woolworth would be worth a rock-bottom minimum of $41 a share if it were to liquidate tomorrow, lock, stock, and barrel. The stock was trading at $26 when Brascan, a Canadian holding company, made a $35-a-share initial bid that Woolworth beat off after seven weeks of stormy litigation.

Values like that are hard to resist, especially for companies like Sun, loaded with cash and powered by a hyperthyroid drive for diversification. As Sun chairman Robert Sharbaugh noted, it's always faster, cheaper, and less risky to buy into a going business than to start one from the ground up. As the Sun executive explained the rationale, "We would be putting fresh inflated today's dollars in to build from scratch and it would make better sense to acquire a going interest rather than start from scratch." The pickings have been particularly enticing for foreign buyers, who through much of the last decade have had the double whammy of cheap stocks *and* cheap dollars working for them. The sweetness of the arithmetic helps to explain the willingness of Grand Metropolitan, a British conglomerate, to tough out a $570 million bidding match with Standard Brands for control of the Liggett Group, one of the biggest distributors of its J & B Scotch in the United States; and the $615 million Great Britain's Imperial

Group, the world's largest tobacco company, laid out for the Howard Johnson motel and restaurant chain.

The virtues of diversification, even into the comparatively more hospitable economic climate of the United States from abroad, can be oversung. Behind the customary rhetoric of how well two companies "fit," there is usually the hard, irreducible diamond of financial advantage. Yes, Becton, Dickinson was one way—certainly the fastest way—for Sun to tap into the growth potential of the health-care field. But there is little incentive for any businessman to make a move that doesn't show an immediate improvement in reported earnings. Hence Robert Sharbaugh's insistence on acquiring a minimum of 20 percent of B,D's stock, with the concomitant right to include a corresponding proportion of the medical instrument producer's profits in Sun's own statement through so-called equity accounting. The 34 percent stranglehold it succeeded in clamping on B,D increased Sun's primary earnings from $6.78 to $6.83 a share. Sharbaugh's original target of at least 25 percent was shaped by the worry that B,D might be able to do something nasty that would dilute Sun's equity below the all-important 20 percent benchmark.

Accounting gimmicks of one kind or another have pumped oxygen into the flames of every merger blaze, including this one. In the conglomerate burst of the sixties, it was the "pooling" of earnings, which permitted companies to combine their profits statements as if they'd always been one. The accountants tightened up on that one, but other quite legitimate—if somewhat misleading—ploys like equity accounting are still very much in evidence. The bookkeeping conventions have made it easier for gung-ho managers to wring the instant gratification of higher reported earnings from onslaughts like the Sun move on B,D.

B,D was in many respects a classic takeover victim, as Richard Rosenthal quickly perceived when he totted up the big chunk of the company's stock held by institutions. While individuals have been net sellers of common stocks for years now, the balance of ownership has tipped in the direction of the institutional investors. The flood tide of new money pouring into pension funds, for example, has pushed them deeper and deeper into equity ownership. Many companies like Becton, Dickinson, because of their quality and growth prospects, are heavily owned by institutions—and likely to become more so. Thus, along with the sick stock market, the huge cash flow of such restless, venturesome companies as Sun, and the vagaries of accounting principles, the phenomenon of spreading institutional ownership has had its effect on the lushness of the takeover climate. The phenomenon has made life simpler for such technicians as Richard Rosenthal by making it easier to locate big blocks of stock. The strategy is simple. At a high enough price, the fiduciaries who run individual investment advisory accounts, trust funds, pension funds, and mutual funds have no alternative except to sell.

Trustees of every description are under a heavy charge to exercise "prudence" in handling the assets entrusted to them. A bad judgment call—or the slightest hint of conflict—leaves them open to the threat of personal liability suits. The prospect of having to dig deep into one's

[79]

personal pockets to salve some irate beneficiary's wounds, like the prospect of hanging, wonderfully concentrates the mind. Thus, in practice, when a bid comes along, fiduciaries really do not have much latitude. No one understands that better than the takeover strategists.

The new wrinkle of pressuring the fiduciaries is one more example of how flexible takeover tactics have become. The tactic cuts against the grain of the old doctrine that companies with sizable family and/or wide-spread institutional holdings are tamper-proof. B,D (and a number of firms in somewhat similar situations) illustrates that is no longer the case. Fuqua Industries, for example, tried to make hay out of a family falling-out at Hoover Company, the venerable vacuum cleaner manufacturer; and American Express Company's abortive reach for McGraw-Hill seems to have been prompted in part by the hope that dissident-seeming family guns could be turned on the then-reigning CEO, Harold McGraw, Jr. Philip Morris successfully turned a divided family situation to good advantage in its takeover of 7UP.

The conventional wisdom used to be that "if you had a third of the stock, you were invulnerable," said Morton Siegel, head of Kidder Peabody's merger and acquisition department. "Then it was forty-five percent, but that was before 7UP," continued Siegel. "Now it's got to the point where everybody is vulnerable, except if he's one guy who owns fifty-one percent of the stock and isn't a fiduciary." That might have been just about the only set of circumstances under which Sun would not have taken on B,D.

4

Bear Hugs and Other Offensive Moves

It was early Tuesday now—7:30 A.M.—and Horace Kephart, Sun's man in New York, was on the phone to Theodore Burtis at headquarters back in Radnor, Pennsylvania. Amid all of the celebratory banter at the Rosenthal dinner at "21" the night before, there had been serious talk about what came next. The logistics were formidable. Two-man teams—one operative each from Sun and Martin Lipton's law firm—would call in person on each of the more than thirty institutional investors who had agreed to sell B,D. The institutions were scattered all over the country from Massachusetts to California. Sun was taking no chances on how quickly B,D would respond once word of the Midnight Raid was out. The sale was conditioned on Sun's picking up signed stock certificates and endorsed proxies against payment by cash or note. At the moment,

Sun had nothing formal in hand, and nothing in writing. Some sellers, in fact—the big T. Rowe Price mutual fund group, for one—were still very much up in the air. Working under the gun the day before, the investment advisory firm just hadn't had enough time to get approval on the sale from all of the individual in-house money managers that had to be consulted on the accounts they serviced. That was going to take time. Kephart laid out the details for Burtis. One Sun Executive, for example—Bill Maling—was ticketed to make stops in Minneapolis and Milwaukee before flying on to San Francisco. Even at the rate Maling was moving, the trek was at least an overnighter.

For Burtis' benefit, Kephart recapitulated all the "lawyer talk" of the night before. He and two other Sun people— lawyer Howard Blum and financial man Jack Neafsey—had discussed the problem with one of Martin Lipton's partners, James H. Fogelson. The key question was what, if anything, should be disclosed to the New York Stock Exchange. Fogelson had argued that the Big Board should be called before the opening and asked to suspend trading in B,D until Sun had enough information on the number of shares it had bought to file the required form 13(d) announcing the purchase. So many institutions had been solicited, Fogelson argued, there were bound to be rumors. Uninformed investors might be tempted to sell into a run-up that could carry B,D common from the last previous trade of $33 all the way up to Sun's $45-a-share purchase price and perhaps beyond. Blum didn't like the suggestion and as Sun's inside expert on mergers, his voice carried weight. The Big Board, Blum insisted, would alert B,D to the purchase and the fat would be in the fire. Fogelson wore him down. In the end, Blum agreed the Exchange should be asked to shut down B,D, but with one very important restriction: Sun's name was not to be revealed. That was the bottom line that Kephart gave Burtis in this early-morning phone call. Sun was so worried about a B,D counterattack that one of the first items on the checklist this Tuesday morning was to assign litigation teams to the courthouse where they would get to work immediately on trying to quash any B,D response. Burtis wanted no press releases, either, for the moment, and while calling the Exchange was all right, he agreed with Blum: no names.

With that ratification, Kephart instructed Fogelson to deal with the Big Board and settled down to work himself. He still had to confirm the oral agreements made with several major individual sellers—Fairleigh Dickinson and his daughter, for example—and there was all the institutional stuff hanging fire, too. The impact of the Midnight Raid was still eddying around the country. The T. Rowe Price group, for example, not quite sure exactly how much B,D it owned, had asked to be guaranteed payment against the delivery of around 800,000 shares. Promptly at 9:00 A.M. this Tuesday about twenty investment advisors— eight different teams representing the various Price funds and individual accounts—gathered in the organization's New York and Baltimore offices and listened as Howard P. Colhoun, a vice-president, explained the Sun offer on a two-way telephone hookup. There were so many people at the meeting in Baltimore that Colhoun can't quite remember all those who were there. "It was a sea of faces," he said. Colhoun told his managers to figure out what they wanted to do and to get back to him. Not until noon— some three hours later—was Colhoun in a position to call

Kephart and tell him he could count on the Rowe Price group for 740,000 shares of B,D. There were similar pockets of uncertainty in Hartford, Boston, and New York, and what Martin Lipton called "tremendous confusion" over the exact number of shares Sun would be able to harvest.

Further, though messengers were being moved around like pawns on a chessboard—Bill Maling arrived in San Francisco carrying a now-redundant pair of galoshes that had proved very comforting in Milwaukee—the collection system was overwhelmed by "mechanical difficulties." Martin Lipton recalled Salomon Brothers' registering "great unhappiness" at the shortage of manpower at his firm. Though Kephart's tally showed that Sun had commitments on 34 percent of B,D, James Fogelson was "personally not confident that was indeed the fact. "I was not confident at all," he said, "as to the number of shares with respect to which commitments had been entered into."

None of that detail was mentioned when Fogelson called Richard Grasso, a Big Board vice-president, and announced he represented an unidentified company that would be making a Williams Act filing on B,D "by approximately noon the next day." Fogelson recalls having suggested to Grasso "that the Exchange consider not opening the market in B,D because I anticipated there would be rumors as to various matters which would adversely affect trading." Fogelson argued it "would be in the public interest not to trade the stock until accurate information with respect to the Williams Act filing was made publicly available."

Grasso told Fogelson he needed more information— Who was the client? What was the filing going to say?

When Fogelson declined to answer those questions, Grasso told him flatly the stock could not be shut down on the basis of what had been revealed so far. The Exchange, though, is sensitive to wide, unexplained price swings. Such erraticism clashes with the image of solid, blue-serge capitalism it tries to project, and tends to reinforce the kind of investor suspicion the Exchange has been trying to cauterize ever since the Great Crash—i.e., when there are profits to be made out of rumors, members of the Exchange always seem to have them first. Thus, the Big Board's tendency is to play it safe. Fogelson knew that, and reached for reinforcement. After the turndown from Grasso, he immediately dialed Richard Rosenthal and told him what had happened.

Rosenthal was alarmed. He said he'd just been on the phone with a Salomon Brothers salesman who had been talking to a client who sounded awfully well informed. The client, Rosenthal told Fogelson, wanted to sell some B,D stock to Salomon "because he had heard a private transaction had taken place the night before." Fogelson quickly called Grasso back, told him there "might be rumors circulating in the market," and suggested the Exchange executive could call Rosenthal if he wanted to check things out. Grasso did so. Rosenthal "very strongly seconded the request by the attorneys" that trading be halted. "We felt that some people were aware of certains facts that would have meaningful impact on the price of B,D," he added. Rosenthal conceded some of those people could have been other Salomon employes not directly engaged in the Midnight Raid. Much of the final planning, of course, had been done within sight and sound of the investment bankers' busy trading floor. Precisely who knew what—and was circulating what—didn't matter too much to Grasso. Time was beginning to run out; the market opening was almost on him. The fact was that Rosenthal, one of the canniest traders on the Street and a partner in a major member firm, had warned that investors might "get the hell banged out of them" if B,D wasn't shut down.

Grasso tried without success to get more information out of Rosenthal, who noted only that "he and his senior partners [the highly respected John Gutfreund and William Salomon] were staking their credibility" on the fact that a "material development" involving B,D would be announced. That was a considerable amount of membership weight for a paid Exchange employee to match his judgment against. Grasso checked with a floor governor, who reported "unusual interest" in the crowd at the B,D trading post. Grasso recommended that the stock be shut down, and at 10:40 the official word moved over the tape. Trading in B,D had been halted, "news pending . . ."

James Fogelson later argued with some heat that for Sun to have made any disclosure at that point would have been "misleading." Even a press release simply describing what it had done—and was in the process of doing—might have been "misinterpreted by the SEC, among other people, as an attempt to solicit additional shares." Perhaps. But to the degree it kept Joseph Flom and Wesley Howe in the dark and immobilized B,D's defenses, Sun's silence was truly golden.

It was again snowing heavily now, and the blizzard had put a crimp in Sun's collection efforts. By 10 P.M. that Tuesday, Horace Kephart had in hand only about 2 million of the 6 million shares he hoped to buy. As long as the market was shut down, the institutions had nowhere else to sell their stock. Kephart didn't have to worry about the price running away on him; nor did he have to worry about the prospect of a competing bid from a White Knight. Best of all, he knew there was a good chance the lightning bolt of litigation expected from B,D would be stayed until Sun had all the institutional stock firmly in its grasp. Was shutting down the market an important element in Sun's strategy?

The market reaction had been discussed at perhaps a half-dozen brain-storming sessions over a period of several weeks. One of the givens was the combativeness of Wesley Howe and Marvin Asnes. As Martin Lipton saw it, Sun's strategy had to be shaped in the context of "a management that was determined to protect itself regardless of the interest of the shareholders or anybody else." That put a premium on speed and stealth. Sun wanted to get off the mark at the cheapest price it could, with the lowest possible risk of getting tied up in the courts while it had money on the table. There would be no talking to B,D management until after the blow fell. A straight tender offer was out of the question for several reasons. Any warning at all would give management time to mobilize, and almost certainly mean that Sun would have to pay up to meet a competing bid. The arithmetic, though, was beguiling: Kenneth Lipper and Robert Zeller from the very beginning had seen there was a good chance of putting together at least a 20 percent block by combining the Dickinson stock and allied individual holdings with whatever could be shaken loose from institutional investors. Maybe the package could be enriched by purchases in the open market. What was the best way to go?

As Robert Sharbaugh remembered it, Salomon Brothers'

[87]

initial proposal was to contact a limited number of institutions first in a move that might net about 15 percent of B,D's outstanding, take in another 13 percent from the individuals, file the requisite acknowledgement of the purchases with the SEC, and then go into the open market for perhaps another 6 percent or so.

Going into the market *after* paying a sizable premium to take out the institutions and individuals, though, could get very expensive. And going into the market beforehand in any volume might tip Marvin Krasnansky and the other wary tape watchers at B,D that something was up. The refinements were war-gamed in terms of three variables— the time it would take to get control, the risk of discovery, and price. The final decision was to solicit the individuals first on the ground that they would be less likely to leak the deal. "Institutions," said Robert Sharbaugh, "have frequent and regular communications." Hence "there was more of a risk that word would leak and there would be an injunction or a request for a hearing, and you'd get hung up while the deal was still in the making." Among the many potential legal complications was the question of whether the purchase, as structured, amounted to a tender offer requiring under the Williams Act immediate notification to the SEC, the Exchange, and B,D.

Not as Martin Lipton interpreted it. First of all, because the SEC preferred to regulate on a case-by-case basis rather than by statutory fiat, there was no flat definition of exactly what constituted a tender offer. And as Lipton read it, all of the case law seemed to exempt "private transactions" between sophisticated buyers and sellers from the early warning stictures of the Williams Act. Sun would certainly have to file a form 13(d) within ten days of having acquired more than 5 percent of Becton, but not before.

"The basic concept of going to Mr. Dickinson and a number of institutional or sophisticated investors to purchase the stock in a short period of time was something that I specifically focused on," said Lipton. "Specifically, I said it was our firm's opinion that it was perfectly legal, proper, and an appropriate method of accomplishing the acquisition."

As far as anyone could tell, the approach was unique. No one had ever done a deal in quite that way before. There was novelty, too, in Sun's willingness to do an unfriendly deal, when American Home Products and a half-dozen other companies Salomon Brothers tried to interest backed away from the uncompromising hostility of B,D's management. Sun had never done an unfriendly deal before—indeed had never invested in another company without first making sure its presence would be welcome. Sharbaugh was clearly willing to take the heat on this one. B,D was one of the most glittering prospects on a Sun "shopping list," which had been pruned from several hundred candidates to no more than ten really strong possibilities. Kenneth Lipper had underscored the need for a quick decision by telling Horace Kephart that three other companies were also interested in B,D. "Intensive study" had shown that B,D fit all the criteria for the "new legs" Sun needed to become a "multi-legged stool." As Kephart wrote in a proposed checklist to Sun directors on a "major acquisition opportunity," B,D had everything: no antitrust problems, a good growth pattern, a clean balance sheet, a strong market position, and probably could be bought at a "reasonable premium." It had everything, that is, except an acquiescent management.

Sharbaugh expected a fight, but he wasn't worried over the prospect. Things were "unfriendly but manageable." "I am not saying I expected that the management of B,D would look friendly toward Sun for our having purchased thirty-four percent," he noted. "All I am saying is that when we talk about are we willing to do a friendly or unfriendly kind of acquisition, I never put that in the context of what we are doing."

That willingness to do an unfriendly deal is a comparatively new element in the takeover scene—new, at least, for top-rank companies and investment bankers. "Our policy for quite some time had been that we thought hostile takeovers were somehow immoral and probably not very nice things to do, until we really began thinking about it," noted Felix G. Rohatyn, the number-one merger and acquisition man at Lazard, Frères. "Now," he continued, "our policy is that we will work with any one of our clients with respect to the possibility of a hostile takeover, provided we have a high degree of confidence that he can win and that he's not starting something he can't afford."

As Martin Lipton suggests, the trend to hostility springs from one of the elements that has made acquisitions so attractive. Nobody is eager to sell out at the low, low valuations the stock market has been putting on corporate earnings. Few executives worth their salt are anxious to bear some other CEO's choler, of course. Resistance is all part of The Game—sometimes only to exact a higher bid, but often, as in the case of B,D, because the incumbents truly feel they can do better by stockholders than any outsider.

It's hard to find an aggressor who would not rather do a friendly deal than storm the barricades, but approaching a target management olive branch in hand can pose something of a dilemma. For one thing, unfriendly takeovers tend to be rushed and that can be risky. The aggressor may not have access to enough information to get a comprehensive reading on the quality of the operation he is about to buy. In a friendly deal, on the other hand, there is usually enough leisure—and cooperation—for the buyer to get solid, inside answers to all his questions. The bargaining on price, conducted in a non-crisis atmosphere, tends to be more informed, too. Friendly deals by definition also foreclose the appearance of White Knights and the sort of wild-card bidding likely to throw even the most flexible pricing strategies into disarray.

The friendly approach, however, is easy to brush off and sometimes leaves the pacific acquisitor vulnerable to "sandbagging." As Martin Lipton suggests in his *Takeovers & Freezeouts,* the technical bible of the business, talking beforehand can give the target too much of a chance to stall for time. Consider this letter, cited by Lipton, that one slippery target devised to tie up a raider: "The proposals contained in your [communication] of March 28 raise very substantial and difficult financial and business antitrust and other legal issues. We will study these issues and the other questions raised by your [proposal]," the letter continues, "with our investment bankers and legal counsel and we will consult with the various federal and state agencies as required. In this connection, we may ask you to furnish to us detailed information about you and various of your businesses and products and future plans. . . ."

Further, any campaign promises made to the target management in early palaver—long-term employment

[91]

contracts, for example—can be challenged as "bribes." The target, in a calculated burst of candor, might even make a quick public announcement of an approach in the hope of driving the market price of his stock above the raider's offer. Thus, much offensive strategy, like Sun's, tends to lean heavily on speed and surprise. Hit first, talk later is often the doctrine of choice.

When there is talk, the objective is to frighten management into acquiescence. The first step, says Joseph Flom, is "to determine how to get the attention of the target's management, to make sure they are going to focus, that they know you are serious and that no matter what happens, the company is going to go to someone else— either you or another bidder." Raiders not infrequently demonstrate their seriousness by first buying up part of a target and then trying to open a dialogue. An equity tends to give the aggressors more standing. Buying stock in advance of a tender is a good way to test the market, and provides a bit of insurance, too. If the target in the end does go to a higher bidder, the raider at least has the solace of cashing in his chips at a profit. The bigger the equity, the better the chance that the raider will have the target's full and undivided attention. Sun, for one, certainly did not want to get caught in the zany kind of auction that took place a few years ago when Tyco Laboratories made a run at Leeds & Northrup, a producer of electronic instruments and controls. In an effort to dilute Tyco's 22 percent hold, Leeds & Northrup sold 10 percent of itself to Cutler-Hammer. Tyco shrewdly retaliated by selling the 22 percent of Leeds & Northrup it owned to Cutler-Hammer, and then buying up 32 percent of the latter. Cutler—three times Tyco's size—tried to escape that lock by calling on

Koppers Company for help. When 21 percent of Cutler found its way into Koppers' hands, Tyco sold its 32 percent of Cutler to Eaton Corporation. As part of the deal, Eaton agreed to sell Cutler's big block of Leeds & Northrup to Tyco—provided that it, Eaton, got control of Cutler. Cutler thereupon sold its L&N stock to General Signal. When the dust settled, there was a general armistice under which Eaton took over Cutler-Hammer, and General Signal took over L&N. Tyco, which started the whirligig, wound up with a bunch of cash, proving once again that it never hurts to have a piece of the action.

Short of showing that the aggressor is utterly beyond redeeming social value—a subsidiary of Cosa Nostra, Inc., for example—or is acting illegally, the target-company management and directors are bound by their fiduciary responsibilities to at least give the offer a fair assessment. As Joseph Flom says, "When you put the offer on the table, the [target] board has the monkey on its back." The threat of personal liability is a very heavy one. At an Institute for Securities Regulation seminar a while ago, Flom mentioned a case where a director asked him, "What do I have to do on this?"

Flom told the director, "If you believe that the offer is inadequate or if you believe there would be a better time down the road to sell the company, you can reject it."

"Supposing I get sued?" the director asked.

"I'll give you ten to one that you will not suffer any ultimate liability," answered Flom.

"The premium is a hundred million dollars over the market and ten to one odds are not good enough," said the director.

"So there was negotiation," recalled Flom. "The target's

management got the price up and the situation was resolved."

Management's vulnerability to that sort of squeeze has led to the formulation of a variety of "bear hugs." They often evolve out of a casual pass, such as the suggestion for a merger James D. Robinson III, chairman of the American Express Company, made in a telephone call to his then opposite number at McGraw-Hill, Harold W. McGraw, Jr. The courteous, self-effacing McGraw, according to friends, tried to let down Robinson gently with the observation he did not think merger was "appropriate." There was already a link between the companies in the person of then Amexco president, Roger H. Morley, who was also a McGraw-Hill director. There was no mention of price in the phone call, and McGraw regarded it as nothing more than a pass—"completely exploratory." One evening six months later, McGraw discovered Amexco had been doing a lot more exploration than he knew. Robinson and Morley came by McGraw's office for what he at first thought was a purely social visit. That illusion vanished when the two executives began to draw McGraw a picture of how beautiful life could be together, and invited him to share in a joint press release indicating McGraw-Hill was studying the $34-a-share offer Amexco had just made in a "Dear Harold" letter. Putting a price tag on the pass of six months earlier meant the offer would have to be considered by the McGraw-Hill board—by definition a "bear hug." The press release Amexco put out the next day announcing the bid upgraded the tactic into a "strong" bear hug. American Express ultimately got hung up on the barbed wire of a surprisingly strong McGraw-Hill defense, but its offer was artfully constructed to encourage negotiation.

The threat implicit in the bear hug and all-cash opening bid of about $830 million was balanced by the kind of soothing alternative that often leads to a friendly deal: a bid to do 49 percent of the deal in cash, and the balance in a tax-free exchange of securities.

Two-step acquisitions—a combination of cash and stock—are particularly appealing to aggressors who have to watch their pennies. They can be equally appealing to big individual stockholders of the target (members of the McGraw family, for example) who don't like the idea of sharing their capital gains with the IRS. When it comes to competing offers, though, the momentum tends to be with cash. The Liggett Group, for example, spent more than a month fending off a Grand Metropolitan cash offer of $50 a share. It was all set to combine with Standard Brands on a cash and preferred stock package valued at $65 a share when Grand Metropolitan came roaring back with $69 a share in cash and picked up all the marbles. Cash is the great solvent. It is quick, easy to understand, and much to the taste of venturesome *arbitrageurs*, whose participation is a make or break element in most big takeovers.

Almost every offer, in fact, is structured with an eye to getting the arbitrageurs behind it. The professionals hope to make money by picking up stock below the tender price and turning it in to the aggressor at the tender price. The spread between those two prices is the arbitrageur's profit, often sweetened by dealer fees ranging from 1.5 to 2.5 percent of the offer price. Because they are cloaked in fearsome power, the arbitrageurs—there are probably no more than twenty-five of them in the Street—are often damned by corporate stockholder-relations people as the most amoral of opportunists. The arbitrageurs do have an economic function, though, and quite an important one. There is usually no certainty, at least in the early stages, that a deal will go through. Thus, though the market usually rises, the price of the stock rarely goes to the full tender price. The difference between the tender price and the market reflects the degree of uncertainty in the deal. The arbitrageurs provide liquidity by their willingness to buy from those cautious stockholders who would rather take the money and run than hang around only to find that the deal has evaporated. The arbitrageurs work out the price they are willing to pay on a shrewdly formed estimate of how likely the deal is to go through. The bigger the risk, the lower the price they are willing to pay.

The arbitrageur's enthusiasm—or lack of it—is partly a function of the size of the premium the aggressor is offering, and the possibility that a richer competing bid will materialize. A lot of what makes Richard Rosenthal and his buddies run, however, is buried in the fine print of the offer.

From the arbitrageur's point of view, the most satisfactory bid is for "any and all" shares of the target. The alternatives—a bid for a minimum or maximum number of shares—raise the level of risk. If more than the number of shares requested pours in, the arbitrageur faces the unhappy prospect of being "pro-rated." Only a portion of the shares he has scooped up will be accepted. That puts the arbitrageurs in the same boat with other stockholders, of course—not a very attractive proposition for professionals who measure their rewards in terms of the time value of the cash they have invested.

Any adolescent floor clerk of three days' standing at Merrill Lynch knows that you have to stay on the sweet side of the "arbs." Their enormous purchasing power, measured in the millions of shares, puts them at the spearhead of every successful tender. The aggressor's strategy is to jolt as much stock as possible out of the portfolios of individual shareholders, who might have some sentimental attachment to management, into the more clinical hands of arbitrageurs who, in the nature of things, look to the raider for their profits.

The key is setting a premium—sometimes as much as 100 percent over the market—that sets the arbitrageurs' adrenaline to pumping. Like almost everything else in The Game, the business of shaping the premium is more an art than a science. Robert Sharbaugh, for example, bluntly conceded that Sun felt it didn't have "enough knowledge to price Becton, Dickinson right or properly" if the strategic choice had been for an outright tender. "Because of the possibility of competing offers and a bidding contest," the Sun executive continued, "we would have had a damn difficult time establishing a proper price at which the result would have been above twenty-five percent of the company and below forty, forty-five percent, certain."

It helps for the aggressor to lead with a premium that lends itself to easy dramatization. The more dramatic the premium—"one hundred percent over the highest price of the last ten years"—the harder it is for the target to explain the offer away. Still, no aggressor wants to pay more than he has to. In most hostile situations, the strategy is almost always to keep something in reserve for such contingencies as quixotic White Knights. "The question of how much to keep back in a hostile takeover," said Felix Rohatyn, "is a matter of judgment. Should it be five percent, seven

[97]

percent, or ten percent? When we're dealing with sizable companies where the competition is likely to be very limited, we tend to go up to the higher reaches of the range because the possibility is that you might just cut it off right there. Of course, it's other people's money so it always seems somewhat simpler," laughed Felix Rohatyn. Like most merger and acquisition (M & A) professionals, the Lazard Frères partner takes the long view. "If you've picked the right target and it fits with your client and your client has the financial capability of doing it comfortably," he said, "whether you pay five percent more or less really doesn't make any difference in terms of the economics over a decade of a company."

The rising level of premiums and the number of fiercely competitive White Knights entering the jousts suggests a shortage of good target material—and that indeed seems to be the case. Some analysts argue that The Game has a salutary Darwinian effect on industry. In that survival-of-the-fittest scenario, strong managements root out the weak. Maybe, but rare is the aggressor who knowingly buys an out-and-out dog. As the Sun attempt on B,D shows, the emphasis is very much on quality—so long as the price is right.

5

The Peddling of Becton, Dickinson

It was May 10, less than three weeks since Fairleigh
Dickinson had been ousted as chairman, and the Salomon
Brothers–Eberstadt campaign to do a deal with his B,D
stock was in full swing. The talks with Avon Products—
dropped several months earlier when word of B,D's ill-fated
attempt to acquire National Medical Care broke—were
resuscitated, only to be dropped again when Avon shied
from what it diagnosed as an untractably hostile situation.

Now Fairleigh Dickinson himself was on the phone to
William Laporte, the hard bargaining chairman of American Home Products Corporation. Laporte was on a
business swing through the Far East and Dickinson caught
up with him on a stop at the Philippine Plaza Hotel in
Manila. Though the two men are not close, Dickinson had
known Laporte socially for more than thirty years. Ken-

neth Lipper urged Dickinson to use this connection to break the ice. The Salomon Brothers partner had his own shopping list of companies that could fit with B,D, and American Home was high among the possibilities. Along with a hodgepodge of such household familiars as Black Flag, Easy Off, Sani-Flush, Wizard air fresheners, and Woolite, American Home has a sizable position in anti-hypertensives, tranquilizers, oral contraceptives, and other prescription drugs. The product line hints at some kind of marketing compatibility, so Fairleigh Dickinson was reaching out for his old acquaintance, Bill Laporte. He told Laporte how "deeply troubled" he was by the "trend of affairs at Becton, Dickinson." Dickinson also remembered saying that "there had been some discussion about the possibility of affiliating Becton, Dickinson with another company and that American Home [looked like] a logical one." The conversation lasted only three minutes, and Dickinson recalled Laporte as being "noncommittal," but the phone call did what it was supposed to do. It opened the door for Kenneth Lipper, who put a call of his own through to Laporte a half hour later.

The merger and acquisition business is a tight little world. Kenneth Lipper had good connections to Fairleigh Dickinson through his brother Jerome, who has been Dickinson's personal attorney since the late sixties. Jerome had introduced Kenneth to the B,D chairman sometime in the early seventies. Kenneth Lipper was Phi Beta Kappa at Columbia and was graduated from the Harvard Law School in 1965. He'd done graduate work in law and economics at both the University of Paris and New York University with the help of a two-year Ford Foundation grant, added a year in Washington to the résumé, and then joined Lehman Brothers as a partner in corporate finance. He moved on to Salomon in 1975 and it was somewhere around then that Dickinson remembers being introduced. The approach was flattering. Kenneth Lipper, Dickinson recalls, had come to him "for advice as to whether he should stay in finance," or do something in the academic world.

Deferential as he was to Dickinson, a "friend of the firm," Lipper made no effort to hide the fiercely competitive spirit that burns behind his flawless credentials. He defined his mission in elemental terms—"to create interest on the part of major corporations in acquiring B,D"—and felt a certain urgency about the approach to Laporte. "Everything I do," he said, "I would like to do as soon as possible." That was all right with Laporte. Listening over the satellite line from New York, the American Home chairman took a series of detailed notes that filled four sheets of hotel stationery as Kenneth Lipper laid out the arithmetic that Dickinson had touched on in his earlier conversation. Eberstadt and the mutual funds it managed—the Chemical Fund and the Surveyor Fund—controlled about a half-million shares of B,D. That stock, combined with the Dickinson and allied holdings, amounted to about 13 percent of the company. The remaining 17.5 million shares were spread among a mere 813 holders. The numbers suggested that it would not take too much effort to get control of B,D. The stock was selling at a discount and Laporte sensed opportunity. The growth rate in some of his major product lines was slowing. B,D could give AHP entrée to new medical markets that might help to reverse the trend.

[101]

When the American Home chairman got back to New York two weeks later, he and Dickinson met for lunch at one of the favorite executive haunts on the east side, the River Club. Dickinson emphasized again how unhappy he was with B,D management. It would have to go. There was some talk about stock prices, and Dickinson was impressed with the amount of homework Laporte had done on B,D since their phone conversation, particularly on such abstruse items as the level of cash contributions to the pension fund. "I was impressed and interested," recalled Dickinson. The two men parted with an agreement to continue the conversation the next day at Salomon Brothers in the company of Robert Zeller, John Gutfreund, and the rest of the investment banking team.

Kenneth Lipper was doing his homework, too. A couple of hours after the River Club lunch, he, his brother, and Fairleigh Dickinson met for "beer and peanuts" at the Williams Club. Kenneth Lipper didn't want any surprises the next day. The conversation was, Lipper recalled, "mostly a description of Mr. Laporte for my benefit, the type of person he was, Dickinson's college and social relationship with him. It was a short meeting and a tough meeting, and it was basically a discussion of the characteristics of Mr. Laporte."

Things got even tougher the next day. Laporte insisted that he would not accept any merger terms that gave American Home an increase in earnings of less than three cents a share. Kenneth Lipper thought Laporte's position was absurd. So did Eberstadt's Robert Zeller. Zeller remembers telling Laporte that "it was customary in these deals to pay a premium over market and that if he persisted in his three-cents-a-share position, there would be no premium."

Laporte also asked what sort of role Fairleigh Dickinson expected to play in the merged company. He wanted "continuity of management," while Dickinson wanted Howe and Asnes out. Kenneth Lipper repeated an earlier statement that Fairleigh Dickinson was not looking for an "operational role." "As a friend," Lipper continued, Laporte might want to "dignify Dickinson with some kind of honorary post, like a vice-chairman or something like that."

Laporte replied that would be "satisfactory," but countered that he was "really concerned about operational management." The best way to resolve that problem, the AHP chairman argued, would be to approach management directly. "In that way," Laporte continued, "I can get a lower price and also continuity of management, and do a friendly deal."

Zeller and Lipper quickly threw cold water on that idea. "We said that probably wouldn't be successful, that it would be relatively unproductive," recalled Lipper. Salomon from the very beginning had insisted there was no point in stirring up Howe and Asnes, presumably because to do so would only give them more time to reinforce their defenses. Laporte, however, was adamant and—much to the investment banker's distress—equally ungiving on the subject of fees. Laporte is a hard-line devotee of the cheese-paring school of management. At AHP, *Business Week* noted in a recent article, "Penny pinching is cultivated as an art form." Thus, when it was suggested that $2 million would be an "appropriate fee" to have Salomon represent AHP in the proposed takeover, Laporte

[103]

predictably enough "blanched" and allowed as how, at that point, he didn't owe anybody anything.

The bankers tried without very much success to soothe Laporte's exposed pocketbook nerve. As Kenneth Lipper recalled, "We said, 'Look, we are not here for any particular deal. We want to become your investment banker and we will do such a good job that you will pay us whatever you think is fair.'"

Laporte said flatly that he didn't operate that way, that he wanted to have things in writing. When John Gutfreund and Kenneth Lipper said, no, no they'd be happy to work on a handshake, Laporte once again snapped, "I don't do business that way." It was a slur on a deeply felt ethic. Handshake deals are quite common on Wall Street—every time a share of stock is bought or sold, in fact—and William Laporte was about to be given a lesson in deportment. "John got up, and the rest of the delegation got up, and we all walked out," recalled Kenneth Lipper. "It was our definitive way of saying, 'Tough, we don't do business with you, either.'"

Lipper thought Laporte "a very strange man, to say the least." Fairleigh Dickinson was perturbed, too, that so promising a deal might founder on the rocks of anything so mundane as investment banking fees. He agreed to act as middle man for Laporte in a move the bankers just could not derail—a direct approach to B,D management.

Fairleigh Dickinson was charmed to learn that Bill Laporte and Henry Becton had gone to the Collegiate School in Passaic together. That link somehow apparently made it easier for Dickinson to talk to Becton, who had very definitely come down on the management side of the power struggle. Dickinson recalled the conversation as being "very brief—to call it a discussion is to over-dignify it. I just said that Bill Laporte wanted to discuss things with him and I thought he would be hearing from him."

With that third-party introduction, Laporte braced Becton and Wesley Howe directly on the subject of merger. When they gave him the cold shoulder, Dickinson set up meetings for Laporte with several outside directors, including Fairleigh's old friend (and major B,D stockholder), J. H. Fitzgerald Dunning. Laporte followed up that initiative with a modified bear hug in the form of a letter outlining his proposal that was sent to each member of the B,D board. Fairleigh Dickinson again provided an assist by pushing Henry Becton on the question of when the board was going to put the AHP proposition to a vote. On June 22, some six weeks after Fairleigh Dickinson's phone call to Manila, the B,D board did exactly that. The vote came on a resolution that said, "At this time, the board believes the best interest of shareholders . . . would be served by the continuation of this company as an independent enterprise. Accordingly," the resolution continued in a parting shot at Fairleigh Dickinson, "the management and its employees are hereby instructed not to seek or enter into discussions or negotiations with potential acquirers of the company without further action of this board." Dickinson voted against that declaration of independence and Dunning abstained, but Laporte got the message. Shortly thereafter, he formally notified Howe and Becton of his withdrawal from the field.

For all his disenchantment with the investment bankers' fee structure, Laporte did not cut the connection with Salomon Brothers. As the end game was played out, there were continuing talks about the strategy to follow with

B,D's unyielding board. Kenneth Lipper kept trying to persuade Laporte that an outright takeover—either a direct tender, open market purchases, purchases from major holders, or some combination of the three—would not be "classified as a raid, as such." It might be different if AHP had "come out of the blue just to take over this company," Lipper argued, but that really wasn't the case. Laporte would only be "taking one side in what might be considered a family dispute." The act of resolving a family dispute, Lipper continued, "would give a tremendous amount of credibility and acceptance to any offer [Laporte] would make." In the end, it was No Sale. Laporte wasn't sure he could get 100 percent of Becton, and in any event sensed such hostility on management's part that he did not want to take over a smoking ruin.

Lipper's sales talk was all part of The Game. Almost everybody in it talks about the intellectual satisfaction of shaping strategy—and psychology—when there is big money at stake. Salomon Brothers' blueprint for AHP was a classic attempt to panic B,D directors into putting Laporte's proposition to a shareholders' plebescite.

As outlined by Kenneth Lipper, the scenario went like this: There was no doubt B,D would "oppose vigorously" a bid from American Home. "Whatever the fairness of the price, it was often a natural instinct of management not to lose its independence, irrespective of the stockholders' interest." Thanks to the split in the company, however, "some, if not all, of the outside directors could demand that shareholders be permitted to vote on it.

"Hopefully," continued Lipper, "people such as Fairleigh Dickinson, Dunning, or Stillman, or whoever, would come out and demand that shareholders be given a right to vote, if there is a good premium in it, saying it is for shareholders to decide and not entrenched management. It would be particularly potent," added Lipper, "if someone such as Fairleigh Dickinson, whose name is on the door in the name of family, founding family, came forward and demanded this." Forcing an offer to institutional investors would "add even more effectiveness and potency to such a situation," continued Lipper. Consider the Chemical Fund, "an old-line investor in B,D, associated with the founding family, [which] must have felt very uncomfortable to see Dickinson ousted from the company, and also . . . normally motivated by a great desire to get a premium and get out of a stock that had not shown great performance over the past couple of years.

"A fund like that, or more funds," the Salomon Brothers partner said, "might come forward . . . demand, and perhaps even sue the management, to make them negotiate on the offer, and we hoped that directors who owned shares would say they were going to go along with this. That they themselves would tender their shares and this would create such pressure on the management of B,D that, even if it wanted to resist because of its own personal desire to maintain itself, they would have to capitulate.

"In effect," added Lipper, "it was a good offer for shareholders and we even thought Mr. Becton would join in those wanting to sell their shares because he would want the premium, and I thought he needed the money." The theory was that the landslide, gathering speed and mass, would carry everything before it. "I would hope Mr. Becton would sell his shares," said Lipper. "We hoped Mr.

[107]

Dickinson would sell his shares and we even thought that maybe Mr. Asnes would be materialistic enough that he would sell his shares if the price was right."

Robert Zeller, on his own at first, and then reinforced by Salomon, had been trying to sell that concept (or variations on it) since 1975. Like most M & A strategy, it showed an opportunistic grasp of the dynamics. The strategy of bonding highly mobile outside stock to the nucleus of the Dickinson and Dunning family holdings emerged early on. Zeller took great pains to disassociate himself as the chairman of F. Eberstadt & Company from any portfolio decisions that might be made by the mutual funds the firm managed. But there were times when the disclaimer seemed to be a subliminal form of advertising, coupled—as it often was—with the statement that a 20 percent block of B,D could easily be put together in one way or another. The sales appeal of a 20 percent block and the placebo effect of equity accounting on the aggressor's income sheet was all part of the strategy.

As in most other games, though, creative flashes rarely catch fire in the merger and acquisition business without the help of a foot-slogging sales effort. It was an effort that Robert Zeller, Kenneth Lipper, and Richard Rosenthal were more than willing to make. They got turndowns from at least ten companies before connecting with Sun. Some of them (like Sun) were already Salomon clients. Kenneth Lipper barnstormed Pepsico, for example, even though he thought "there was a low probability of interest," because the soft-drink producer ranked as an important client. "We like to keep them open to all our ideas," said Lipper. Part of the sales spiel to Pepsico was that there "was a management split in B,D, and if ever there was an opportunity to acquire such a company, this might be a good time to do it."

Other prospects were approached through personal connections. Robert Zeller, for example, a former director of Warner-Lambert, had known Burke Giblin, then chairman of the drug company, for a long time. Zeller got on the phone, told Giblin that B,D might be up for grabs, and suggested that he "take a look." Giblin got back to Zeller several days later with word that too many potential antitrust problems stood in the way of a deal. Zeller, who had been a top-flight Wall Street lawyer before joining Eberstadt, also used the Warner-Lambert connection to canvass Ciba-Geigy. The president of the drug company had been chief financial officer of Warner-Lambert when Zeller was on the board there. "I didn't need to identify myself to Don MacKinnon," said Zeller; "I asked him to please take a look." MacKinnon called back a couple of days later and told Zeller he thought B,D was "too big" for Ciba-Geigy to handle.

Fairleigh Dickinson was going through his tickler file, too. At the suggestion of his wife and Paul Stillman, he called a neighbor and "old friend," Richard F. Furlaud, who just happened to be CEO of Squibb. Dickinson asked Furlaud if he thought it would be "worthwhile looking into a possible joint effort in some form or another," and at a subsequent meeting raised the possibility of selling his stock to Squibb. Furlaud, according to Dickinson, said he didn't think a deal was possible because of differences in the two companies' capital structures. At about the same time, Alan Lowenstein, Dickinson's New Jersey lawyer, made an approach to Hoffman-LaRoche through his friendship with Robert Clark, then head of the Swiss-owned American operation. That didn't work either.

One company that gave a good deal of thought to B,D—Monsanto—was drawn into the tent as the result of a routine call by one of Salomon Brothers' new business people, who learned the chemical producer "was interested in buying health-care and drug companies," and immediately got back to Kenneth Lipper with the news. "He knew, as was generally known," recalled Lipper, "that we were trying to put together some kind of deal to sell B,D, and said it would help him in his business effort to be able to expose Monsanto to the idea of acquiring B,D." Those talks died because Monsanto wasn't interested in an unfriendly deal, but the cold-turkey prospecting went on, with Robert Zeller setting an example for everyone. Eberstadt had been B,D's first investment banker and, as an old friend, Robert Zeller began testing the merger market when the first signs of Fairleigh Dickinson's disaffection began to manifest itself in 1975. There had been the approach to Eastman Kodak and, when that didn't work, a phone call to Procter & Gamble, which netted Zeller an appointment with a vice-chairman of the company. Preparing for the trip to Cincinnati, Zeller asked one of his analysts to "make up another sales kit" on B,D. "This should include Becton's most recent annual report," the analyst was told, "its most recent quarterly report, and your recent write-up on Becton." The result: "Nobody from Procter & Gamble ever said no, but nobody ever said yes. They just dropped it."

That didn't discourage Zeller. "I have not had the

pleasure of meeting you before," he subsequently wrote the chairman of the 3M Company, but "I would very much like to come to St. Paul to talk about a possible acquisition by your company. . . ."

For all the high strategy and hard sell, the Sun–B,D combination may, perversely enough, have been a historical accident. The names of both companies, independently of each other, had been popping in the minutes of Salomon partners' meetings for months. As late as August 29, for example—more than four months after Fairleigh Dickinson had been deposed—the minutes of the corporate finance partners meeting for that Monday morning carried the two companies on separate lines that said:

SUN OIL CO.—NOTHING NEW TO REPORT

BECTON, DICKINSON—PROCEEDING

Exactly when the juxtaposition hit the flash point is not clear. Kenneth Lipper had been working on both accounts. It was November 28, the first Monday after Thanksgiving, when he handed Horace Kephart annual reports on two different companies with the suggestion that they be studied for possible fit into Sun's diversification plans. One of the two was Becton, Dickinson.

Becton, as Salomon Brothers saw it, was a hot idea in search of a buyer. A few investment bankers don't operate on speculation—or at least they say they don't. They don't like to move without a firm commitment from a buyer or seller. Goldman, Sachs, for example, tends to specialize in defense. It doesn't go prospecting for buyers (except for

[111]

White Knights in the heat of battle) because most of the firm's clients simply don't want to be sold. Morgan Stanley & Company, partly because so much business gets brought to it, also tends to steer clear of working on speculation. For most of the Street, though, "concept" deals are an important source of fees. "If we know there is a major buyer out there for a given product," said J. Tomilson Hill III, director of mergers and acquisition at Smith, Barney & Company, "we would attempt to come up with an idea and sell that idea to a particular buyer. If he buys the idea," Hill told Geoff Smith of *Forbes*, "then we will be retained to execute that transaction. All we have is the idea. We don't have either side. We don't have the seller. We are trying to be hired by the buyer."

The bankers are the middlemen in what has become a worldwide bazaar. "It's a lot like any market," said Hill. "It's like trading stocks, only here we are trading companies. You've got buyers of companies, and you've got sellers of companies. Sometimes sellers are willing, and sometimes they are unwilling because they have been placed in a situation." Becton, placed willy-nilly in a "situation," was the object of a sales campaign that has become commonplace in the M & A business. Tom Hill, for example, who did graduate work in Japanese studies at Harvard before moving on to the Business School, talked matter of factly about his own marketing skills and how they have developed. If you go down the Fortune 100, he said, "pretty much every company, I could give you a sense of what it is they've bought in the last five years, who it was in those companies that made decisions, what it was they were interested in, whether or not they would do an unfriendly deal, how fast they can move, whether or not they have got something on their plate so they would not be a buyer in this particular deal. That kind of knowledge is critical," he added, "when you are trying to target in very short order."

Much of that kind of information, of course, gets banked in the computers and is available at the punch of a keyboard. It is the hard-won accretion, though, of endless hours in the marketplace. "Take an example like the Hoover Company," said Hill. "It gets raided, Smith, Barney is retained, and what we're trying to do is develop alternatives. I'm on the phone with top Fortune One Hundred decision-makers," continued Hill. "The guy says either I'm interested or not interested. But since I've got him on the phone, I say, 'If you are *not* interested in Hoover, *what* are you interested in?' So you begin to develop over time a sense who the buyers are, what products they are interested in, and whether or not, under different circumstances, they can move effectively. Plus the fact that we're constantly calling on these companies, giving them ideas."

The seven months or so Kenneth Lipper and company put into the selling of B,D suggests that even the hottest of concepts don't fall into place by themselves. "The probability of any one deal going through is relatively remote," said Hill, "so the objective is to have a lot of balls in the air." Though the mortality rate among target companies is very high, most of Tom Hill's colleagues agree that the odds against getting a specific deal done are long. "We're in the business of making miracles," said George Wiegers, a partner at Lehman Brothers Kuhn Loeb. "Maybe five ideas out of ten make sense and if one sensible idea gets done, that's a good batting average."

The batting order tends to shift from year to year, depending on the size of the deals they've handled, but the top M & A hitters include Morgan, Stanley; Lazard Frères & Company; Goldman, Sachs; First Boston; Lehman Kuhn Loeb; Kidder, Peabody & Company, and Salomon. The numbers are hard to get at, and not always consistent, but one idea of the scale involved comes from Lazard Frères. The firm probably won the most recent annual award for the biggest number of deals when it figured in forty-five transactions totalling around $12 billion. Two out of every three of those situations involved $100 million or more.

Investment bankers, of course, do a good deal more than play the acquisition angles. Salomon Brothers, for example, founded in 1910, has evolved into the Street's (and maybe the world's) biggest and most sophisticated trader of government and corporate securities. Though a major underwriter, Salomon has yet to break into "The Club" dominated by Goldman, Sachs; Lehman; Merrill Lynch, and their long lists of blue-chip regular investment banking clients. For all its manifest strengths, including one of the biggest capital positions on the Street, Salomon is still regarded by many conservative corporate money men as more of a "trading firm" than an investment banker—an image it is in the process of upgrading by hiring its share of "three-piece suits" from the top-ranked business schools. In its own way, Salomon is a symbol of how competition is sharpening. While the firm has been pushing deeper into underwriting at the expense of some of its older establishment rivals, it has been meeting increasing pressure in some of its traditional preserves—institutional trading, for one—from aggressive rivals such as Morgan, Stanley and Merrill Lynch. The rising tide of competition has put a premium on the development of high-profit ancillary services that require solid technical skills but not much more capital than a desk and a telephone—to wit, merger and acquisition.

As Smith, Barney's Tom Hill noted, the M & A business is pretty much a "closed shop, with maybe seven or eight individuals within the investment banking firms who are, in effect, key decision makers." Most of them are highly visible and articulate, beginning with the man most of his peers think of as the most effective operative in the business—Felix Rohatyn of Lazard Frères. Born in Vienna, the soft-spoken Rohatyn joined Lazard as a trainee in 1948, became a partner in 1960, and is probably best known for the efforts he put into helping keep New York City just this side of bankruptcy as chairman of the Municipal Assistance Corporation.

As a director of ITT, Rohatyn helped structure that omnivorous conglomerate's acquisition of such major companies as Avis, Continental Baking, Grinnell, Hartford Fire Insurance, and Rayonier, among others. Rohatyn has also worked on such billion-dollar ventures as RCA's takeover of C.I.T., Exxon's buyout of Reliance Electric, and United Technologies' battle for Carrier Corporation.

Though relatively modest in size, Lazard probably brings in more merger and acquisition profits per partner than any house on the Street. Access and ingenuity go a long way to explain why. "What they have," said Tom Hill, "is a

[115]

bunch of individuals who are very transactional oriented. Some of them have been in industry, guys who used to run companies who have contacts at the chief executive level. When they come up with an idea, they can sell very effectively to the CEOs of major corporations."

"Lazard doesn't have a lot of bodies," added George Wiegers of Lehman Brothers, "but in many cases they are dealing with the person at the top, many times with institutionalized companies with only one strong guy at the top. No one else comes close to Lazard in productivity."

Though still only in his early fifties, Felix Rohatyn laughingly describes himself as the "old man" of the M & A business. The Game is indeed heavily populated with men in their thirties and early forties, but they don't have a monopoly on sensitivity. Most of the movers and shakers in M & A agree with Tom Hill's diagnosis that "the ability to be successful in this area depends a lot on your ability to change personalities, to read nuances. In some situations," the Smith, Barney executive continued, "you have to scream and there are others in which you have to be very calm to put the client at ease. It's all studied, it all has purpose, it all has a deliberate end." The Salomon Brothers mass walkout on William Laporte after he got testy on the subject of fees may have had an element of gamesmanship in it, for example, and the urgency Kenneth Lipper injected into Sun's calculations when he told Horace Kephart that two other companies were in the running for B,D also carried a whiff of psychological gunpowder.

It may be that sheer physical stamina has almost as much to do with the youth movement in the M & A business as psychological finesse. Like their confréres in the law, the M & A wizards tend to zip from crisis to crisis against time restraints that rarely permit the luxury of getting the 5:05 home to Greenwich every night. For example, Lehman's Steve Schwarzman was researching a merger in Chicago late one Friday afternoon when he got a phone call that despatched him to Florida. There was a merger proposal (Beatrice Foods' bid for Tropicana) that had to be evaluated before a board meeting scheduled for nine the next morning. It was snowing heavily in Chicago, though, and air traffic was so fouled up that Schwarzman didn't get to Florida until four A.M. He didn't get a look at the merger proposition until eight, but by the appointed hour of 9:00 A.M.—after hasty consultation with Lehman partners in New York—Schwarzman had his recommendations ready. As Karen M. Arenson reported in the *New York Times*, Schwarzman fielded questions on the proposal for two hours and by 5:00 P.M. an agreement between the two companies was drafted and signed.

That's not atypical. An ordinary working day in the life of Tom Hill starts at 8:00 A.M. with a breakfast meeting on a possible deal, then fans out into a series of other meetings, most of them to do with defending a client who has come under attack. "I started in on a deposition at a lawyer's office around four P.M., which lasted until ten P.M. After that, it was back to my own office for a couple of hours," said Hill. "It all goes with the territory."

The territory is endlessly interesting. Part of the fun is "the excitement; it's really exciting work," said Hill. "It's almost impossible to plan. The best laid-out schedule of the day changes, simply because you are dealing with events that are beyond your control, and you've got to be there to take advantage of the changes." Like so many people in the Street, Hill's eye span keeps shifting from a visitor to the march of events across the ticker screen that dominates his life. "You get an announcement of a major oil company attempting a takeover of a big insurance company coming across the tape," said Hill, "and you have to spring into action. You have to make calls to find other buyers just like that," he added with a snap of the fingers. The excitement of the game is matched by its financial rewards. It is a rare M & A partner who, counting base pay and profit sharing, does not make well into the six figures and up. One of the many attributes the M & A operatives share is a heavy dose of the entreprenurial itch. "I'm an implementer," says Stephen Schwarzman. "I have a tremendous need to succeed."

The crude measure of success is how much money a deal brings in. Sometimes fees are negotiable, and sometimes they are shaped in the classic laissez faire tradition or whatever the traffic will bear. Before submitting Eberstadt's bill to B,D for the study the firm had done on the proposed National Medical Care merger, for instance, Robert Zeller first called Fairleigh Dickinson. "Dick," he recalls saying, "it's time to fix the amount of the bill. It's a bill to an individual and I don't know quite—it's unusual for us. What do you think you want to pay?"

"What do you think you ought to get paid?" asked Dickinson.

"Somewhere between thirty thousand and fifty thousand," replied Zeller.

"Suppose we fix it at thirty-five thousand," said Dickinson, and that was the size of the bill Zeller mailed to the chairman for transmittal to the B,D board. For its study on the same subject Salomon billed B,D a whacking $250,000. Zeller was left breathless. "Congratulations," he told Kenneth Lipper, "you fellows know how to bill better than I do."

B,D management refused to pay either bill on the grounds that the NMC studies were "not authorized by the company," but the episode dramatizes how upscale—and flexible—the fee structure can get. In general the size of the investment banker's reward is keyed to the size of the deal—with a little trimming and tucking here and there. Most bankers work against a comparatively modest minimum and get paid in full only if the proposition gels. When Robert Zeller pitched B,D to Eastman Kodak, for example, he talked in terms of ¾ to 1 percent of the market value of the deal. Talking to Procter & Gamble, he said "the norm for a large transaction was one percent," but considered that amount "excessive in this situation." A fee in the range of five-eighths to three-quarters of one percent," Zeller continued, "would be [more] appropriate." Though the fee ordinarily comes out of the buyer, in his dealings with Merck & Company Zeller said Eberstadt would look to Becton, Dickinson for its commission. "I would expect to work that out on a mutually agreeable basis with Mr. Dickinson," he told Merck executives. Thus, Zeller seemed to be tailoring his suit to fit the cloth.

Robert Greenhill of Morgan, Stanley has indicated that his firm fixes its charges on sliding scale, depending on the size of the deal—about ⅝ percent on $300 million, for example; ½ percent on $600 million and ⅖ percent on $900 million. Sometimes the situation calls for a flat fee, so the buyer won't get hit for a higher charge if he gets caught in a bidding match and has to pay up to achieve a target. Flat fees are far less common on the sell side of a deal, however, where the incentives are scaled to insure that the

[119]

banker will bargain for absolutely the highest price he can get. For arranging the uncontested marriage of Exxon and Reliance in a billion-dollar deal, Morgan collected $3.75 million. For representing Pullman, on the other hand, in a knock-down drag-out bidding war that brought $52.50 share instead of the $28 first offered, First Boston pocketed $6 million—a fee of about 1 percent of the purchase price.

As the deals have gotten bigger, M & A rewards have gotten richer—so rich, in fact, that old hands like Felix Rohatyn are beginning to worry that runaway incentives are enticing the Street into doing some deals that might be better left undone. "It's a very seductive business," he said. "The fee you get when a deal closes, compared with the minimum processing fee you get if it doesn't, is so enormous. The incentives to do a deal are much too great. There is a dangerous push, conscious or unconscious, to get the thing to go."

The real danger, of course, is that viable companies are being railroaded out of independence into shotgun marriages as a kind of reflex to the Street's pursuit of higher profit margins. The M & A operatives are sensitive to the issue. Felix Rohatyn, for example, said that Lazard is "a small firm with low overhead," and noted flatly that "our people know it is far better to say no to a client and walk away from a deal than to go with something marginal."

Robert Greenhill makes much the same point. "We are in business a long time," he said. "What really is basically at bottom in every one of these things is the firm's long-term reputation. There is no single deal worth doing, something we do not believe in, just in order to earn a fee."

Still, the business is rife with ethical dilemma. Part of it involves what one merger maker calls servicing "the egos of chairmen." As the Becton, Dickinson history demon-strates, it is sometimes hard to divorce egos and internal power plays from the economics of acquisition. And that is true not only of management, but the Street as well. Is it really possible for a highly motivated M & A operative preoccupied with the niceties of a deal to resign himself to a nonviolent solution that might be better for the com-pany? Both Martin Lipton and Joseph Flom, for example, hoped the trigger would not be pulled at B,D and worked hard at trying to arrange for the company to buy out the Dickinson stock. The attorneys couldn't manage that, but they certainly got no encouragement from Kenneth Lipper. "Salomon Brothers," he said, "would not participate in any discussion of this type because we were not representing Mr. Dickinson and it was my intention to sell the entire company. I had no interest in these discussions," he added, "because I was going to find someone to buy all of B,D."

That is as good a synthesis of the strive-and-succeed ethic of M & A as any. "There is a lot of anxiety," said George Wiegers of Lehman Brothers, "because the banker's skills are on the line and our business grows or reduces on the perception of our competence." It's push, push, push all the time. When Dan Lufkin, who had long since severed connections with the brokerage firm of Donaldson, Lufkin & Jenrette, conveyed his sympathies to Fairleigh Dickinson on having been stripped of the B,D chairman's job, for example, both Robert Zeller and Kenneth Lipper were alarmed. Zeller was worried that Lufkin was "trying to get an investment banking position in this matter." Lipper was even more concerned. He called Lufkin and got himself invited to the meeting with Dickinson. Why? "I thought Lufkin might be proposing some sort of deal," said Lipper. "I wanted to insert Salomon Brothers into the deal."

That sort of jockeying is typical of a field in which almost everybody starts off with the same level of technical skills, and the concept is all.

Thus, when Zeller made his approach to 3M, he told the company it was "particularly important" to him that Peter Peterson "not be brought into the matter until very late in the discussions, if at all." Peterson, a 3M director, is also a Lehman partner. Lehman had tried to work out a deal between Merck and B,D before Zeller arrived somewhat belatedly on the scene with the same proposition. It was good business sense to keep Peterson and Lehman in the dark on 3M. "I didn't want any more competition than I could avoid," said Zeller.

Fairleigh Dickinson, of course, for a time kept both Eberstadt and Salomon in the dark. Unbeknownst to either of them, both firms made separate approaches to Avon Products on B,D. Zeller put as good a face as possible on things when Dickinson finally broke the news, but it is clear that he was put out. Zeller was even more unhappy when Eberstadt and Salomon Brothers learned that Morgan, Stanley was very much in the Avon Products picture, too. As Avon's investment banker, Morgan had been told right along all there was to know about the B,D proposals.

The three investment bankers met at Salomon Brothers to sort things out. John Gutfreund, according to Kenneth Lipper, opened the session by outlining for Robert Greenhill, Morgan's acquisitions chief, how Fairleigh Dickinson had come to them for help. Gutfreund allowed as how Salomon would be happy "to join Greenhill in being a co-manager of an [Avon–B,D] deal in exchange for bringing him the idea."

Greenhill had his own territorial imperatives. He recalled telling Gutfreund that "Morgan, Stanley is the sole representative of Avon and that the only advisory relationship we have in this meeting is to act for Avon. If you have any different understanding, you will have to discuss that directly with Avon." Gutfreund "immediately got off that track," Greenhill remembered, "and the meeting proceeded."

Kenneth Lipper, however, remembered the dialogue as being a lot sharper: "Greenhill said we weren't bringing him any idea. He had had the idea already and done a study on B,D. He said, in any case, Avon would do only a friendly deal because Mr. Mitchell [Avon chairman] didn't have the stomach for an unfriendly one after he had lost the Monarch Life unfriendly tender, and his reputation couldn't stand another loss like that."

The Salomon partners came back with the argument that it wouldn't be an unfriendly deal "because hopefully people such as Fairleigh Dickinson and others who share his opinion could step forth and say, 'Avon is a great company, there is a runaway management [at B,D], and it's in the best interest of shareholders to be exposed to this offer.'"

Greenhill parried with "What are you guys bringing? It's my client. I put the work in on the study. We don't need Salomon for that, we can do it ourselves."

"We can help you get the shares on the marketplace, we can talk to Dickinson and hope to get him to get his side to us and add this kind of friendliness to the deal," countered the Salomon partners.

Whereupon Greenhill said, "Look, all you guys have got, at best, if anything, is Dickinson, and if Avon were to make a tender exchange offer, I think Fairleigh Dickinson would tender his shares anyway, so we don't need you guys to work on this."

It was on that note, recalled Lipper, that the meeting "broke up in a rather unsatisfactory huff on everybody's part because we felt [Greenhill] was stealing our idea, and because he wanted to keep us away from Avon. Several of us were unhappy."

In the end, of course, Avon backed off and Salomon did the deal. Who was the first White Knight to surface before there was even any public notice that Sun had bought a big chunk of B,D? Avon, of course, and Robert Greenhill had barely urged David Mitchell into action when the Avon chairman got a phone call from an investment banker at Merrill Lynch. His suggestion was that Avon might want to jump into the bidding for B,D. Anybody who stands still in the M & A Game has a good chance of getting run over.

6

Those Hyperactive Arbitrageurs

The highly public nature of the management split at B,D was bound to attract a certain amount of opportunistic attention from the rest of the Merger and Acquisition community no matter how close to the vest Salomon and Eberstadt tried to play their cards. In the Street, even the most muted corporate quarrel is the sound of opportunity knocking. The close secrecy clamped on Sun's strike on the institutions, and the speed at which it moved, though, caught another of the Street's tightly knit groups—the arbitrageurs—absolutely flat-footed. Had those agile middlemen sensed what was going on, they would have bought heavily into B,D. On past form, their scramble for a quick premium would have forced the price of the stock up. Sun almost certainly would have had to pay more than $45 a share, perhaps in a bidding match where the prize might have been lost to a White Knight.

No one had a deeper appreciation of the perils an infiltration of arbitrageurs might bring than Richard Rosenthal, himself one of the Street's most talented traders.

One of the architects of the Sun strategy, Rosenthal played a considerably broader advisory role in the B,D deal than his title as head of Salomon Brothers' equity department might suggest. What he brought to bear in working out such technical details as how much of a premium it would take to shake loose the institutional holdings is a superb set of market skills—skills he began developing in his teens at Ira Haupt & Company after dropping out of a high school curriculum he felt had nothing to offer him. They are skills shared by less than a dozen other major arbitrageurs at such big trading firms as Bache Halsey Stuart Shields; First Boston, and Goldman, Sachs.

Arbitrageurs, said Rosenthal, must have a good sense of supply and demand. "The best of them," he added, "are people who can sort of detach themselves from the emotional arena that is going on around them at all times, and be just that—an arbiter of supply and demand. It takes a certain risk orientation—somebody who is not afraid of being wrong." All of the top investment bankers are in arbitrage to one degree or another, primarily for their own account. Other more public-oriented firms specialize in arbitrage accounts for individual customers.

"Risk" (or merger) arbitrageurs are truly middlemen, operating in what has become largely a professionals' no-man's-land between the aggressor and the target. When news of a takeover breaks, the buy side on the target stock consists almost exclusively of arbitrageurs willing to take the "risk" that the deal will go through at a premium. On the sell side are individuals and institutions who would rather not take that risk. They profit by capitalizing on the instant run-up in price that word of a tender almost invariably brings. Much of that profit, of course, is generated by heavy arbitrage demand. The arbitrageurs maximize their profits by operating largely with borrowed capital, and reduce their risks by spreading that capital over a portfolio that at some of the big firms—depending on what is going on in the market—can amount to as many as fifty or more situations. There is a lot of money at stake, well into the hundreds of millions—but the potential returns are big, too. One arbitrageur's rule of thumb is "to try for an average return on investment of forty percent, but be willing to settle for thirty percent."

In classic bidding matches, such as J. Ray McDermott's successful fight for control of Babcock & Wilcox—or its unsuccessful fight for control of the Pullman Co.—the arbitrageurs may come away with an annualized return of 100 percent or more on their money. Their massive buying power, in fact, often determines what the market price is going to be, and into whose hands the target will fall. When the Babcock & Wilcox struggle came down to the wire, for example, the arbitrageurs held about a third of the company's outstanding stock. In the Pullman fracas, they may have held as much as 45 percent of the outstanding stock. As those numbers suggest, the arbitrageurs are truly the balance of power. "Did you say the balance of terror?" laughed Joseph Perella, co-director of mergers and acquisitions for the First Boston Corporation.

Terror is not quite the word you would associate with

Richard Rosenthal or any of his fellow arbitrageurs. As a group, they are pretty much like the M & A guys down the hall—young, for the most part in their thirties or early forties, with a heavy admixture of Ivy League background, and very, very entrepreneurial. Simultaneously juggling telephone calls, sopping up intelligence from the broad tape, and coaching a couple of the eighteen traders he supervises, Richard Rosenthal speaks with deep conviction of the "meritocracy" of Salomon Brothers. He wears three-piece suits himself now, with the casually rumpled panache of a man who has arrived but isn't making a big thing of it. Very few other major firms would have taken him on without a high school diploma to his name, said Rosenthal, and he is grateful for the gift of an environment in which his talent could flourish. "He who can do the job gets the responsibility regardless of background," the Salomon partner continued. It is all delivered in a relaxed cadence. The only clue to the fierce kinetics behind Rosenthal's unemphatic style showed in the chain-smoker's mound of Benson & Hedges butts rising in the ashtray in front of him. Like the world of M & A, arbitrage is a tidy cosmos in which everybody knows everybody else. Rosenthal sits on the board of Mt. Sinai Hospital along with Robert Rubin, "a good personal friend," who runs the Goldman, Sachs arbitrage operation, but the Salomon Brothers partner doesn't think of himself as belonging to "the Club." He said that he is rarely on the phone with other arbitrageurs. "We like to keep our own counsel here and make our own decisions," added Rosenthal. "The old girl network is really something I don't want to be part of."

Guy P. Wyser-Pratte, on the other hand, who heads the

Bache Halsey Stuart arbitrage operation from his ground floor office in the shadow of the Brooklyn Bridge, is uncommonly explicit about the advantages of belonging to the Club. "The community is extremely cliquish," he wrote in a monograph on arbitrage that was part of his M.B.A. thesis at New York University. "Each member of the Club has his own particular set of friends within the Community with whom he will freely exchange ideas and information, often via direct private wires." There are times when the French-born Wyser-Pratte, who put in a couple of years as a Marine Corps Officer after graduating from the University of Rochester, tends to the grandiloquent. His father was a trader on the Paris Bourse before bringing his family to the United States in 1948, and Wyser-Pratte thinks of himself as literally having grown up in arbitrage. "I learned from my father, who was considered one of the deans of the business," he noted, "and if it is not too presumptuous to say of one's own father, I would call him a master." Wyser-Pratte, who has a sly sense of humor, calls his fellow arbs "Les Girls." He says they are on the phone all the time—to one another, to company officials, and to the M & A operatives—trying to draw out what Wyser-Pratte called "the hard cold facts about the real state of affairs." He regards much of what filters through his phone with appropriate cynicism, but makes it clear that the arbs, in one way or another, manage to keep fairly close tabs on who is buying and selling what.

As in any club, there are some standing gags. Talking about the complexities of the communications link, a deadpan Wyser-Pratte notes that "some arbitrageurs" had taken to playing small jokes on one of their fellows—Ivan

Boesky of Ivan F. Boesky & Company. A lawyer who has lectured on arbitrage at New York University and who for a time kept a press agent on retainer to publicize his winnings, Boesky is renowned for some of the highly leveraged risks he has taken in such competitive situations as Babcock & Wilcox—a play that is said to have netted him $7 million. "It is a little sad," says Wyser-Pratte in what is clearly a grudging accolade. "I have heard that some of his friends have been so uncourteous as to call Ivan from time to time and make pig-like 'oink, oink' sounds into the telephone." Wyser-Pratte, himself an outstanding example of how rich the rewards of arbitrage can be, gets a certain amount of chaffing, too. Over the last three years his salary, based on a percentage of his department's earnings, has ranged from a low of $864,855 to a high of $1,374,197. The source for those numbers is the Bache annual proxy statement, a document that is always scanned on its arrival with deep interest by the rest of the arbitrage community. "It's too bad they have to make information like that public," cracks one arbitrageur. "Wyser-Pratte must be mortified to have everybody know he's one of the lowest paid guys in the business."

Irony, of course. The bottom line in such storied plays as Babcock & Wilcox can be dramatic. The bidding match between United Technologies and J. Ray McDermott for control of B & W pushed the price of the stock from around $35 to $65 a share. With UTC and McDermott slugging it out toe-to-toe, the arbitrageurs couldn't lose. They started buying at around $40, shortly after UTC offered $42 a share for B & W, continued to buy when the aerospace company jacked up the bid to $48, and hit the stock again when McDermott countered with an offer of $55. *Fortune* has estimated that the "Four Horsemen" alone—Richard Rosenthal, Wyser-Pratte, Ivan Boesky, and Robert Rubin of Goldman, Sachs—had a total of about $100 million at risk and netted $30 million—all in a period of less than six months. The returns were equally gratifying in the Pullman extravaganza in which the stock was alternately bumped by J. Ray McDermott and Wheelabrator-Frye from $28 to $43; from $43 to $43.50; from $43.50 to $52.50 to $54. Holding what Joseph Perella of First Boston estimated at "between four and five million shares" of Pullman, some of it bought at prices as low as $39 a share, the arbs cleaned up.

There are also plenty of situations in which the arbs have taken a bath. Many of the arbitrageurs lost money, for example, on such abortive bids as Anderson-Clayton's move on Gerber; Marshall Field's attempt on Carter Hawley Hale; and the American Express bear hug on McGraw-Hill. On-and-off-and-on-again deals like RCA and C.I.T. can hurt, too. Sometimes the chemistry goes wrong in ways no one can anticipate. Richard Rosenthal cites one example where two chief executives, good friends, signed a preliminary agreement on a merger and went out with their wives to celebrate. The two women got into a knock-down, drag-out fight, said Rosenthal, and "the two guys called off a very major deal. They looked at each other and said, 'I love you and you love me, but it just ain't worth it.' That may sound obscene," continued Rosenthal, "but it's a very real world attitude. Most deals fall apart for people reasons more than any other, and there's no way to predict that."

[131]

There has been a tendency to romanticize the arbs as "river boat gamblers," and they do take significant risks, but risks that are carefully weighed. "What I don't do is speculate," said Wyser-Pratte. "I want to get a return on the firm's capital, but when a deal does look do-able, then I'm in up to my ears." Robert Rubin makes the same point. "Our job," he told an American Bar Association seminar on takeovers, "is to assess risk, reward, and probability, and try to make judgments enabling us to win often enough to absorb the inevitable large losses and on balance come out ahead at the end of the year." The risk profile in friendly deals, for example, is often quite low and while the arbs prefer cash, they can turn securities into money in a variety of dazzling ways—selling the aggressor's stock short, for example, and capturing the premium by buying the target company's stock.

The arbitrageurs also reduce their exposure by spreading their talents around. "Tenders can be exciting," said Richard Rosenthal, "and certainly they fill up a lot of space in the newspapers, but there is a whole world out there of liquidations, reorganizations, and traditional amalgamations. People who have been involved with Penn Central for five years during the reorganization, acquiring and trading the securities," he continued, "have done very well in life. Some of those securities were trading at nine percent of face value and they're getting paid off at over a hundred percent. But it took five years and a lot of fundamental work to determine if the values were there and if the case was going to be settled."

In non-cash situations where they are dealing with two (or more) sets of securities, the arbitrageurs can usually hedge against the vagaries of the market. The only real risk is that the deal won't go through. Thus, as Wyser-Pratte explains it, the arbitrageur's first question always goes to the business logic of an offer. Does it make enough sense to fly? Are there potential antitrust problems? Will the proposition have to pass muster with other regulatory agencies—the Federal Communications Commission, for example—as well as the FTC and the Justice Department? Most arbitrageurs keep antitrust attorneys on retainer to provide answers to those questions. What is the timetable? How long will my capital be tied up? The latter is not always an easy question to answer, but it has a vital bearing on how large a return the arbitrageurs can expect. How much of a return is there in the spread between the market and the aggressor's offering price, or between securities that might be exchanged in a straightforward consolidation? What is the downside risk if the deal falls through? Often the answers have to be hammered out in the half hour or so between the point at which trading in a stock is halted on a takeover announcement and the point at which the issue is permitted to open again. The answers all go to determine the price at which the arbs will jump into the market. If they bid the stock above the aggressor's offer, as in the case of Pullman, it's a sure sign the arbs are betting on a higher second bid, or sense a competing bid in the wings. More often, the arbs will come in under the offer price—not very much under if the odds on the deal's going through look good; and at a somewhat deeper discount if the going looks really chancy.

There are other elements in the mix, but the aggressor's strategists usually try to make the risk assessment easier by framing the merger terms in ways that will stimulate maximum arbitrage participation. The arbs are courted because they are predictable. They gravitate to the optimum combination of high reward and low risk. J. Ray McDermott, for example, could never have won Babcock & Wilcox if its investment banker—Smith Barney, Harris Upham—had not worked the arbs brilliantly. Conversely, McDermott might never have lost Pullman if the same investment banker had not at the last crucial moment seemingly miscalculated the amount of risk the arbs were willing to absorb.

In the Babcock deal, McDermott started out with what seemed to be the short end of the straw. True, it had bought almost 10 percent of Babcock & Wilcox in the open market before first declaring itself, but McDermott was offering only 35 percent cash and some unidentified security down the road for the target, while the United Technologies bid was all cash. As Robert Rubin puts it, "Arbitrageurs are very cash oriented and disinclined to wait for paper." Thus, on the early form, it looked as though UTC had a lock on the deal. UTC certainly thought so. As the bidding escalated, it held at the $58.50-a-share mark, while McDermott pushed on to $62.50. The $62.50 looked good, but the arbs complained that McDermott's unwillingness to pay cash for more than 4.3 million shares of B & W left them with a Hobson's choice. Since only a little more than one-third of the 3 million shares they were holding would be taken up for cash, the arbs had only two ways to dispose of the overage, and neither of them was very palatable. They could dump the stock back into the market, but doing so would put heavy pressure on

B & W, which meant the arbitrage shares might well be sold at a loss. The alternative was to wait around for the stock swap with McDermott, but there was no telling how attractive the terms would be, and any delay would add to the interest costs on the huge position the arbitrageurs were carrying. B & W, which wanted no part of UTC, resolved the dilemma with a last-minute surprise. Some twenty hours before the aerospace company's offer was scheduled to close, it declared a special dividend of $2.50 a share, which McDermott promptly announced would be passed on to all shareholders who tendered to it. The effect, thanks to the generosity of B & W's board (and the shrewd tactical sense of Morgan, Stanley, B & W's investment bankers), was to sweeten McDermott's bid to $65 a share. That topped UTC's offer to pass on only half the special dividend, and McDermott—with a gleeful assist from the grateful arbs—carried the day.

There was the same pattern of escalating bids in the battle for control of Pullman—a battle in which Wheelabrator-Frye beat out J. Ray McDermott's bold last-minute bid for arbitrage support.

Some of the arbitrageurs pooh-pooh the idea that their support is essential to the success of a takeover. "I don't think we're crucial," argues Richard Rosenthal. "I think arbitrageurs are peripheral in a transaction. As much as they would like to think they influence the transaction, they do not." Yet the Securities and Exchange Commission raised some questions in at least one situation where a group of arbitrageurs pledged their support to a White Knight, apparently in the hope that doing so might encourage a bidding match.

That kind of activism is not entirely consistent with the picture of the arbitrageurs as remote and clinical technicians. Richard E. Cheney, for one, vice-chairman of Hill & Knowlton, who has handled public relations in some of the biggest takeover fights of the last twenty years, thinks the arbs are "operating with more money and more boldness than ever before." Cheney enumerated the high level of outside expertise the arbs have working for them— antitrust consultants, law firms retained "to assess the possibilities of the target company's injunctive relief," and observers who will cover the courts or regulatory hearings "to make sure a takeover isn't going off the track." The arbs, continues Cheney, are also not bashful "about calling directors, members of management and others, and expressing their point of view. Asked 'Aren't you an arbitrageur?'" said Cheney, "they reply, 'I'm one of your major stockholders.'"

And so they are, though never for the long haul. Tactically, however, some of the arbs have found it advantageous to wrap themselves in the flag of "corporate democracy," particularly in situations where a recalcitrant management elects to fight a bid. Bache, for example, at Guy Wyser-Pratte's insistence, backed a stockholder suit aimed at forcing Gerber Products Company to accept a fat $40-a-share bid made by Anderson, Clayton & Company. Gerber was having its problems. With the contraction in birth rates, much of the growth had seeped out of its line of baby foods. Diversification into other baby products and insurance hadn't helped much, and by almost any standard the Anderson, Clayton offer looked good—it was more than twice book value, and came in at around fourteen times earnings in a period when the market as a whole was selling at around only seven or eight times earnings. Gerber put up a tough defense, arguing that the bid was not in the best interests of stockholders. The rejection manifestly was not in the best interest of arbitrageurs. Wyser-Pratte's suit, aimed at forcing Gerber to reconsider, didn't get anywhere. It was a signal, though, that managements who vetoed a bid had better be prepared to run a gauntlet of single-minded opposition backed by deep Wall Street pockets.

Yet another sign of the growing militance among arbitrageurs came when Wyser-Pratte looked into the possibility of starting a proxy fight that would push McGraw-Hill into a reexamination of American Express's final offer of $40 a share. "Stockholders are getting screwed," said Wyser-Pratte, by entrenched managements whose major concern is in hanging on to their own jobs. "If a lot of companies have 'not for sale' signs on them," he fumed, "when were stockholders told? Who would have bought the stock if a company has a 'not for sale' sign on it? The public has a right to know." Wyser-Pratte hoped his own uncompromising stand would generate some resonance among institutional investors who also held large amounts of McGraw-Hill.

Wyser-Pratte has a lot to say about the virtues of "corporate democracy" and the need to have any reasonable takeover put to a stockholder vote. There is no arguing that shareholders for the most part have benefitted handsomely from the takeover trend. Equally, however, much of what Wyser-Pratte has to say is self-serving. He paid around 31 for the 16,900 shares of McGraw he bought for the Bache account, and took a paper loss of around $150,000 in the sell-off that followed the company's successful brushoff of the American Express bid. The arbs don't like to lose, and their growing militance is a way of narrowing the risks of the game. Ivan Boesky emerged as such a large shareholder in several situations where he was able to call the tune almost on his own. His firm owned just under ten percent of ERC Corporation, for example— a stake that helped to steer the reinsurance company past two other competing bids into a highly rewarding union with Getty Oil.

Still another arbitrageur, Carl Icahn, has pushed the perimeters of the arbitrage to the horizon where his confrere, Wyser-Pratte, also seems to be heading: the proxy fight aimed at dictating a sellout. Icahn is a fortyish one-time med student who heads the New York Stock Exchange member firm that bears his name. He went to work at Dreyfus Corporation in 1960, made quite a lot of money trading for a couple of years, and then learned the hard way that the market is a two-way street. "I lost everything I had in one week," he told Edwin McDowell of the *New York Times*. "It was so bad that I sold my white convertible Galaxie for twenty-five hundred dollars to eat and pay the rent. That's what hurt the most; I really loved that car." The bottom line on that experience was "never to play the market."

That, in a nutshell, is the arbitrageur's creed. The market is unfathomable—a blind, capricious end product of hundreds of thousands of individual greeds, hopes, and fears. Not so a single deal. There may be risks that the idea won't work, but they are for the most part foreseeable, and can be adjusted for in an assessment of the downside risk. And when you happen to be an aggressor holding all of the cards in a carefully chosen situation, the risks are minimal. Thus, short of the company's going bankrupt, there was little that Carl Icahn had to lose when he started buying into the Tappan Company, a Mansfield, Ohio, producer of stoves and other home appliances that had fallen on lean times. "It was selling way the hell below book and management had made some mistakes," says Icahn. Trading at around $8 a share, with a liquidating value of more than $20 a share, Tappan was grossly undervalued. Icahn saw the "potential for better earnings" and a property "appetizing enough to be taken over." He quietly bought up more than 300,000 shares of the company and then ran up the Jolly Roger. His proxy fight for a seat on Tappan's board was keyed to the pledge that his first order of business would be to scare up a buyer for the company. Within a year, Tappan was sold to AB Electrolux, a Swedish-owned home appliance producer, for $18 a share. Icahn cleared about $2.3 million on the deal. "You can't beat that kind of return," he said.

The big profits being made from takeovers have added immeasurably to the speculative tone of the market. "A lot of dumb individual speculators are trying to play this game now," said Guy Wyser-Pratte, "and all they do is make things more volatile; they're just asking to get hurt." The rumor mills work overtime. A market letter hints that a medium-sized manufacturer of steam-generating equipment is up for grabs and the thinly traded shares of the company jump from 32 to 49 in a matter of hours. Management knocks down the rumor and the stock immediately sells off to 39. Alert brokers hustle to stimulate commission business by putting out lists of companies that look ripe for the picking. Robert Metz of the *New York Times* reports on a mysterious "newsletter" that pops up on the Street quoting the odds on specific merger prospects. It is sent to top traders with a personalized note that goes something like this: "Dear Jim, I also sent a copy to so-and-so, but you can still get on the bandwagon." "No one seems to know who the writer is," Metz warns his readers, "or whether he is long or short on the basis of his own tips."

Can the intelligent investor with an analytical turn of mind really sniff out takeover candidates before the professionals are on the scene? Not likely. All of the brokerage-firm computer screens are set to register pretty much the same supposedly telltale characteristics. Companies sitting on big cash positions or otherwise selling at a deep discount from asset values tend to turn up on all the hit lists, and so do such so-called "special situations" as Becton, Dickinson where major stockholders might be eager to sell. Many takeover candidates share some or all of these financial earmarks. On the basis of their own experience, though, the pros insist that there is no predicting where the lightning is going to strike next. "There is no simple matrix of factors you can look at to find an acquisition target," insisted Robert Greenhill of Morgan, Stanley. "I used to do statistical tabulations on takeover candidates," said Rollins Maxwell of E.F. Hutton, "but I found that very few of them wound up being taken over."

A number of mutual funds—the Over-the-Counter Securities Fund, for one—have done nicely out of takeovers, but their gains seem to be more the result of solid, basic investment policy than any particular search for takeover candidates as such. There may be a moral there. Buying into a company that looks undervalued in terms of earning power and assets is probably the best way to play the investment game anyway. If some aggressor wants a piece of the action, too, so much better; but don't buy into anything that looks like a takeover prospect unless it can stand as an investment on its own two feet. You may have to live with your hopes for a long time to come.

The arbs, of course, never buy on rumors, and they never bet on the hope that some Good Samaritan—somehow, sometime—is going to take a mistake off their hands. The pros don't move until a concrete offer has been put on the table. Can the ordinary investor really play that game with any hope of success? With a little help from his friends—Maybe. Oppenheimer & Company, for example, over the last three years has made 126 buy recommendations to retail clients who subscribed to its "special transactions" service. More than one hundred of those deals worked out for a success ratio of 85 percent.

One measure of the bullish enthusiasm with which some well-heeled investors are chasing arbitrage opportunities shows in the heavy demand for shares in a limited partnership Oppenheimer closed recently. The partnership, which concentrates exclusively on arbitrage deals, raised more than $20 million in a very short time despite a stiff minimum investment requirement of $250,000. Still, the backing of high quality research like Oppenheimer's is no substitute for common sense—or humility.

The pros, after all, operate with the best research money

can buy, and even they take their lumps from time to time. Further, the ordinary investor can't hope to duplicate the arbs' cost structure. The pros don't have to worry about the drag of commissions on their profit margins, nor about the tax impact of short-term capital gains in the way that individual investors do. Diversification is critical. Betting on a number of situations spread over the risk spectrum is the only way around the very real threat of getting wiped out by one bad loss. That means capital—probably no less than $100,000 of true risk capital, for openers. Anyone who tries to play the arbitrage game should be smart enough to know he is playing with pros who know all the moves, and often a lot more—inside information, for example.

One of the most striking—and disconcerting—features of the takeover phenomenon is the way in which the stocks of so many target companies begin to move up in price before the aggressor shows his hand. The pattern crops up in study after study. *Forbes* took a sample of forty takeovers and found only four in which there had been no run-up in price for thirty days prior to a formal bid. *Business Week* did a study of fifteen takeovers and reported that prices have jumped anywhere from 14 percent to 37 percent in the month before a public announcement. Frederick Klein of the *Wall Street Journal* checked out thirty such deals and noted that all but three stocks climbed in the two weeks before an announcement was made—some by as much as 20 percent. Klein even turned up the venerable Arthur Murray, who after selling his chain of dance studios began trading stocks full time for his own account. Murray, in his eighties, concentrated on takeover deals and claimed to have doubled his money. The former dance master said he gets "very good tips from stock brokers," and then told Klein: "There are always leaks when a deal is in the works, directors telling their friends, and that sort of thing. My goodness," continued Murray, "if you wait until a deal is announced, you can't make any money at all these days."

Some of the early price movement, of course, may reflect nothing more sinister than aggressors buying into a company before making their interest officially known. That sort of buying, however carefully masked, sometimes causes enough of a ripple to catch the eye of technicians who make their living out of spotting changes in trading volume. A rise in trading volume can sometimes confirm good analytical intuition that a company is up for grabs and cause a chain reaction that generates still broader buying interest.

But yes, Arthur Murray can still teach us all something about the dance. The easy inference is that many of the early run-ups are the result of leaks and insider trading. Sometimes a leak can be a carefully planted defense tactic—an attempt on the part of a target to torpedo an aggressor's pricing strategy, or to squeeze a higher bid out of him through the pressures of the marketplace. Leakage rarely works to the advantage of the aggressor—unless he is doing something unethical, such as trying to lure a White Knight into the game so he can unload his own shares at a profit. Hence the use of code names for target companies, a prevalence of paper shredders, and the restriction of intelligence on a "need to know" basis. The planning and execution, though, can involve scores of individuals: management, directors, investment bankers, lawyers, consultants, public relations people, secretaries, and printers.

There have been just enough SEC enforcement actions to support one broker's contention that "corporate inside information may be one of the worst-kept secrets in the United States."

A consultant, for example, is charged with trading on inside information in seven acquisitions he helped to put together; a lawyer admits to profiting on inside information that a corporate client is going to buy in some of its stock at a sizable premium; a physician quickly adds to his holdings after learning a bid is about to be made for a company on whose board he sits.

One example of how quickly the good news can spread from "tipper" to "tippee" shows dramatically in still another case the SEC put on the record—the case of an allegedly wayward chief executive whose company was about to be taken over at a comfortable premium. The executive told his brother about the deal while they were having dinner one night, mentioned it to a friend while they were playing golf, and then dropped the word to still another friend in a telephone conversation. The brother, in turn, told his investment advisor that the shares of the target "appeared to be a good investment." One of the chief executive's friends bought some stock for himself. The other bought some for a family foundation, and in turn recommended the company as a buy to one of his own friends. The friend, in turn, put a charity he advises into the stock. Then there was the accountant whose wife was related to someone who was married to an executive of the target. . . . And so the word of mouth flies, giving insiders who trade on what they know a significant advantage over the innocents from whom they buy or sell.

The doctrine that insiders must abstain from trading on

information that might affect the price of a stock—or disclose what they know before trading—has been growing on a case-by-case basis out of the antifraud provisions of the Securities Exchange Act for almost a half-century now. Much of that accretion, though, is still swathed in ambiguity. It's pretty clear that an executive, his press agent, and his press agent's secretary are insiders. But what about the lawyer whose eyes begin to sparkle Mammon as he learns about a coming merger from a conversation overheard in the seat alongside him on the 5:05 to Greenwich? Or what about an intrepid journalist who fortuitously trips over a hot memorandum in the men's room while researching a piece on what Felix Rohatyn, Joseph Flom, and those other bigwigs talk about during all those high-level black coffee–and–grapefruit breakfasts at the Regency? Or what about such seeming outsiders as Vincent F. Chiarella, whose job as a mark-up man in the composing room of a financial printer included helping to put together tender offer announcements? The security appeared to be tight enough. The identity of the targets was shrouded until the very last moment, but Chiarella was able to put bits and pieces together and get buy orders off to his broker on at least five proposals before word of them broke into public print. Did the fact that the printer regularly handled "material" information—information that would affect the investment decisions of others—make him an insider?

The SEC thought so, and in an effort to push the interpretation of the law into new territory, prosecuted the hapless Chiarella on criminal charges of fraud. The case went all the way to the Supreme Court, which overturned Chiarella's conviction on the narrow technical ground that there was no fiduciary relationship between the printer and the individuals from whom he bought stock. The Court never got to the question of whether Chiarella had breached a fiduciary duty to the companies that entrusted confidential information to his employer, Pandick Press. That so-called "lost theory" was left open because the prosecution failed to present it to the trial jury. Chiarella did not get off scot free. The printer was fired from a job he'd held for twenty years and, under an agreement with the SEC, was forced to disgorge the $30,000 profit he'd taken out of the market. Pandick Press had gone to the trouble of posting warnings that using information gained on the job for personal ends was both illegal and a breach of company rules, including a big sign over the time clock where Chiarella had punched in more than six hundred times a year. The printer argued that he had done nothing criminal. "I was guessing," he said. "It could have gone wrong. The offers might not have gone through, or I might not have guessed right," he told Karen Arenson of the *New York Times*. "They were only calculated guesses."

Chiarella did not get the SEC as far along the enforcement road as the agency would have liked, but the case is only one manifestation of its growing interest in the reaches of insider trading. At roughly the same time the Chiarella case was working its way through the courts, the SEC adopted a tough new rule under the Williams Act that seemed to slam the door the Supreme Court was just about to open. The rule forbids "any person"—insider or no—to buy or sell at any stage of a tender offer on material, non-public information the trader knows or "has reason to know" has come "directly or indirectly" from the aggressor, the target, or *anyone* acting on their behalf. The rule doesn't require the SEC to show a breach of a fiduciary relation. Thus, it seems by fiat to stand the Chiarella decision on its head, and presumably extends to such potential miscreants as the eavesdropping attorney on the 5:05, the journalist in the latrines of the Regency, printers like Chiarella—and maybe even to arbitrageurs and their often well-placed sources. New litigation may change the shape of the rule, but it is so sweeping in intent that Wall Street is worried. There is so much money in The Takeover Game that none of the players wants to see it piled up on the rocks of regulation. That is one of the reasons why two cases questioning the solidity of the Chinese Wall at Morgan Stanley kicked up such a furor.

The first case broke when Tim Metz, one of the *Wall Street Journal*'s most enterprising reporters, dug out of the fine print of a couple of merger statements an indication that Morgan Stanley had: (a) taken a 149,200 share arbitrage position in Olinkraft shortly after Texas Eastern Corporation announced an offer of $51 a share for the company; and (b) used confidential earnings projections on Olinkraft received during a completely different set of merger talks in an evaluation that led to a bidding war for control of the West Monroe, Louisiana, forest products company. Thanks in part to the bullish tone of the earnings projections, reported Tim Metz, Morgan Stanley client Johns-Manville Corporation felt safe in pushing the ante for Olinkraft to $65 a share in a bid that drove Texas Eastern out of the running. Morgan Stanley's evaluation certainly benefitted Olinkraft shareholders, who got a much higher price for their stock than they might have otherwise. And since the arbitrage department loomed large among those shareholders, Morgan Stanley benefitted, too.

The confidential information the investment banker got from Olinkraft, which was not a client, had been given to the firm under tight restrictions. It was to be used only for the limited purpose of merger talks with Kennecott Copper Corporation, a Morgan Stanley client, in a prospective deal that never materialized. Tim Metz reported that the subsequent use of the Olinkraft material to the advantage of a different client had "set some Wall Street sources wondering whether Morgan Stanley may have compromised its integrity." Further, reported Metz, "the issue raised" by the firm's big arbitrage profit "is whether Morgan Stanley's Chinese Wall," which supposedly sealed off privileged investment banking intelligence from the trading room, had "somehow failed." The *Institutional Investor*, Wall Street's most influential trade magazine, followed the *Journal*'s lead with a hard-hitting cover story by John Thackray and Gary Reich. It asserted that "by slicing the doctrine of confidentiality paper-thin, by fumbling its arbitrage disclosure obligations, and by omitting key elements of its explanation until the eleventh hour, Morgan Stanley had created an unflattering image that would be a blow to the reputation of any investment banking firm." But "because Morgan Stanley is Morgan Stanley, a firm that has relied as much on its mystique as on its undeniable talent," the magazine continued, "the blow is that much more shattering."

The *Wall Street Journal*'s disclosures also touched off a suit in which two Olinkraft stockholders alleged that

Morgan Stanley had breached the Chinese Wall by taking its arbitrage position "upon the informed conviction that a competing offer at a higher price than $51 a share would be made for Olinkraft"; and then, in effect, using that same confidential information "in an effort to induce [Johns-Manville] to make a substantially higher offer."

The suit got nowhere. The District Court threw it out on the grounds that the shareholders were unable to show that Olinkraft had been injured. Indeed, there was no such allegation in their complaint and Federal Judge Morris E. Lasker ruled that the shareholders consequently had no standing to sue. A three-judge appellate bench took a somewhat different tack. It, too, with a dissenting opinion from Judge Oakes, dismissed the case, but on the ground that the shareholders "failed to state a claim upon which relief may be granted." The majority opinion accepted Morgan Stanley's argument that it had dealt first with Kennecott and then with Johns-Manville "under circumstances that clearly placed it in an arm's-length position regarding Olinkraft." There was no breach of fiduciary duty, the Court said, because the investment banker wasn't acting on behalf of Olinkraft. "Although, according to the complaint, Olinkraft's management placed its confidence in Morgan Stanley not to disclose the information," the majority opinion said, "Morgan Stanley owed no duty to observe that confidence."

In his dissent, however, Judge Oakes argued the stockholders should be given permission to amend their complaint in a way that would sharpen the issue of exactly what the relationship between the investment banker and Olinkraft was. Oakes said he thought a broad reading of

the complaint would establish "a sufficient relation between Morgan Stanley and Olinkraft so as to prevent the
former from utilizing non-public material information
obtained from the latter for its own profit. I think
acceptance of such information by Morgan Stanley on the
confidential terms, along with its understood role as
intermediary in a cooperative takeover," the judge continued, "imposed a duty on the investment banker under
well-established common law principles not to use that
information for its own profit."

Since the case was never litigated, the facts will remain
forever frozen in dispute. Morgan Stanley argues that the
Chinese Wall was never breached. The investment banker
says its arbitrageurs moved into Olinkraft on the technical
merits of the Texas Eastern offer, ignorant of any earnings
projections that were in the M & A files, and with no
knowledge that Johns-Manville would come along with
another offer. Johns-Manville, in fact, had backed away
from Olinkraft after an earlier look at the company and
belatedly jumped into the bidding only because it was
agreeably surprised by what seemed to be a comparatively
low first offer from Texas Eastern. That in a nutshell was
Morgan Stanley's position. The firm was on the defensive,
though, and the headlines had hurt.

The *Journal* and the *Institutional Investor* stories, coming
as they did in an environment saturated with suspicion that
some insiders were doing awfully well, left the Street with a
sense of malaise. "The Morgan Stanley thing means those
enforcement guys will be watching investment bankers
closer than ever on takeover deals," one source told Tim
Metz. "There's nothing they like better than taking on a

nice juicy target like a Morgan, Salomon Brothers, or Goldman, Sachs." Metz's man could not have been more prophetic.

Not long thereafter the government alleged that two M & A specialists, Harvard M.B.A.s both—one formerly employed by Morgan Stanley, the other by Lehman Brothers Kuhn Loeb—had been leaking inside information on takeovers to three outside confederates and sharing in the profits for more than five years from behind a facade of secret foreign bank accounts. The indictment charged the group with gross violations of the "fiduciary duties of honesty, loyalty and silence . . . owed directly or indirectly to Morgan Stanley, Lehman Kuhn Loeb and their clients."

Other investment bankers may well find themselves in the same embarrassing predicament, as the hunt for other illegal insider activity broadens. Does that mean the odds in the Takeover Game are going to shift from the pros to the public? Not very likely. As Wesley Howe, Marvin Asnes, and the rest of the management team at Becton, Dickinson discovered, when information is in the wind, the pros are always the first to pick up the whisper.

7

The Defense Strikes Back

Becton, Dickinson, on that snowy Tuesday morning in January, literally did not know what had hit it. The first report, like an intimation of some horrible street accident, was fragmentary. It had come in the shape of two phone calls from Jerry Sullivan in the stock list department at the New York Stock Exchange. Sullivan had told B,D secretary Robert Butler and then Marvin Krasnansky that an unnamed law firm, acting on behalf of an unnamed client, had requested that trading in Becton common be temporarily shut down. The client was about to file "under the Williams Act," indicating that a large-scale purchase of B,D stock—perhaps a tender, perhaps a preliminary to a tender—was in the works. A heavy imbalance of buy orders had already begun to pile up on the floor of the exchange and rumors of a buyout were beginning to build. Did Krasnansky know what was going on?

An alarmed Krasnansky told Sullivan he would have to check with B,D management and rushed past Dottie Matonti's desk into Wesley Howe's office. Robert Butler had already told Howe and a hastily summoned Marvin Asnes what he had heard from the Exchange and then repeated the dialogue for Krasnansky. Krasnansky broke into the recital with the rumor he had picked up from Norton Simon's securities analyst, Mary Ann Beck, the day before—notably that somebody, perhaps through Salomon Brothers, was about to make a bid for B,D at somewhere around $40 a share.

What almost everyone remembers of those first few hours was the blur of motion and confusion. "It came as quite a surprise at that moment that anything was going on," said Wesley Howe. "There were no meetings in the sense of people convening around a table or sitting down and having an agenda," recalled Krasnansky, "but conversations. There might be several conversations in a room with five or six people, two or three conversations going on. I might have been in and out of one office, taking a phone call in an adjacent office. A rather jumbled scene, as you can imagine."

What came through was a sense of outrage. If somebody was about to make a Williams Act filing explaining who they were and what their intentions were, nobody at B,D had heard anything. "The company had not contacted us. We did not know who the company was, or if indeed there was such a company," recalled Krasnansky.

B,D was a captive of its own ignorance. To get its defense cracking, B,D needed more information and it needed it quickly. Krasnansky, ever the activist, was seething with frustration. On the basis of his own experi-

[153]

ence working in the Big Board's public relations department, Krasnansky felt that the Exchange was "not tough
enough on companies in forcing them to come up with
information in cases in where there has been unusual
activity in a stock." He was convinced that the exchange
"was sometimes influenced by pressures applied by important members."

After talking with Howe and Asnes, Krasnansky got
back on the phone to Sullivan at the Exchange. Howe, as
chief executive officer, Krasnansky said, had authorized
him to "strongly object" to the delayed opening in B,D.
"We are officially asking the Exchange to demand further
information and that this information be disseminated
rapidly so that trading can resume," he said.

When Sullivan responded that the Exchange should be
able to get some information "soon," Krasnansky peremp-
torily cut him off. Howe was not satisfied with the way
things were going, Krasnansky said; "We'll have to turn
the matter over to our attorneys." The embattled group at
B,D, in fact, had already sounded the alarm to its lawyers.
One of them was Arthur Liman, a partner in Paul, Weiss,
Rifkind, Wharton & Garrison. "At that time," recalled
Liman, "I had two telephone lines in my office and they
both went off at the same time—Mr. Krasnansky and Mr.
Howe." Another SOS had gone out to Joseph Flom's law
firm. It was answered by his partner Robert Pirie, who had
been visiting another client in New Jersey and so was able
to make his way quickly to B,D headquarters.

The strategy was to prod the Exchange to get out more
information. At the moment, the best guess was that B,D
faced a tender offer. Aggressors, as part of their own
strategy, typically try to shut down the market in a stock so

as to cut off arbitrage action that almost always has the effect of raising market prices. Nobody wants to have his bidding strategy scrambled. But at the moment, B,D was shadow boxing. Without something tangible to hang its hat on, such as an SEC filing, it could not lay down what is often a first line of defense—a court action alleging inadequate disclosure, a breach of margin requirements, or some other violation of the securities laws. Unable to put so much as a name to the aggressor—let alone any estimate of its holdings—B,D couldn't seriously get into a second line of defense, a search for a White Knight and a potentially better price.

There was one thing Wesley Howe did know—a serious tender offer would almost certainly mean that control of B,D would shift . . . if not to the first bidder, then to a second or a third. "There was obviously a price and we didn't know what it was. But at some place, there has to be a price the board would have to recommend to the shareholders that they accept," said Howe. No less an authority than Arthur Liman—a top litigator whose firm had been retained to handle the growing problems with Fairleigh Dickinson—had warned Howe to be realistic. "The management of B,D," he said, "had been schooled in the fact that if someone was going to make a tender offer at a full enough price, there was nothing they could do to preserve the company's independence."

At the moment, however, price was just one of the many elusive facts that had to be smoked out. The mystery surrounding word that trading in B,D had been shut down "pending developments" left the Street abuzz. There really wasn't much that Krasnansky could tell the securities analysts and newsmen who were keeping the buttons on his phone winking. About noon, though, he picked up a call from Martin Schwartz, an analyst at E.F. Hutton. Schwartz told Krasnansky he'd heard that Sun had bought about 3.2 million shares of B,D through Salomon Brothers from Fairleigh Dickinson and several other institutions and individuals. There was also a call from Dave Allen, a financial reporter for the (Newark, New Jersey) *Star-Ledger*, who guardedly told Krasnansky "Wall Street sources" were saying that Sun was attempting to acquire B,D and had already picked up 25 percent of the company.

Word was getting around. "When the stock was closed," said Robert Greenhill, "Rumors came to Morgan Stanley almost immediately that somebody was buying from institutions. We heard a price of 40, 42 pretty quickly." Greenhill called Joseph Flom's office. "It turned out we knew more than he did," recalled Greenhill. "First we heard an oil company, then Sun, then a price, then a higher price—40 to 42, then 45."

Wesley Howe was also working the phones in search of information. He had called J. H. Fitzgerald Dunning, Fairleigh Dickinson's old friend, and talked to him "as a [fellow] director." "When I asked him directly if he had sold the stock," remembered Howe, "he said he couldn't tell me because he had been sworn to secrecy or some such words. I had to infer from that, that it was something he and Dickinson had been involved in together." By then Robert Pirie, the Skadden, Arps partner who had been within quick commute of the B,D executive suite that morning, had reached Martin Lipton. Pirie told Lipton he understood Sun had bought "a large number of shares" and asked if a tender was going to be made. "I told him it was my understanding that no tender offer was going to be made," recalled Lipton.

By late Tuesday, B,D had no more than the dimmest outline of what it was facing—and still nothing tangible on which to base a defense. Sun's couriers, fighting a blizzard and erratic plane schedules, were traveling the entire country for possession of the stock that had been committed in the Midnight Raid of the day before—fearful they might be stopped dead in their tracks by some lightning stroke from the opposition before the shares were gathered. Production of the Williams Act filing, which had been promised the exchange "by approximately noon the next day," receded another twenty-four hours.

The first formal word B,D got from Sun came late Wednesday, when Robert Sharbaugh, the oil company's CEO, reached Howe in a strategy meeting at Skadden, Arps. Sharbaugh, Howe recalled, "indicated they were going to file and that they were about to, or would by the next day have something like . . . thirty-three, thirty-four, thirty-five percent." A consensus on the defense was beginning to form. "The upshot was," said Marvin Asnes, "that we were going to present our case to all possible forums—the public, the Congress. There was a tentative question of the regulatory agencies that might be involved and there was some tentative discussion of a lawsuit."

The fact that Sun had popped up as the aggressor was truly a surprise. A number of other names, most of them in the medical or related fields, had been raised as potential threats by the investment bankers at First Boston and Paine Webber, but Sun's appearance was a wild card— something that no one had anticipated. The fact that an aggressor had surfaced, though, presumably armed with at least the Dunning and Dickinson stock, was in itself no great shock. Wesley Howe and Marvin Asnes had known for months that the Dickinson block was being shopped, and had taken some precautionary defense measures to blunt its thrust. Did they have the right to fight a bid that might enable shareholders to cash in their stock at a profit? Yes. A tough defense can sometimes help keep a target independent, and, perhaps equally important, force a raider into raising his initial bid price. One of B,D's first moves had been to retain Joseph Flom, a month or so before Fairleigh Dickinson was ousted as chairman, at the suggestion of the M & A people at First Boston. "If something like an unfriendly takeover was in the works," said Howe, "our board would want to be advised by the best people we could find." Flom's reputation, perversely enough, helped to shape Sun's strategy. The great stress laid on secrecy was a tribute to that reputation. As Martin Lipton said of his old friend and antagonist, "A threat from Mr. Flom is indeed a significant event in an investment banker's life."

There were other defense moves. Two of the Street's proxy solicitors had been put on retainer to help get the stockholder vote out, if that proved necessary. Hill & Knowlton, a public relations agency with considerable expertise in takeovers, was also put on retainer. Outside directors of some stature were added to the board—a move frequently aimed at demonstrating management is more than willing to subject itself to independent judgment. There were some structural changes in the works, too. A management proposal to increase the amount of stock B,D was authorized to issue from 22.5 million to 35 million shares was scheduled to be put to a vote at the upcoming stockholders meeting, over the violent objection of Fair-leigh Dickinson. Dickinson saw the proposal as an "obscene" effort on the part of B,D's management to water down his equity.

Marvin Krasnansky had initiated a stock-watch program, an early warning system designed to flag such takeover telltales as increases in the number of shares held in anonymous broker nominee (or "Street name") accounts, or changes in the geographical pattern of stock ownership. He arranged for B,D to get a monthly tabulation of shareholders of record owning a thousand shares or more from Irving Trust, Becton's transfer agent. It all helped, said Krasnansky, to "tell us where our stock was, what kind of investor relations activity would be appropriate, and frequently simply to have a better idea of who was doing what in the stock." In the jargon of the takeover trade, it all added up to "shark repellent"—a package designed to show that B,D was prepared to fight to preserve its independence. There had also been some discussion with First Boston about a couple of other standard defenses—staggered terms for directors, which would make it difficult for an aggressor to get control of the board, for example, and a requirement that a merger could go through only with an 80 percent "supermajority" of the stock voting. Both proposals required stockholders' approval and neither was adopted by the board, perhaps because doing so might draw attention to B,D's vulnerability. Shark repellent, as Martin Lipton notes in his *Takeovers & Freezeouts*, really doesn't pack enough wallop to deter a determined ag-gressor, and with so well-heeled a contender as Sun in the field, Howe and Asnes knew that something stronger might be needed—a White Knight, for example.

Robert Greenhill had lost no time in letting it be known he thought his client, Avon Products, would look good in shining armor. "As soon as the stock was closed and the Sun purchases were under way, I called David Mitchell and David, in turn, communicated with Mr. Howe to make it clear Avon was ready to sit down and discuss things with them," he said.

The White Knight option had to be explored. Advisors such as Joseph Perella and Greg Doetsch at First Boston had suggested as much to Wesley Howe. So had Ray Troubh, a former Lazard Frères partner and one of B,D's newest directors. Troubh was in Egypt on business. Howe had cabled him there that snowy Tuesday and within hours the sturdy advice had come back: File a lawsuit, look for a White Knight. In essence, the search for a White Knight is a search for top dollar—and a farewell to independence. Wesley Howe was convinced that B,D was worth more than the $40 to $45 a share the Street was talking—a good deal more, probably as much as $60 a share. He agreed, however, that it would be useful to screen some potential suitors and "contact at least a few of them to get a rough idea as to what their opinions might be."

David Mitchell and Avon Products were right at hand. One of the prime rules in the Takeover Game is never to slam any doors on a friendly deal. You can never tell when you're going to need an ally; you can never tell when *no* will become *yes*. Mitchell months before had left Howe with the thought that if B,D "should find itself in a position where it was going to, in effect, have to seriously consider a merger proposal," Avon would be delighted to sit down and talk. Howe, moving through his part of the pavane, had made it "clear to Mr. Mitchell if a White Knight was needed at some future time, he would probably be in touch." With Sun knocking on the door, the time seemed to be now. Howe had dinner with Mitchell and the investment bankers went to work. As Robert Greenhill recalled, they "put together confidential projections of how the two companies would look." It turned out that David Mitchell, though "favorably disposed" to a combination on the basis of the projections, really wasn't interested in getting into a slugging match with Sun. Nothing could be done as long as B,D was pinned by the oil company's looming presence. By now Sun, true to Robert Sharbaugh's promise, had made its Williams Act report. It had filed not under Section 14(d) of the law, indicating that a tender offer was to come, but under Section 13(d) showing that 5.3 million shares had been acquired. Subsequent amendments put the total at 6.4 million shares—34% of B,D— bought at a cost of about $290 million in cash and notes. Though the block carried a veto on many of B,D's actions, the oil company insisted it was not a takeover. Sun described itself as an investor. That didn't mean Sun might not change its mind, pick up more stock, and move for full control. The company said only that it "intends to continue to study Becton and its industry and to take such action as Sun considers desirable in the light of its evaluation and circumstances then prevailing." Williams Act filings quite legally permit the aggressor to leave his intentions shrouded in seven types of ambiguity, but the defense at last had something concrete to work with. Sun, in effect, had reported buying a good chunk of its stock from what looked like a group—Dickinson, Fitzgerald Dunning, and the two mutual funds (Chemical and

Surveyor) managed by Eberstadt & Company.

It was certainly a group in the general sense of the term. The key question from the point of view of Joseph Flom and the B,D defense was when and if it became a "group" in the restricted sense of the Williams Act—a number of individuals owning more than 5 percent of the stock and looking in concert to a change in ownership. That, whenever that happened, was the point at which a form 13(d) had to be filed with the SEC. If Flom could show the group had coalesced months before any filing, there was a possible breach of the securities laws. That was the beginning of a defense, anyway, one that might sterilize the Sun stock and at least buy some time—time, maybe, to coax a White Knight other than the cautious David Mitchell into play; time to develop other defenses that might succeed in driving Sun off.

The nucleus of a possible 13(d) action against an aggressor who acquired the Dickinson block and its satellite shares had been developing for months. The prospect, not surprisingly, was first spotted by Martin Lipton way back in April, shortly after Fairleigh Dickinson had been deposed as chairman and taken his troubles to Salomon Brothers. Like any good advocate, Lipton wanted to keep his own client, Salomon, out of trouble. When he learned that Eberstadt was working with Salomon, Lipton focused on the Chemical Fund's B,D holdings. "The obvious concern, if Eberstadt was working in this capacity, was whether there would be an aggregation of the shares which would require the filing of a schedule 13(d) under the Williams Act," said Lipton. The lawyer discussed the problem with Robert Zeller, and was told that Zeller himself had already talked it over with Eberstadt's law firm,

Sullivan & Cromwell, and gotten a clean bill of health. As long as the funds' investment decisions were independently arrived at by their directors and insulated from the regular flow of business at Eberstadt, said Zeller—himself a lawyer of long experience—then the group question didn't arise.

That wasn't Robert Greenhill's opinion. The group concept was one of the first things he hit on during the meeting at which he waved Salomon off from trying to do a B,D deal with his client, Avon Products. The Morgan Stanley managing director remembers asking Richard Rosenthal and Robert Zeller "how much stock is represented" in the so-called block of B,D they could deliver. "We are talking about twenty percent" was the answer he remembered. "I was a little nonplussed by this. I said, 'Do you mean that you are in a position to, quote, deliver twenty percent of the stock, end quote?' They said they were talking about twenty percent of the stock." The figure nine percent was also mentioned.

To Greenhill, that seemed like a group in the restrictive, technical sense of the Williams Act. "I was curious about this so-called block of stock and whether any steps had been taken to file as to their forming a group," recalls Greenhill. "There wasn't really any response to that."

It's possible, of course, that the highly competitive Greenhill was using every weapon he could find to beat interlopers off what he regarded as Morgan Stanley turf. He continued to press the question with Martin Lipton in the cab ride back uptown after the meeting. "Obviously if there is this kind of block of stock," the investment banker remembered telling the lawyer, "the whole issue of filing a 13(d) has to be dealt with." The rejoinder, according to

Greenhill, was that "basically those were the matters [Lipton] was looking into."

Joseph Flom had been pondering the group concept, too. It was hard not to with news of the Salomon-Eberstadt shopping effort coming back on almost every wavelength. Flom, on at least four separate occasions between June and November, warned Lipton that Salomon Brothers was heading for trouble.

"Look, Marty," Flom recalled saying, "one thing we both don't need is to have Salomon get into gear, and you really ought to make sure as to what they are doing. If they don't have a group," he continued, "they should not be representing that they do because that has its own consequences. And if they do have a group—well, you have an obligation to file." Every time Flom raised the question, Lipton checked on what the investment bankers were saying. He warned them that it was one thing to express to potential buyers an "opinion" that a block of B,D could be acquired from a variety of sources, and quite another to represent that twenty percent could actually be delivered. Each time Lipton quizzed the bankers, he got back to Flom and told him his allegations were "not factually correct." It got to be so much of a ritual, in fact, that Lipton at one point twitted his good friend and told him "to go right ahead and file suit," if that's what he wanted to do. There had been "great difficulty in finding a buyer for Becton, Dickinson stock," said Lipton, and a "well-publicized lawsuit might well alert those people who had not been contacted with respect to the opportunity and they might well show up on the scene and make offers."

Lipton also told Flom that "if he wanted me to, I would

be happy to advise [Kenneth] Lipper that he should get together with Mr. Dickinson with respect to Mr. Dickinson putting out a press release to the effect he would very much like to see somebody come in and make an offer for B,D's, since he has no confidence in the management and thought the best solution would be that it be acquired by somebody else." It was a good lawyerly thrust—a challenge—and Lipton remembered Flom's mumbling that he did "not intend to bring a lawsuit at that time."

Lawsuit or no, the group theory was solid enough to bring to the attention of the SEC, which is what Flom and Arthur Liman of Paul, Weiss did by telephone shortly after Sun filed its 13(d). Flom's strategy was no different from that of any other lawyer for the defense. He hoped to raise enough provocative questions about breaches of the securities law to get the SEC in on his side. The ploy of complaining to the government agency was so "endemic," said Joe Flom, that the SEC staff was "jaundiced." "They are very careful," he added, "not to get into a position where they could be accused of bailing anybody's chestnuts out of the fire."

The SEC grilled both Lipton and Flom. Flom, arguing that he wanted the government agency to get the "full flavor from day one of the history of this transaction," took the SEC staff all the way back to what he termed the "one-million-dollar bribe offer" to get Howe to quit his job. But the group theory was at stage center. So was the contention that Sun had gotten its B,D stock not through a series of private individual transactions that did not have to be disclosed until after the fact, but through a tender offer that demanded immediate disclosure—and an illegal one at that. As Arthur Liman saw it, Sun had wanted to get the stock as cheaply as it could and had damaged B,D shareholders by cutting them off "from the auction process that takes place in a normal tender offer." There was also the contention that Sun had deliberately shut off trading in the stock while mopping up its purchases in secret.

At the same time, Marvin Krasnansky and Richard Cheney were working quietly behind the headlines. The *New York Times,* the *Wall Street Journal,* and the *Washington Post* had already begun to focus on Sun's "secret buying program." The characterization angered Martin Lipton. "It was a deliberate red herring," he said, "deliberately misused in order to create a furor" in the press. "The trading was not halted to affect the purchase of shares," he continued, but to keep shareholders from getting hurt in an uninformed, rumor-spooked market stampede. The group theory was all wrong, too, and so was the contention that Sun had bought its stock through anything more than a series of private transactions from sophisticated investors who did not need the mantle of Williams Act disclosure to protect them from harm—all quite legal, and by no means a tender offer. The issues were sharply drawn once again between the two good friends who are the nation's two top takeover lawyers—Joseph Flom and Martin Lipton.

Flom, in his mid-fifties, is short, with a scholarly hunch to his shoulders, and almost always has a well-chewed pipe in his hands. Lipton is eight years younger, well over six feet tall, his working uniform invariably made up of a black suit, white shirt, and silver tie. Flom is Brooklyn College and Harvard Law. Lipton did all of his undergraduate and graduate work at New York University and still teaches at the law school there. Both men seem to thrive on crushing work loads. Flom boasts that he once flew the Atlantic twice in the same day in the line of duty, and wryly remembers the year when he and the family took a place in Spain for what was supposed to be a long vacation. Flom is never beyond reach of the telephone, however, and recalls that he made "seven round trips in two months" between his Spanish retreat and his office in New York. Flom now tries to get a winter vacation in St. Croix, but his description of the place is a better guide to his own workaholic character than to the character of the island. "The phone system isn't very good when the sun is out," he says, "and when it rains, the phones don't work at all." Martin Lipton describes his own lifestyle in somewhat similar terms. "When the bell rings," he says, "you have to jump into your boots and slide down the pole."

One professional who worked with both men under the stresses of several bitterly fought takeovers thinks of them as "prodigious workers." He sees Flom as an "intuitive genius" with an "instinctive grasp of human behavior," and Lipton as the more cerebral of the two. Lipton, says this professional, "zeros in on an issue and has the capacity to focus energy on it the likes of which I've never seen. It's like holding a magnifying glass to a piece of paper and letting the sun shine through. The heat builds up until you have a fire."

The lawyers' own descriptions of what they do are considerably less romantic. Both are strategists rather than litigators. It's rare to find either of them in a courtroom. "I'm just sort of the name up front," said Flom, "and so is Marty Lipton. The world is very complex and what we do is analyze things. We have a lot of talented people working for us."

"We just hold the client's hand. We're opposing field

marshals or war ministers," said Lipton.

It wasn't always that way. When Flom got out of the Harvard Law School in 1948, he went to work at Skadden, Arps for $3,200 a year. The firm wasn't doing an awful lot of business, and it wasn't "until 1954 or 1955" that Flom got his first exposure to the world of the takeover. "Bill Timbers," recalls Flom, "a former counsel of the SEC, came into the firm and brought a proxy fight with him. I had a lot of time, and I decided I better get to learn what it was all about." Flom stopped the flow of reminiscence with a grin. "Believe it or not," he said, "the guy on the other side of that proxy fight was Marty Lipton."

Flom learned fast. As his reputation began to grow, he got called into many of the big proxy fights of the fifties and sixties, primarily on the defense, fighting such heavies as the Murchison brothers in the battle for control of Allegheny Corporation, and such lighter weights as the late Victor Muscat in the struggle for control of American Hardware. "They were real free-for-alls," recalled Flom.

By the mid-sixties, though, the game began to change. The tender offer—faster, less messy, more efficient— became the weapon of choice. Skadden, Arps did not have the field entirely to itself, and what it did have came mainly by way of sufferance from the big Wall Street law firms who were not eager to get bloodied in the highly specialized art of street fighting. They left a vacuum that Flom was more than happy to fill. "Basically," he says, "I was growing in the field and contributing a little of the mystique." Flom, who by the mid-sixties had emerged as his firm's dominant partner, broadened the base for his professional growth with a very smart management call. He began to develop the firm's litigating capabilities in a move that made Skadden, Arps more than just an outside counsel dependent on the needs of the big Wall Street names. Skadden, Arps became a force in its own right. "Joe is enormously resourceful," said a professional who has worked with him for years. "One of his sayings is 'If you've got a lemon, make lemonade.'"

Martin Lipton, meanwhile, had been prospering as a self-styled "academic securities lawyer," who in his spare time carpentered articles for the learned journals that, on at least one occasion, focused on the virtuosity of a Flom defense—a recollection that pleases Flom mightily. "By accident," though, Martin Lipton got catapulted into Loews' assault on CNA, a brawl that was fought through the insurance departments and courts of six different states and raged through almost all of 1974. The documents in the case, bound in red with the title picked out in gold letters, take up almost a foot of shelf space in Lipton's office. The generalship that finally brought CNA to heel gave the investment bankers a new perspective on Wachtell, Lipton. "Hey, they said," noted Lipton, "there's an alternative to Flom."

There are, in fact, now a number of alternatives to both Flom and Lipton. The upsurge in both the size and number of takeovers was bound to attract new talent, but Skadden, Arps and Wachtell, Lipton dominate the field. A little over a decade ago, Skadden, Arps was crammed into a dim suite of offices in the Fred L. French Building (Forty-third Street and Fifth Avenue), where the decor can best be described as work-a-day utilitarian. The firm's internal directory listed about forty-five lawyers—thirteen partners and thirty-two associates. Now Skadden, Arps occupies the equivalent of seven full floors on Third Avenue in the fifties, a high-rent district where the three glass sides of Joe Flom's office command one of the most breathtaking cityscapes on the east side. The in-house directory now lists 240 lawyers—68 partners and 170 plus associates.

The growth at Wachtell, Lipton over the last decade has been exponential, too, but on a much smaller scale—from 25 to 50 lawyers. Part of the difference in size between the two firms reflects a difference in philosophy. "We have to continue growing so we can keep getting good people to make partners," said Martin Lipton, "but we don't want to be dominated by the takeover business. We want to keep the firm like a family where we can still recognize everybody in the hall." There is another difference. Wachtell, Lipton does not accept retainers, while Skadden, Arps does. Many companies hire Joe Flom as a kind of double-edged insurance policy—a way of having real muscle to call on if a takeover threat does surface, and at the same time a way of denying the use of Flom's services to any aggressor who might pose a threat. Wachtell, Lipton has always been broader-based than Skadden, Arps. Martin Lipton says that unfriendly takeovers account for about 15 to 20 percent of the practice, with the balance spread over friendly mergers, securities, and general corporate law. Skadden, Arps has been diversifying into securities, labor, and antitrust law, too, but the big money still comes from the takeover side of the practice. How big Flom will not say. "I really don't pay much attention to the management side of the firm," he says with lawyerly evasion.

An estimate that Flom's share of the firm's earnings in 1978 amounted to a whacking $1.1 million comes from Steven Brill, editor of the *American Lawyer*. A conscientious, energetic digger, Brill based his findings on talks with Skadden, Arps associates and clients. He reported that even partners at the low end of the pecking order—those in the "third tier," ranging in age from thirty-eight to forty-two—"made in excess of $450,000 each." On the whole, wrote Brill, the firm "far outpaced all [others] in the country in earnings per partner." The basic economics, if not the scale, are probably much the same at Wachtell, Lipton. High productivity and high volume are the key to profitability in any law firm.

The volume starts with the investment bankers. B,D's retaining Joseph Flom at the suggestion of First Boston is typical and one more illustration of the tight little world of the takeover professionals. Robert Greenhill, for example, often works with Martin Lipton, says he has "great respect" for him and describes him "as the kind of fellow, at least when he is advising me, who is always very cautious."

Joe Flom also sees "a great deal of" the Morgan Stanley managing director, "both working with him and against him. There are periods of time," Flom continued, "when I will be talking to him almost daily on matters [in which] we are working on the same side, or on the opposite side." Many of those who work together play together. At one point after the Sun purchase, for example, Flom recalled "various partners of Salomon Brothers being at the Marty Liptons and we were all kidding around about it." Flom also remembers at some point swapping banter about the B,D struggle with Ira Harris, one of Salomon's best known deal-makers, in the steam room at La Costa, the posh resort outside San Diego where even the vapors are perfumed with the smell of burning money. The socializing didn't mean that Flom was going to pull any punches, but the realist in him always knows which side of the bread is buttered. "I think I mentioned to Marty," he said of the Sun–B,D fight, "that the last thing in the world I want to do is sue investment bankers. I've got to live with them."

Flom and Lipton live well mainly because they bring a particularly sharp set of analytical skills to The Game—skills by now honed razor-sharp with constant use. "Every deal is different," said Flom, "and the real satisfactions come from doing something innovative." One professional described both Flom and Lipton as having an uncanny ability "to come to the chessboard and work out almost every conceivable scenario. They are superb," he continues, "at figuring out this very complete conceptual development where they can anticipate all the options that are open to the other guy and prepare their own contingency thinking."

Some securities lawyers argue that anybody with a mind to can be as good as Flom or Lipton "because we all read the same books, we all go by the same rules and regulations." That's a little like saying that anyone who reads the right books can bat with Reggie Jackson. It's not just the technical virtuosity that makes Flom and Lipton so good. As Flom noted, "Nobody can do this all by himself." Both men are backed by solid organization. They can throw platoons of lawyers into the fight. "Flom and Lipton are so disciplined," said one professional, "that they have figured out the options, they have the litigation in preparation, and they can file it like clockwork. That's why a target company—or an aggressor—can move so fast with them."

It's the technical virtuosity that catches the headlines, of course. Flom is famous for such imaginative ploys as the "Jewish Dentist" defense he brought to bear when Magus

Corporation, a foreign-based conglomerate, attempted to take over the Sterndent dental supply company. Zeroing in on what he argued was "incomplete disclosure," Flom argued Magus had failed to inform shareholders of a couple of highly material facts: (1) that Magus was 10 percent owned by a group of Kuwaitis; and (2) that the Jewish dentists who made up an important segment of Sterndent's clientele would never do business with a company controlled by Arabs. Flom could also lunch out forever at the Sky Club (the customary order is fruit salad and a split of champagne) on his recounting of the "Vanishing Author" defense—a strategem in which a posse of Houghton, Mifflin's top authors were encouraged to threaten to take their work elsewhere if the publishing company was absorbed by Western Pacific Industries. No slouch at the one-liner himself, Howard A. Newman, the CEO of Western Pacific, cracked that the author's well-orchestrated manifestation had "all the spontaneity of a demonstration in Red Square." Newman did back off, though, worried that he might win the battle only to lose the war for some of Houghton Mifflin's most important assets. Flom deprecates the gee-whiz press coverage of the Jewish Dentist and Vanishing Author gambits with a shrug and an airy wave of the hand, but they help to dramatize what he says is one of the main objectives of the defense: "to show that the aggressor is going to hurt the business; to make him reexamine the real cost of what he's trying to do."

Any second-year law student can run through the manual of standard defense moves—a flurry of counterpunches alleging breaches of securities laws, breaches of the antitrust laws, breaches of state takeover laws, "negative research" attacking the aggressor's credibility. The trick is to put it all together in virtually no turn-around time, as Martin Lipton did in defending McGraw-Hill against the importunings of American Express—and Joe Flom. Starting from scratch on a weekend, the Wachtell, Lipton team worked out a three-pronged strategy. In the space of eleven around-the-clock working days, it (a) helped to draft a sixteen-page request to the FCC asking that the proposed takeover be blocked, pending a full hearing on whether American Express should be permitted to operate McGraw-Hill's four television stations; (b) filed a thirty-seven-page request with the New York State Attorney General requesting an investigation of the legality of the American Express offer under the state takeover laws; (c) filed a complaint in New York State Supreme Court alleging that the takeover attempt was illegal; and (d) put forward a series of requests for hundreds of internal documents and the immediate deposition of top American Express officers. The decision early on was to strike at what Martin Lipton saw as an "embarrassment"—the contention that Roger H. Morley, then president of American Express, had hatched the takeover plot with the help of inside information gathered in his role as a director of McGraw-Hill.

There were also threats, reminiscent of the "Vanishing Author" scenario, that McGraw-Hill's writers wouldn't be caught dead working for a big financial conglomerate that might impinge on editorial freedom. "In a publishing company," says Lipton, "the inventory walks in the door every day." Flom didn't take any of that lying down. He staged a counterattack of his own in Federal Court, alleging—among other things—that a self-perpetuating McGraw-Hill management was "conspiring" to keep other shareholders from voting on a solid cash offer. In the end, American Express sweetened its original bid and then walked away from it, unhappily persuaded by an unyielding defense that the deal just wouldn't work. Flom apparently anticipated—and briefed American Express directors on—all of the moves that Marty Lipton would make, but he speaks with admiration of the quality of his friend's "scorched earth" defense. And why not, since it contained tested ingredients that Flom himself had used on other occasions. "You dream up something one day," he says, "and the next day somebody else is trying to shoot you in the ass with it."

Lipton and Flom are both highly competitive, and there are definitely times when they try to upstage each other. Their friendship, though, is deep enough to have withstood some of the most bitter rough-and-tumbles in the annals of American business. As Flom put it, "In my relationship with Marty, we talk about a lot of different subjects, both socially and on a business level, and some that are just evanescent." During one of their Saturday lunches at "21," Flom let drop a subject very close to his heart. Sun had not yet surfaced as a buyer, the Becton, Dickinson situation seemed stable enough, and Flom was about to head for St. Croix. He's had enough vacations cut short to last a lifetime, and remembered saying to Lipton, "I hope you're not going to rap me in the tail while I'm gone." The answer, as Flom recalls it, was that there was "nothing hot on the fire."

A couple of days later, though, Lipton learned it was very likely that Sun's Midnight Raid would be launched during the time when Flom hoped to be sunning himself at St. Croix. Lipton didn't like the idea of having "inadvertently misled" his friend and didn't want to put him at a disadvantage. At the same time Lipton certainly didn't want to breach the confidentiality he owed a client.

What to do? After thinking carefully about the "narrow path" he had to tread, Lipton called Flom with a trumped-up question on whether there was anything new in the talks they'd been having about the possibility of B,D's buying back Fairleigh Dickinson's stock. When Flom said he "didn't think anything would happen" until after his vacation, Lipton dropped one of his veils with what he thought was a really leading hint.

"I said to him, 'Well, as you know, Salomon Brothers continues to seek a deal for B,D and the matter may not await your return from vacation.' I didn't pursue it beyond that," added Lipton, "and he didn't ask any questions."

The lack of response didn't stop Lipton from another try at getting a subliminal warning through to his friend. Lipton had dinner the next night with Robert Pirie, one of Flom's partners. Pirie said Flom was looking "tired and worn out" and told Lipton how grateful Joe was for having been told "it was unlikely that anything would happen the following week that would interfere with his vacation."

"Didn't he tell you about the telephone conversation I had with him yesterday?" asked Lipton. Pirie didn't pick up the signal, and so it was that Flom had to fly back from the sunshine to the snows of New York to pull together the threads of the B,D defense. The big question was how the SEC would react to the group and illegal-tender theories that Flom and Arthur Liman were urging on the government agency. Had they made enough of a case to get an investigation—and maybe a lawsuit—going? Arthur Liman wasn't sure. The SEC meeting, he thought, had ended on the "usual note of frustration. They were interested and concerned that this kind of transaction could be done, but they wouldn't tell us what they planned to do."

Three weeks to the day after the Midnight Raid, Becton filed suit on its own in Federal Court for the Southern District of New York, charging Sun with an "illegal acquisition." The complaint also cited Fairleigh Dickinson, J. H. Fitzgerald Dunning, Salomon Brothers, and Eberstadt as defendants acting "in concert and conspiracy." There was still no inkling of where the SEC was going to come down, but B,D went into court backed by a brilliantly engineered public relations campaign aimed at giving Sun a bloody nose and forcing the SEC to act.

8

Press Agents, Politicians, and the Press

It was D-Day plus two and B,D was beginning to regroup. The outlines of a counterattack had begun to emerge and Joseph Flom was seized by one overwhelming argument: "If the Sun transaction was permitted to stand," he said, "the Williams Act would be hollow. It would be emasculated. No one would ever make a public tender."

Thinking aloud at this strategy meeting now, Flom told an intent caucus of B,D executives and investment bankers that there might be pay dirt in hammering at the public policy question. If Sun got away with it, "control of the largest industries could pass overnight." Further, at the very moment Sun was spending "hundreds of millions of dollars" to snuff out B,D as an independent entity, "it's fellow members in the oil industry were supplicants before Congress, saying they needed money in order to look for new sources of energy." Sun's Midnight Raid was "totally inconsistent" with what Congress was being told. The raid just couldn't stand moral or ethical scrutiny.

The investment bankers, Arthur Liman and several other Paul, Weiss partners, warmed to the discussion. Congress in its recent debate on the Hart-Scott-Rodino bill had expressed its intention that all big acquisitions be submitted for scrutiny on antitrust grounds to the Justice Department and the Federal Trade Commission. The Midnight Raid had been ratified only by big institutional investors who had profited at the expense of other shareholders. Control of American industry, if it didn't slip into the grasp of oil companies "sitting with huge reserves of cash," could very well "pass overnight to OPEC or other foreign nations—Korea, for example."

The brainstorming went on. It was a typical Flom production—an orchestration rather than a solo performance, based on a strategic doctrine that says that what happens in a court of law is often determined by what happens in the court of public opinion. "It's impossible to say where an idea comes from," said Flom. "It may start with the lawyers, investment bankers, or the client—but no matter where it starts, you have to have really good public relations people on the team. You have to get the message out."

The message, as seen by the public relations people—Marvin Krasnansky inside B,D, Richard Cheney at the Hill & Knowlton agency outside—had to be directed at both Capitol Hill and the press. Yes, the public at large had to be told, but the ultimate audience was small and very select. It consisted of Harold Williams, then chairman of the SEC, and the board of the Sun Company. "Our first objective," recalled Marvin Krasnansky, "was to bring the

SEC into the picture by focusing attention on what we believed to be gross violations of the securities law. The underlying strategy was to raise the discomfort level for Sun's management, its board, most particularly, the pub-licity-shy Pew family" that controlled Sun. Putting Sun through the wringer—really damaging the company's im-age—might persuade the Pews that B,D was a very poor investment indeed. The shortest route to both the SEC and the Pews lay through Congress, and Arthur Liman had drawn into the B,D strategic planning a technician who knew first-hand every twist in the road, Theodore C. Sorensen. A special counsel to and speech writer for the late President Kennedy, Sorensen had been a partner in Paul, Weiss for a dozen years. He specializes in interna-tional law, but at the moment had some time open to deal with B,D's singularly domestic problem.

Sorensen reinforced Flom's lead. He thought Congress certainly would be "disturbed at the implications" of the Sun purchase if it was brought forcefully to the legislators' attention. He added yet another count to Flom's presenta-tion—the question of what outside acquisitions might do to the sensitive subject of the "health-care industry and cost containment." The rising cost of medicine is chron-ically a hot issue on the Hill. Acquisition by outsiders with a different set of values might strip such purveyors of health-care items as B,D of cash in a way that could mean higher prices, or siphon off profits that should be plowed back into vitally important spending on research and development.

Sorensen suggested that the public policy issues could well create a stir among key legislators interested in the major headings that had been mentioned—health care, stockholder protection, antitrust, and energy. A pointed, tightly organized position paper might help to bring the powerful committee chairman over to B,D's side. Sorensen said he would draft the paper after making a quick reconnaissance of the Hill. He sounded out, among other movers and shakers, William Proxmire, then chairman of the Senate Banking Committee; Harrison A. Williams, Jr., then chairman of the Senate subcommittee on securities, and their top staff people. In a memo to Arthur Liman, Sorensen said the legislators had asked for a draft of "a strong letter" they could sign and send on to SEC chairman Harold Williams demanding an immediate investigation of the Sun deal. "We should urge," suggested Sorensen, "that the letter be prompt and public."

Sorensen reported that he had also made the rounds of shareholder-protection subcommittees in both houses, and conferred with the chairman of the Senate antitrust subcommittee, his old friend Edward M. Kennedy. Herman Schwartz, counsel for the subcommittee, should be contacted immediately about the possibility of conducting public hearings on the Sun purchase. The cast for the hearing, said Sorensen, might include the head of the SEC enforcement division; "small, unhappy B,D stockholders"; and an investment banker "or other market specialist who will testify that all shareholders could have done better." There was also a possibility that Senator Kennedy might press the Federal Trade Commission to make a public statement as to where it stood on the Sun purchase. Franz Opper, counsel for the House Consumer Protection and Finance subcommittee, should also be followed up on the possibility of a public hearing, or at least the production of a public statement that the SEC should move on the Sun matter.

The direct lobbying approach to the committee chairmen, Sorensen urged, should be backed with an aggressive grass roots campaign. B,D plant managers throughout the United States should be instructed to protest the Sun takeover in personal visits to their Senators and Congressmen, or at least by telephone, with followup by telegram. Sorensen's blueprint was quickly translated into action.

The draft of the letter to the chairmen of three Congressional committees with primary jurisdiction over the SEC and the securities laws—Proxmire, Harrison Williams, and Representative John E. Moss, head of the subcommittee on oversight and investigation—went out almost immediately. With only modest changes, the letter was sent over their signatures to SEC chairman Harold Williams. It was an echo of almost everything that had been aired around the B,D strategy table.

The legislators underlined their "great concern" over Sun's "sudden and surreptitious purchase" of a controlling position in B,D in a fashion that deprived some thirteen thousand stockholders of "the most fundamental benefits" of the Williams Act.

Public shareholders, the letter continued, were not furnished with information mandated by the Act; they were not permitted to share in the premium offered the institutions; management was deprived of the opportunity to seek competing and presumably higher bids; and B,D holders were deprived of access to a public market. It all added up to what appeared to be an illegal tender offer.

If the Sun purchase was allowed to stand, the Williams Act would be nullified. Other big companies, the legislators told the SEC chairman, would be subject to instant takeovers through the action of financial institutions or foreign investors without the public's receiving the protection of the Williams Act.

After thus impressing on the SEC chairman B,D's legal theory and its potential consequences on U.S. industry generally, the legislators focused on the public policy issues. The Sun purchase raised questions about the size of the oil industry's cash flow and its potential impact on health-care costs. "How is the oil industry's claim that it needs higher prices for new energy exploration and development consistent with Sun's expenditures of nearly $300 million to purchase B,D stock?" demanded the legislators.

Like the scorpion, the letter had its sting in the tail. It ended on this note: "We most strongly urge that the Commission promptly investigate." The committee chairmen would "appreciate a prompt reply," and "would also appreciate your keeping us informed of your actions in this matter."

It was a ten-strike that demonstrated, said Marvin Krasnansky, how useful Sorensen was "in singling out names on the Hill, and suggesting approaches that might strike a chord in the breasts of certain Congressmen." Krasnansky himself was on a first-name basis with only two members of the New Jersey delegation on the Hill; his exposure to the workings of Washington was comparatively limited. Hill & Knowlton, on the other hand, had lots of experience working the Capitol, which was one of the reasons why the agency had been retained at a fee of $4,000 a month. The major attraction though, as Krasnansky put it, was the demonstrated expertise of the agency's vice-chairman, Richard Cheney, "in advising on the best defensive measures against unfriendly takeovers." Cheney, who has retained the corn-pone purity of his central Illinois accent against all of the linguistic assaults of three decades in New York, has a lively sense of humor. He'd been asked to contribute to the B,D Washington strategy and broke up the meeting with his response to Theodore Sorensen. "I told Mr. Sorensen," recalled Cheney, "that for us to help him in talking to Congress struck me as telling Noah about the flood, and unless he directed me to do something, I felt I could leave it in his good hands."

Tactical command of the grass roots campaign Sorensen had recommended was put in the hands of B,D's public affairs director, James R. Tobin, who had gone to work for the company as an industrial engineer not long after graduating from the College of the Holy Cross more than twenty years earlier. The big, gregarious Tobin had spent more than fifteen of the years since articulating B,D's views on tax and health-care legislation in both Trenton and Washington. Thanks to his long exposure to Washington, Tobin said he knew a "majority" of both the House and Senate by "acquaintance," and "quite a few of the members on a first-name basis. I am a very first-name type of person," he added. "Always have been."

Tobin thinks the best approach to a legislator is to "tell him what his constituent interest is." Tobin started with the basic arithmetic. B,D has more than twenty plants and offices in the United States, located in some twenty-odd Congressional Districts in eighteen states. For openers, Tobin figured that meant talking to forty or fifty legislators about the potential impact of the Sun purchase on the folks back home. He put together a master list and grouped the legislators by priorities. Those who were members of six key committees—energy, banking, commerce, appropriations, judiciary, and ways and means—definitely had to be called on in person. Others who "might be beneficial because of constituent interest, even though not on a particularly relevant committee," were marked as "worth a visit." Legislators of the third priority—those representing areas where B,D had only small sales offices or warehouses—were put down for followup by telephone and telegrams.

Tobin's list had twenty-five representatives and thirteen senators in the first priority. They (or their top aides) were to be given copies of the Proxmire-Williams letter to the SEC, a copy of the B,D annual report, and a copy of the Sorensen position paper. It described the Sun purchase as "a lightning covert operation" that raised questions about (a) the oil industry's need for higher prices to support exploration; (b) Congressional intent, explicitly stated in the Williams Act, that all shareholders—large and small— should be treated fairly; and (c) the escalating costs of health care. Tobin's mission was clear. The lawmakers were to be asked "to look into the situation and to use their offices as legislators to represent their constituencies by petitioning for speedy redress of the problem." The SEC should be urged to act "expeditiously and effectively."

Tobin recruited a task force consisting of six plant managers and B,D's director of labor relations. He ran a quick briefing for them in B,D's Washington office. The "gang of seven," as they were baptized, were given maps so "they could tell Cannon from the Rayburn building," and injected with a bit of protocol. Tobin explained that "you call a Senator 'Senator,' that you can call a Congressman either 'Congressman' or 'Mister.'" He also recalled telling the gang that "you are always courteous, that you are always responsive, open, and above all, that everything you say is absolutely accurate and true, to the best of your knowledge." The seven were then loosed on the Hill with some startling results. Tobin described the results with a throwaway line and a grin. "Generally everybody we met was cordial," he said. "We didn't get thrown out of any place." John Huber, for example, B,D's plant manager at Sumter, South Carolina, to his eternal astonishment, found himself in a chummy tête-à-tête with Senator Ernest F. Hollings, a former Governor of South Carolina. Hollings, upset by what he had heard, almost immediately got Harold Williams on the phone and then wrote the SEC chairman asking—among other things—for the "legal basis" on which the government agency had shut down trading in B,D stock. Hollings said that if he didn't get an answer by weekend, he would personally contact the Attorney General "and have him investigate." When Williams informed Hollings it was not the SEC but the Stock Exchange that had shut down the stock, the Senator apologized, but made it clear that when "constituent interest" was at stake, he was not to be trifled with. Maybe the SEC hadn't ordered the trading halt, but it had certainly acquiesced in it, and what was the explanation for that? Representative Toby Moffett of Connecticut put out a press release questioning the "legal and ethical implications" of the Sun takeover. Representative Benjamin Gilman of Orangeburg fired off a letter based on the B,D survival kit demanding that the New York State

Superintendent of Banks look into the actions of state-chartered banks that had sold B,D stock to Sun, and Senator Edward Brooke asked the Comptroller of the Currency to do the same with federally chartered banks.

Tobin himself called on "eight or nine" legislators or top committee staffers and, between appointments, persuaded eleven members of the New Jersey congressional delegation to sign a letter demanding the by now familiar "prompt and thorough investigation from the SEC." The letter was drafted in the office of Representative Harold C. "Cap" Hollenbeck, in whose district B,D's East Rutherford plant lies, but Tobin was more than happy to midwife the document's birth. He saw it "several times before it was fully signed and sent."

There was a modest show of force in Trenton, too, when Tobin talked to both the Governor's counsel and Bergen County legislators in an effort to stir up some action against Sun under the New Jersey takeover statute. His primary mission, though, was to follow up on the committee staffers Theodore Sorensen had touched base with in his reconnaissance. They were cordial and promised "to look into things," but the prospect of the immediate hearings that had been raised in the earlier talks with Sorensen seemed to be evaporating. Franz Opper, counsel for the house subcommittee on consumer protection, for example, told Tobin that his members—now that B,D had gone to court—were not interested in airing the subject. A number of other legislators took the same line, and it would be another four months before Wesley Howe would be asked to testify before the Senate antitrust subcommittee. On balance, however, the gang of seven had carried the message to almost all of the legislators on Tobin's master list and succeeded in energizing quite a few of them. The real coup had been the Proxmire-Williams letter, which predictably enough got solid coverage in many of the nation's major dailies. It was by now clear that the SEC had started a formal investigation of the Sun takeover. The government agency almost certainly would have done so even if B,D hadn't pulled out all the publicity stops, but that didn't mean the pressure was going to let up. Sun was taking a pounding in the press, an advantage that Krasnansky and Cheney did not intend to lose.

Sun was laboring under a terrific handicap. Part of its difficulty with the press lay in its basic strategy. In the crucial days before Sun filed its form 13(d), when its hard-pressed couriers were struggling to bring home the B,D shares, the oil company was literally locked into silence. Marvin Krasnansky and Richard Cheney, on the other hand, were not. They were talking to reporters all the time, and the coverage reflected it. The New York Times and the Wall Street Journal were quick to piece together the presence of Fairleigh Dickinson, Jr., Salomon Brothers, big institutional sellers, and Sun. By D-Day plus three, the New York Times' Robert Metz was saying in his widely read "Market Place" column that "the mysterious halt in trading in the shares of B,D has raised questions as to whether the interests of individual shareholders are being served."

Citing unconfirmed reports of "massive off the board" institutional sales "through Salomon Brothers," Metz said "the remaining individual shareholders have been left out in the cold." Speculating that the size of the purchase may have precluded the prospect of B,D's eliciting a competing bid from a White Knight, Metz said that "in the long run, the individual may get less for his shares than he might otherwise receive. That, according to one cynical observer," the *New York Times* columnist continued, "could explain all this secrecy."

Metz in the same column cited an anonymous lawyer as noting "it is inconceivable that a group could have come together for purposes of such a coordinated sale in the last 10 days. Under the Williams Act, filings are required in 10 days and there may be violation here." The lawyer was also critical of the Big Board for, in effect, cooperating in takeovers by unnecessarily shutting down trading in a target's stock for more than the "few hours" it takes to get an explanation on the trading tape. The column anticipated much of the B,D counteroffensive and drove into public consciousness the possibility that Sun might have breached the Williams Act—all without a word of contradiction from the oil company.

Even when it filed the 13(d) and was presumably somewhat more free to talk, Sun came off badly. Reporting on the filing, Robert J. Cole of the *New York Times* said there was a "question being raised on Wall Street." The question: "Whether Sun's highly secret accumulation of Becton stock . . . at a time when trading in the stock was suspended could be construed a violation of Federal securities laws; or as an unofficial tender offer that deprived small shareholders of a chance to sell their Becton stock to Sun on the same terms."

There was no indication in the story that the question was put to the Sun spokesman who told Cole that the abbreviation of the subsidiary through which the B,D stock had been purchased—L.H.I.W.—stands "for nothing." The spokesman did not improve on his credibility a couple of days later when Cole asked him point blank whether the initials stood for "Let's Hope It Works." "The spokesman scoffed," reported Cole, and reiterated that "the initials had no meaning, having been chosen so they could not possibly be the name of an already existing company, and thus cause delay."

That colloquy occurred in a telephone conversation after a Krasnansky press release charged that the Sun purchase was "secret" and "illegal." Sun did for once manage to get across the argument that the stock had been bought "as a result of contracts with sellers made prior" to the trading shutdown requested on its behalf. Cole also reported Sun's contention that the stock had been bought "privately," but in general the oil company seemed unable to get the press to convey to readers the heart of its rebuttal—i.e., the contention that there is a significant legal distinction between a tender offer and a series of private purchases.

When Stephen M. Aug of the *Washington Star* put together one of the first step-by-step recreations of the deal from Sun's 13(d) and other sources, Salomon Brothers had "no comment," and by the time word of the Proxmire-Williams letter to the SEC broke, the Sun defense—if it ever existed—was dissolving through most dailies like the smile of the Cheshire Cat.

The good press that B,D was getting didn't just happen. Many editors tend to think of stories in categories. For them, B,D *versus* Sun was one more recounting of David against Goliath, and even the dullards on the copy desk know who won that one. Simple mind-riveting concepts such as "Mysterious Halt" and "Illegal Purchase" make headlines; legalistic distinctions between private purchases and tenders don't. Somehow the denials never seem to catch up with the charges. Sun was hurting. The company did try to interdict B,D on Capitol Hill in the form of a one-man truth squad by the name of Horace Kephart, and it registered enough of a complaint with Wesley Howe for him to take the precaution of consulting with his lawyers on how long a leash his PR men should be given. The Sun board may have been prepared intellectually for a tough lawsuit, but some of the oil company's directors were apparently shocked by the idea that B,D would stoop to using poison gas.

In Krasnansky and Cheney, Sun was up against the very best in the business. Cheney, who has a master's degree in psychology from Columbia, worked on *Tide*—that long-defunct journal of the advertising world—before taking the public relations veil three decades ago. Like Krasnansky, he has a highly developed sense of what makes a good story. Equally important, he knows which reporters like what kind of material. He describes Robert Metz of the *New York Times*, for example, as "interested in articles about matters where small individual shareowners or individual owners of companies have gotten a bum deal, or any stockholder, where one group of stockholders gets a bum deal at the expense of another." Stephen Aug of the *Washington Star*, on the other hand, "based on his stories, is concerned about concentration of economic power and misuse of it; the ownership of American companies who abuse their fiduciary responsibilities."

Cheney and Krasnansky make it their business to get around and talk to reporters. Each of them does some entertaining. Cheney counts Bob Metz among his personal friends and cracks that he "bought him dinner once before he got married." Krasnansky "may go out socially with some people on occasion, have them for a guest at a football or a soccer game." He sometimes "takes a newspaper person to lunch" and on occasion is even taken to lunch—a happening he described with no evident surprise as "a more recent trend in the newspaper business."

Long, liquid lunches, says Cheney, were a staple of the PR trade "twenty years ago," when the business news departments at some big dailies were heavy with vinous rejects from other sections of the paper who tended to slip down the copy chute by late afternoon. No longer, says Cheney. "Business writing has improved enormously," and the trade is attracting "bright, shrewd reporters who are much better educated and much more independent. A lot of reporters like food," he adds, "but you're not going to buy a reporter with a nice lunch." Gershon Kekst, who owns Kekst & Company, after Hill & Knowlton probably the most experienced PR firm in the Takeover Game, makes the same point. "There is absolutely no similarity between the financial writers of twenty-five years ago and those of today. None. Today they are younger, they are brighter, far better educated, far more aggressive, and far less likely to take handouts over a bar."

The most toothsome item Cheney can think of is a good story idea and in the Takeover Game that often as not means "negative research." The term is drawn from politics and starts with the assumption—or at least hope—that there is a skeleton to exploit in every aggressor's closet. "You try to put his credibility in jeopardy some way," said Cheney, find "some huge bomb you can throw into his operation that you can suddenly spotlight to make an impression." Though Sun seemed unprepared for the beating it was taking on the secrecy and public policy issues, the attack on credibility is a common ploy. Gershon Kekst, for example, who represented McGraw-Hill in its battle with American Express, had a made-to-order issue in the alleged "conflict of interest" posed by Roger H. Morley's dual role as a director of the publishing company and president of the company that was trying to take it over. Kekst also had a number of made-to-order issues for him when he represented the Mead Corporation in its epic four-month-long struggle with Occidental Petroleum Corporation. Occidental, led by that inner-directed octogenarian Armand Hammer, had controversy aplenty in its background—problems with the SEC, questions about illegal personal campaign contributions, and a tangle of litigation over environmental violations sitting on the doorstep of a major subsidiary, Hooker Chemical Corporation. An outside director of Occidental conceded to the *Wall Street Journal* that "the vehemence of the personal attacks [in the press] contributed to" his company's decision to call off the attack on Mead. The material was all in the files, just waiting to be mined.

The search is always for what Hitchcock called the "McGuffin"—a pivot on which the plot can turn; a concept simple and easy to dramatize. The search usually starts with newspaper clips and public documents on file

[193]

with the SEC. "We sit down with the investment bankers and go through the financial statements," said Kekst. "Then we sit down with the lawyers and go through all of the legal and regulatory implications. We go through it with them looking for material that is either interesting or relevant and try to find a pattern."

The pattern is sometimes quick to emerge. Cheney, for example, recalled on one occasion picking up the genesis of a counterattack out of a fast reading of an aggressor company's proxy statement. It showed that the CEO's salary and bonus were keyed to earnings. The company's earnings, however, were in a down trend. One inference was that a takeover would enhance the aggressor's earning power all right, and call for bonus payments to the CEO as well. Cheney put it all together in an advertisement that ran in the CEO's hometown newspaper, the *Greenwich* (Connecticut) *Times*. "I love to do that," laughed Cheney. "I learned it from Saul Alinsky. You don't picket in front of your own building, you go picket the landlord's house."

The ploy can be overdone. Cheney on another occasion was fighting an aggressor who, in a résumé given to stockholders, announced he had gone to the "University of Northwestern." The reversal of what should have come out as "Northwestern University" caught Cheney's eye. On a hunch, he checked Northwestern and found the aggressor "had gone there for only three non-consecutive semesters and he claimed to be a graduate." Cheney says he also found out the aggressor "had left this company and set up a competing business that went bankrupt." All of that was put in an ad that ran in the aggressor's hometown newspaper. There was trouble. "We were trying to work out a settlement with him," recalled Cheney, "only somebody forgot to tell me. They were just about to sign when the ad ran. It blew the settlement for the moment, and it took three weeks to get this guy down from the ceiling. They gave him a seat on the board," added Cheney with a shudder, "but he could never forgive me. He's still on the board right now, and he'll never forget it."

Cheney doesn't think of himself as running a department of dirty tricks. "There's never any falsification," he says. "We stick only to the verifiable truth. You can't call a reporter and tell him things that aren't true. Good reporters see right through that and they resent it. They resent that kind of an arm bend."

Much of the negative research technique, in fact, revolves around giving—or pointing—a reporter to the germ of the story and letting him do the verifying himself. Cheney says he milked the "Vanishing Author" ploy at Houghton Mifflin for maximum publicity by giving carbon copies of the authors' protesting letters to Robert Lenzner at the *Boston Globe.* "I found out where Lenzner could reach Schlesinger and Galbraith, both of whom were Houghton Mifflin authors," continued Cheney. "He called them and they told him their views on leaving Houghton Mifflin if Western Pacific took over and he had a story."

The story was subsequently followed by the *New York Times* and the *Wall Street Journal.* "It was only partly out of published documents," said Cheney, "but it was creative and fun. No big deal, but perfect because it was a rifle shot."

Sun got the blunderbuss. At one point, for instance, Krasnansky thought the point B,D was trying to establish on Capitol Hill could be reinforced by an overall piece on the menace of takeovers. Hill & Knowlton produced a long list of companies with heavy institutional ownership, ranging from Air Products & Chemicals to the Upjohn Company. Included with the list was a background account of the B,D experience; it got good pickup all over the country, including a piece by Stephen Aug in the *Washington Star* headed "59 Big Corporations Appear Vulnerable to Overnight Raids." The article scrupulously noted that the list of fifty-nine had been prepared by B,D from "publicly available sources," but inexorably went on to say that the Sun deal had been "strongly criticized by several influential Congressmen and Senators . . . for apparent lack of fairness." As Cheney candidly admitted, the concept was to accentuate the negative. There was no attempt to put pressure on Sun, he says with a grin. "It's all disclosure. Everything should be out in the sunshine."

Becton's sunshine boys were particularly anxious to put a psychological burn on Sun's directors—a standard defense tactic. For reporters who like to spit and whittle with him on the subject of the engineering of public opinion, Cheney has a favorite saying: "Companies whose directors don't like to be interrupted at garden parties ought not to be in the takeover game." Acting on that principle, B,D executive vice-president Marvin Asnes called William F. Pounds, dean of the Alfred P. Sloan School of Management at Massachusetts Institute of Technology and a Sun director, a few days after the raid. Asnes, an M.I.T. grad, is on the visiting committee of the Sloan School, and minced no words describing his own feeling about "a prominent member of the academic business community being associated with a move" that had "no redeeming economical or social value."

Asnes came on very tough, indeed. He asked the M.I.T. dean how he "justified his participation in this affront to public policy." The Sun raid, Asnes continued, had caused unrest at all levels of B,D management, enriched thirty stockholders to the impoverishment of eleven hundred others, and breached the Williams Act. Asnes closed on a chilling note, telling Pounds that he "might have an interesting time on the witness stand justifying his posture as the dean of a major business school in associating himself with such an effort."

Cheney recalled talking to the *New York Times* Robert Metz about Pounds' being "not altogether sure whether this [Sun] transaction was a good one. I have a vague feeling I might have mentioned Dean Pounds," says Cheney. "It is conceivable I even had his phone number, but I don't remember." Metz called the Dean and reported in his "Market Place" column that the academician "said he did not consider himself to be an expert on the Sun transaction itself." He quoted Pounds as saying, "I was informed and inquired as best I could of the effectiveness and appropriateness of the way the transaction was undertaken. I was obviously relying heavily on the advice of others." The Metz piece went on to say Pounds indicated "a lawyer spoke on these matters at a meeting of Sun's directors. He did not know who the lawyer was. He said that his attitude toward the transaction—which he approves—had not changed. He spoke of it in the context of the petroleum company's long-term efforts to diversify. . . . Rumors that some directors of Sun have had second thoughts about the takeover attempt," reported Metz, "could not be confirmed."

The idea of dissension on the Sun board had been

planted, though, and Cheney followed it up with another brainstorm keyed to a reading of another of those ubiquitous public documents, a Sun quarterly report. As Cheney recalled, it "had an elaborate discussion of the big plans for the Sun annual meeting with inside TV and all the rest." Now suddenly the meeting had been postponed. The Hill & Knowlton executive called Bob Metz, and suggested he might want to look into why, given "all this lavish effort," the meeting had been delayed. Cheney said he "perhaps gave" the *New York Times* writer the phone number of former Sun chairman Robert G. Dunlop, who, while the planning for the Midnight Raid was underway, had raised a number of questions with Sun management about the benefits of the B,D deal. Providing the Dunlop name and telephone number was all part of the Cheney service: "Anything we can do to help a reporter pursue a story, if he feels he wants to pursue it, is a courtesy." Other reporters were out pursuing the story, too. "Signs of Dissension at Sun" ran the headline in the *Philadelphia Inquirer.* "Internal Split Seen at Sun Over Becton Move" said the headline over the Greer-Kandel Report in the *Washington Star.*

There were indeed signs of dissension, signs that began to multiply after the SEC—on D-Day plus seven weeks—filed suit in Federal Court for the Southern District of New York charging Sun with having breached the Williams Act.

Among the other defendants were Fairleigh S. Dickinson, Jr., J. H. Fitzgerald Dunning, Kenneth Lipper, Robert Zeller, Salomon Brothers, and Eberstadt & Company. The complaint was a PR man's dream—a treasure trove of negative research. Robert Metz has been covering Wall

Street for a long time and Cheney is just one of many sources, but the PR man presumed to give his friend a superfluous suggestion: read the complaint, he said. The column was headed "A Behind-the-Scenes Look at Bid for Becton."

9

Trial and Error

Richard Cheney could scarcely be blamed for urging his
newspaper friends to study the SEC complaint. Artfully
crafted, it read almost as though it might have been tailor-
made for journalistic consumption—a brisk narrative of the
management split at B,D; Fairleigh Dickinson's ouster; the
shopping of his stock; and the deal with Sun that
culminated in the Midnight Raid.

The SEC's legal theories fell pretty much in line with
what Joseph Flom and Arthur Liman had been arguing for
months. They focused on two major contentions: (1) that
Sun had breached the Williams Act by making a tender
offer without giving the requisite warning under Section
14(d); (2) that Fairleigh Dickinson, J. H. Fitzgerald
Dunning, and Eberstadt—through its management of the
Chemical and Surveyor funds—had breached Section
13(d) of the act by failing to give notice they had formed a
group aimed at transferring control of B,D.

From those two basic points there trailed a streamer of other allegations: Robert Zeller, Kenneth Lipper, Salomon Brothers, and Eberstadt had "aided and abetted" Sun's illegal tender offer, while Zeller, Lipper, and Salomon "aided and abetted" the group violation. Fairleigh Dickinson breached his fiduciary duties as a director by not disclosing that he was trying to engineer a takeover. Sun had further breached the tender rules by giving terms to Fairleigh Dickinson and his daughter, Ann Dickinson Turner—an installment sale of their stock that reduced tax liabilities—different from those offered the other sellers. Sun had also breached 13(d) by failing to disclose it was more than a "passive investor" in B,D—i.e., that it had set out to buy "negative control" as a way of pinching off prospective competing bids. Eberstadt broke the strictures of the Investment Company Act against self-dealing by helping Sun put together the B,D purchase for a sizable fee in one of its manifestations, while in yet another serving as a fiduciary to two key B,D shareholders—the Chemical and Surveyor funds. Zeller aided and abetted the violation.

So contended the SEC in an intervention that immeasurably strengthened B,D's position. The government agency's entrance infused B,D's argument with broad public interest. The SEC's presence transformed what some judges might have seen as just one more of those narrow sectarian boardroom struggles between two headstrong managements into an issue freighted with significance for investors everywhere. The SEC jumped into the fight because it agreed with Flom's argument that his good friend Martin Lipton had planned a brilliantly executed flanking move on the Williams Act that got his client exactly where it wanted to go with speed and secrecy to burn. That new route, if not blocked, could well become a superhighway through the heart of the Williams Act leading right back to the bad old days of the "Saturday Night Special," when raiders could stampede shareholders into giving up their stock for a pittance.

That was not the way Sun saw things. Horace Kephart told reporters that he was "baffled and upset." The SEC, he said, "is trying to write law rather than enforce existing law." And so the issue was joined. Sun may have been baffled, but it could not have been too surprised. Some of its own lawyers had recognized the virtuosity of the Lipton approach early on, and more or less reconciled themselves to the certainty that novelty was a lot more likely to draw judicial attention than the tried and true. That didn't mean, though, that the oil company was going to take the SEC's incursion sitting down. "It was those gales of publicity, the lobbying effort that got the SEC to act," raged one Sun attorney. "They rarely intervene in a case like this, particularly when you've already got heavyweight law firms representing both sides." That curbstone opinion was elevated during the pre-trial discovery phase of the case to a counterforce strategy. Questioning James Tobin about what he and the B,D gang of seven had been doing on Capitol Hill, Wachtell Lipton partner Douglas S. Lieb-hafsky promised that "this lobbying effort, this politicking is going to be developed in this case, and the court is going to be made fully aware of the manner in which the SEC was induced to act here. The court is going to be made aware of the gigantic political effort." The Tobin deposition, coupled with similar questioning of Cheney and Marvin Krasnansky, became the basis of an argument that the case should be thrown out of court. Because of its effort to blacken the oil company's image, B,D was coming to the bar with "unclean hands," contended Sun, and thus was not entitled to a hearing. As for the SEC, it had caved in to political pressure, and so also forfeited its right to be heard.

For an SEC enforcement action, it was big league stuff. The B,D suit, several individual B,D stockholder suits, and the SEC suit were consolidated for ease of handling into one action. Counting those appearing for Sun, Fairleigh Dickinson, and the other defendants, there were eight top-flight law firms directly involved in the case, while at least one other (Skadden, Arps) did legwork behind the scenes. Lawyers from both sides remember the pre-trial period as a blur of depositions. About 115 people were examined in five months—an average of more than one witness per working day. The witnesses were spread all over the country and a lot of the preparation was done on the run. "You'd have one day to depose somebody," recalls one SEC attorney, "and then go right on to the next. You'd be in Madison on Monday, fly to Minneapolis on Tuesday, move from Minneapolis to San Francisco and then from San Francisco to L.A. It was really a massive effort to get the case to trial."

Making an effort of that scale on its own would have stretched the government agency's enforcement arm to the breaking point. Thanks to the resources B,D, was pouring into the fight, however, the SEC litigating team—five attorneys and one paralegal—was able to draw on the talent and manpower of the three law firms the company had retained—Paul, Weiss; Skadden, Arps; and Parker, Auspitz, Neesemann & Delehanty. "I've never been involved in another action where we had such cooperation from private law firms," said one SEC attorney. One of the firms kept the SEC lawyers supplied with files holding the paperwork—diaries, memos, and minutes of investment company meetings, for example—that is the raw material of the discovery process. Still another of the firms put together a detailed chronology of the Sun–B,D struggle that ultimately swelled to the thickness of the Manhattan telephone book. So massive was the discovery effort that when the issue came to trial in November—ten months after the Midnight Raid—Paul, Weiss literally wheeled its case into court in the form of six filing cabinets. A total of more than thirty lawyers and half as many paralegals made for such a crush that almost all of the spectator benches in Judge Robert L. Carter's courtroom had to be removed to give them elbow room. The pick-and-shovel work of discovery had sharpened the issues. Some of the facts were in dispute, but the case would turn mainly on how Judge Carter interpreted the law.

A strikingly handsome man of medium height and build, Judge Carter received his law degree from Howard University in 1940 and, after four years in the Army Air Corps during World War II, joined the National Association for the Advancement of Colored People as a legal assistant. Carter was general counsel when he left the organization in 1969 to spend two years as a partner in the well-connected law firm of Poletti, Freiden, Prashker, Feldman & Gastner before being nominated to the bench in 1972.

It was not an easy case to get a handle on. Was the SEC stretching the term "group" to cover several diverse interests, which had come to no common agreement at all to sell B,D? Did the Sun raid carry all of the traditional hallmarks of a tender offer—pressure on a widespread number of shareholders to act quickly if they wanted to benefit from a non-negotiable premium, for instance? Or was the deal, as Sun argued, simply a series of private purchases from sophisticated sellers that was anything but a tender offer?

Embedded within those legal questions, like an enigma within a puzzle, were some tough factual considerations: Had Fairleigh Dickinson reluctantly come to a decision to sell his shares only after losing all hope of working out a solution with management? Or had he been intending sale from the very beginning? Had Salomon Brothers, Kenneth Lipper, and Robert Zeller really told prosepctive buyers they could "deliver" 20 percent of B,D? Or had they simply voiced a professional opinion that the right price would shake loose a lot of stock? Had Sun actually set out to gain "negative control" of B,D? Or did Sun simply want to accumulate enough of the stock so that B,D's aggressive management couldn't dilute its position below the all-important equity accounting mark of 20 percent?

Led gently around the group concept by his lawyer, Sheldon H. Elsen of Orans, Elsen, Polstein & Natfalis, Dickinson testified there had been no discussion whatever of the Chemical Fund's holdings of Becton, Dickinson— not in the first war council at Salomon Brothers after he had been deposed as chairman; not at any time before the Sun deal that he knew of. Dickinson was aware that the Fund had owned B,D stock for a long time, but there had never been any kind of agreement, oral or written, involving the sale of his and the fund's holdings.

It was true, Dickinson continued, that he had signed a letter indemnifying Salomon Brothers against any liability that might grow out of their efforts to "seek an offer" for his stock, but the document didn't quite mean what it seemed to say. The circumstances under which he had signed the letter were "a little complicated." Prodded by Joe Flom's threats of a lawsuit against Salomon, Martin Lipton had urged the investment banking firm to get some protection in writing from Dickinson. Dickinson talked it over with his own lawyer, Jerome Lipper, and decided to let things sit. Dickinson told Judge Carter he thought the letter was too open-ended, and exposed him to unknown risks. "It would be against anything I was ever taught to do," he said.

A couple of months later, though, Lipton really began to push. Jerome Lipper, Dickinson continued, had "reflections" and suggested now that he sign the letter. Dickinson did so, he said, because "the loss of Salomon's counsel would have been catastrophic." Besides, he added, Salomon's treatment of him as a friend of the firm was "quixotic." "I would interpret their position," he said, "as having gone far beyond self-interest—they were doing things somewhat idealistic in an area not notoriously idealistic." Actually, continued Dickinson, the indemnity letter did not authorize Salomon Brothers to sell his shares, but to prospect for a company that would come in and take over B,D. "That is, in fact, exactly what they were doing," he told the court.

The examination was friendly and relaxed, but suddenly Sheldon Elsen's tone sharpened. The lawyer's antennae had somehow picked up the disturbing presence of Marvin Krasnansky. Leaving his client hanging in the middle of an answer, Elsen identified Krasnansky as a "potential witness" and demanded that he be "excused from the courtroom." Robert Smith, a Paul, Weiss partner, said he had no plans to call the B,D public relations man to the stand.

"I don't want Mr. Krasnansky in the courtroom," snapped Elsen. "I would ask that he be excused."

Arthur Liman broke into the colloquoy: "I thought this was a public trial, you know. . . ."

Judge Carter suggested that Krasnansky might sit in the back of the courtroom.

"I asked him to sit up there because they have objected every time we have somebody sit in the back, Your Honor," said Liman.

"All right," said Judge Carter, "I don't think they can make that objection now."

Did that flareup suggest tension beneath the matter-of-fact way in which the defense was attempting to downplay Fairleigh Dickinson's effort to market B,D? Take that dinner meeting with the top executives of Monsanto at Kenneth Lipper's Park Avenue apartment, for example. Dickinson remembered expressing "dissatisfaction" with some of the management people at B,D and "satisfaction with others," but there was no conversation about selling his stock. Dickinson did recall mentioning something about the family trusts. Much of the conversation around the table in the Lipper dining room, however, was not about finance, but technology. "I quickly realized I was in over my head," recalled the self-effacing Dickinson. "They were talking about chemicals and petrochemicals and highly sophisticated molecular structures and their use in pesticides, their potential use in medicine."

Led by Elsen, Dickinson also minimized the importance of the conversations he had opened with his "old friend" Richard Furlaud of Squibb. Dickinson remembered asking

[207]

the Squibb CEO whether it would be "worthwhile looking into . . . possible joint efforts in some form or other," but did not recall thinking about the sale of his stock. Dickinson conceded he later heard there had indeed been some discussion of his holdings at a subsequent meeting between some of the Squibb and Salomon people, but insisted he had still been hoping for a "settlement" with B,D management.

Dickinson testified he first heard about Sun in mid-December, when Kenneth Lipper handed him an annual report and asked if he had "any mindsets" against oil companies. Dickinson agreed to meet with Sun management on, "give or take, the twentieth, twenty-first" of December, but from that point on the suggestion was that the former B,D chairman couldn't possibly have been part of a selling group:

Q: In late December, early January, did anything happen to your memory?

A: Well, it didn't get so hot, sir.

Q: Was there any physical condition that affected your memory?

A: Well, truly there was. In the period twenty-fifth December to, oh, I would say tenth January, the sequence of things was very difficult.

Admitted to the Neurological Institute at Columbia Presbyterian Hospital on December 21, Dickinson was out again on Christmas Eve, readmitted on Christmas Day, and testified that he was under heavy sedation into the second week in January. "I do know there was a lot of medication," he told Judge Carter.

By January 13, though, Dickinson felt well enough to make a date with Jerome Lipper, Kenneth Lipper, and Robert Zeller for the next day. Kenneth Lipper, following the script the lawyers had drafted for an "individual buyer," told Dickinson "a responsible corporation" was interested in buying his stock at $40 to $45 a share, on either a favored-nation basis or outright. Dickinson testified that he asked who the company was, and then brought up the question of an installment sale. Some of his stock had a tax basis of "approximately" $1 a share, some about 75 cents a share. Explaining his insistence on an installment deal, Dickinson told the court, "It would have been literally improvident to sell out the entire work of two generations of my family on the basis of the then tax law."

Lipper was telling Dickinson he would have to talk to the lawyers about that when Mrs. Dickinson walked into the room and asked, "Who got the parade permit?" After some conversation with Jerome Lipper, Mrs. Dickinson left to spell her daughter, Ann Dickinson Turner, who was sitting with the Jeep in which the two women had driven from New Jersey. There was so much snow that the driveway to the hospital was blocked. The daughter agreed to consider the same offer that had been made to her father, and Fairleigh Dickinson suggested that it might also be put "to Dr. Fitz Dunning, if that could be done." Could Dunning keep the proposition confidential? asked Kenneth Lipper. Dickinson thought so. He called Dunning and told him that Lipper and Zeller would see him at his home in

Towson, Maryland, the following day.

The nut of Dickinson's testimony was that there had been no group. It wasn't until late in the game that he had given up hope of a settlement and decided to sell. Nor had he been subjected to any pressure, certainly not of the kind the SEC was now associating with a supposed tender offer. Dickinson described himself as "extremely tense" because this "was a momentous matter," and he did get the "impression" of a contingency deal—Sun wouldn't buy his stock unless it got 20 percent of B,D's outstanding—but nobody was pushing. "It was a normal business atmosphere in an abnormal place," Dickinson told the court.

The testimony seemed to be aimed at highlighting Dickinson's ingenuousness, the kind of disarming courtliness that caused more aggressive associates such as Adele Piela and Paul Stillman to wish the founder's son would act "more like a chairman." B,D attorney Robert Smith, in his cross examination, attempted to paint Dickinson in considerably stronger colors. Hadn't Dickinson tried to get Wesley Howe fired after the National Medical Care merger fell through? asked the Paul, Weiss partner. And hadn't he held out the prospect of succeeding Howe to a man who was thought to be the "swing vote" on the board—Dr. Charles E. Edwards, head of research at B,D?

Dickinson conceded that "the subject" of firing Howe "may have come up" at a dinner meeting with Edwards; and yes, he looked on Edwards as a "possible" successor to Howe, but he never thought of the physician as a particularly important ally on the B,D board. The jockeying apparently held painful memories for Dickinson. Smith tried to exploit his ambivalence on the subject.

Q: Is it your testimony that you didn't attempt to fire Mr. Asnes on that day?

A: Yes, sir.

Q: Did you ask him to resign?

A: No, sir. I wanted to discuss the whole matter with him, find out what we could do, where we could go. It's fair to say that I hoped for his eventual resolution outside of the company; but, no, I specifically did not tell him he was fired.

Fitz Dunning, Robert Van Fossan, and Paul Stillman, however, non-management directors all, had all testified that Dickinson had indeed asked for Asnes' resignation. Did that refresh Dickinson's recollection? Had he tried to fire Asnes? "I had not in fact done that, but I certainly hoped for it," said Dickinson. He had talked about firing Asnes: "I know I had such a discussion, but that I would arbitrarily go out and just fire anybody would be more or less inconceivable," testified the former B,D chairman.

Impeaching a witness is all part of the game, but credibility emerged as a major issue in the trial. All the defendants carried impeccable professional credentials, and all had relied on the advice of eminent counsel at almost every step of the way. Part of the Paul, Weiss strategy was to try to establish that the respectability was only a facade, concealing an out-of-control profit motive that would stop at nothing—including illegal conduct—to make a buck. That was no secret to the strategists on the other side, and almost everyone sensed that B,D was going to make a major attempt to shake the story of one of the most outspoken architects of the Sun purchase, Salomon Brothers' Kenneth Lipper.

In his pre-trial deposition, Lipper had made no attempt to hide the fact that his job as an investment banker was to sell B,D. Lipper said he began acting on that premise the very day Fairleigh Dickinson came to Salomon Brothers for advice on how to deal with the management that had just stripped him of his chairmanship. As Lipper saw it, Dickinson left the conference at the firm "saying that he was going to try to get an independent board of directors." Questioned by Judge Carter, Lipper said he thought Dickinson's chance of success was at best a long shot. Lipper's solution was to sell Dickinson's stock to a company that might be encouraged to buy all of B,D. "I thought it was a good opportunity from a business point of view as well as I thought, in the end, it would be in Mr. Dickinson's interest when he failed in his attempt "to regain control of B,D."

"So without being specifically authorized, your testimony is you started seeing what companies would be interested?" asked Judge Carter.

"Yes, sir," answered Lipper.

The Paul, Weiss lawyers tried to establish that Lipper's singleminded dedication to the task of selling B,D was disreputable, even underhanded. That at least appeared to be Arthur Liman's objective in this line of questioning:

Q: And you felt that if you could present this as a situation in which there was a division in management, that would be helpful in encouraging [buying] interest, am I correct?

A: Not so. The division in management as much as the fact that a gentleman of Mr. Dickinson's stature was disaffected, if you want to use that word, from management. Not so much the division of management as . . . there were shareholders who were discontent; the people of reputation were discontent.

Lipper testified that he put both Dickinson and Fitzgerald Dunning among the disaffected, and conceded that Chemical Fund was part of the "sales conception," too. "It was being used as an example of the kind of institution that would possibly sell its stock. It was just, as you say," continued Lipper, "an attempt to present a coherent conception."

In the SEC's lexicon, of course, Lipper's "coherent conception" was just another name for a selling group that should have made its presence formally known months before the Sun raid. The government agency's argument was that the Chemical and Surveyor funds' sales of about 450,000 shares of B,D were really triggered by Eberstadt and Robert Zeller from behind a facade of supposedly independent fund directors. The government agency insisted that they, for the most part, were not even given such vital information as the name of the stock, the buyer, or the price before being asked to rubber-stamp the sale. The SEC contended the investment company holdings were so important to Kenneth Lipper's marketing plans that he described the Chemical Fund as a "bellwether" in his conversations with LaPorte of American Home Products.

Lipper tried to strip the term of the heavy connotation the SEC was putting on it. By "bellwether," he said, he meant only that Chemical Fund was "an example of the type [of] institution disenchanted with the internal squabbling at Becton, Dickinson. . . . Since B,D had shown no growth as a stock and Chemical Fund was . . . growth-oriented, all of these factors would make it—as well as many other institutions—like to sell at a substantial premium."

Did Lipper think of the Chemical Fund as a bellwether in the critical period from a month or so after Dickinson's ouster up to the Midnight Raid? asked SEC attorney Robert Romano.

A: It frankly became completely irrelevant once . . . That was part of the sales conception in terms of getting a company interested in acquiring B,D and getting coherent presentation as to why this was an interesting opportunity for an inquirer, but . . .

Judge Carter: No, Mr. Lipper, answer the question.

The question was repeated. Did Lipper believe the fund to be a bellwether in the period between Fairleigh Dickinson's ouster and the Midnight Raid nine months later?

"I am trying to be as responsive as possible to your question of accuracy, since you want it accurately," said Lipper. The bellwether concept was relevant until just before the Sun deal began to take shape, but "had absolutely no relevance" once the sale was in the works "because then they were just one of a number of institutions and their response would be irrelevant as distinguished from any of the other twenty institutions that were contacted. So the answer is exactly that."

Q: But you considered Chemical Fund to be special in the sense that it was a bellwether institution, didn't you Mr. Lipper?

A: Purely in the sales effort.

Q: Yes or no, Mr. Lipper?

A: Up until the Sun transaction I did consider it to be special, but once the Sun transaction was being implemented it was not special at all. It was a commodity.

Q: It was a commodity?

A: Yes, sir.

Q: Thank you. Nothing further, your honor.

Lipper was on the stand for three days, and even Judge Carter noted that he was under heavy pressure. The investment banker was getting a bit hoarse, the bench on occasion had to remind him to keep his voice up ("I don't think Mr. Kerr is hearing you"), and there were times when the lawyer in him seemed to be rising to the challenge of jousting with the opposition.

At one point, for example, Arthur Liman asked Lipper, "Now, in your business of acquisitions, had you ever participated at a meeting when there was a chart that gave numerical ratings for legal risk?"

"First of all," snapped Lipper, "my business is not acquisitions."

"Your business is an investment banker?"

"Yes, and a small part of it is acquisitions," answered Lipper, who then went on to point out that there was nothing sinister in measuring legal risk. "It's been discussed in every transaction I've been in, including this one."

The SEC stressed the comparatively high risk rating Sun's planners had placed on the Midnight Raid. The emphasis was apparently part of the SEC's effort to reinforce its contention that the takeover scheme was a ploy to get around the Williams Act. Lipper downplayed the importance of the charts Horace Kephart had worked up to assess the risks in the takeover plan. Kephart, after all, was "an engineer" and charts helped him think. As to a numerical assessment of legal risk, "It was an inconsequential and silly discussion," said Lipper. "I really spent my time on things I know much more about."

At another point, Lipper broke into a colloquy on a technical point between defense attorney Sheldon Elsner and Judge Carter. "May I interject a comment?" he asked.

Judge Carter told Lipper to be silent. Lipper's attorney reinforced the admonition. "You're in the witness chair," said Sheldon Elsner. "That's the penalty you pay for giving up the practice of law."

In an aside to the investment banker at yet another point, B,D attorney Liman said, "I take it you have had some disappointments in your life."

"I do everything I can to avoid such things," snapped Lipper.

Sun wanted to avoid disappointment, too, didn't it? Isn't that why it set out to get "negative control" of B,D? Not at all, said Lipper. Robert Sharbaugh had no objection to B,D's making any mergers on its own. In fact, continued Lipper, the Sun CEO hoped B,D would continue to grow at a good pace in any way it could. Sharbaugh just wanted to hold enough stock to guarantee that Sun's position could not be diluted below the all-important 20 percent equity accounting level. "It didn't matter to him whether or not there was thirty-three and a third percent and he wasn't interested in negative control," testified Lipper.

Arthur Liman tried to shake that characterization:

Q: You testified that Mr. Sharbaugh said he wasn't interested in negative control.

A: Correct. That wasn't important.

Q: It wasn't important. Have you ever read the 13(d) that was filed by Sun on Becton, Dickinson?

A: I believe at the time it was filed I might have read it.

Q: Did you ever note that Sun described the fact that it had thirty-four percent and that the affirmative vote of sixty-six and two-thirds percent of the outstanding shares was required for certain transactions?

A: It sounds like a factual statement to me.

Q: And you say that Mr. Sharbaugh said that he intended to vote for the management proposal for an increase in authorized shares?

A: I believe so.

Q: Was there any discussion with the lawyers as to

whether that should be included in the initial 13(d)?

A: I have no knowledge of these things.

There was one other SEC allegation that went to ethical tone—the contention that Lipper had pressured Sun to move when it did by telling Kephart that three other prospective buyers were waiting in the wings. As Lipper explained it, several Salomon people had met with executives of BASF, a big German pharmaceutical company, and talked generally about acquisition possibilities. The Salomon partners thought B,D might fill the bill and talked about "showing it to BASF," but didn't want to do so "without the permission of the Sun Company."

Early in December, when the Sun executives were meeting at Hilton Head, said Lipper, Kephart was told: "We would like to show B,D to a potential buyer if you are not interested, but we are not trying to rush you into making any decision, you could take your time. You are the client. This is just a new business prospect. If you are not interested, we would just like to know, so that we can go forward and show it to someone else."

According to Lipper, Kephart replied: "You can show it if you want to, but let me take it up with the other management people who are down here. We happen to be here for a management meeting and I will take it up with them."

Whereupon, continued Lipper, "We said, 'Look, if you haven't decided what you want to do, we definitely are not showing it to anyone else. Sun is too important a client to Salomon to do that. So take your time and get back to us.'"

Between December and January, Lipper said he also did some talking with the investment bankers for Hoffman-LaRoche, a big Swiss-owned drug company. He told the bankers that an exploration of B,D would have to go on the back burner because he was already working with another client on the company. It was just about that time the Sun board was putting together a consensus on B,D, and Lipper said he told Kephart "precisely the nature of the inquiry" he had received. Under friendly cross-examination, Lipper also related how he had "inferred" from conversation with John Whitehead, senior partner at Goldman, Sachs, that Monsanto might be back in the picture, too.

Whitehead, said Lipper, had told him he would be meeting with Monsanto executives in January. "There were several people he felt that perhaps had not shown enough initiative in reviewing the B,D transaction and he was sure it was going to come up for discussion at that meeting.

"It immediately sparked in my mind, as it would in any professional banker's mind," Lipper told the court, "that this was a highly unusual call; (a) that it was initiated by Mr. Whitehead, (b) that he specifically raised the status of B,D, and (c) that he said it was going to be reviewed at the senior levels of Monsanto in January."

Lipper testified that he called Kephart and said, "'Kep, this indicates that something is up. I don't know what's going to happen or anything is going to happen, but it's clearly of some significance."

Q: What about the SEC contention that Lipper had made "intentionally false statements" to push Sun into a "transaction which ended up being illegal"?

A: It is an absolutely McCarthyite lie that the SEC did for the purpose of getting it into the newspapers, for publicity purposes, has absolutely no truth, and that slander of Salomon Brothers and myself deserves an apology from the SEC.

Q: The answer to the question is no?

A: No.

That friendly tour of the horizon was designed to repair any damage Arthur Liman might have done in his direct examination. It had been a tense couple of minutes.

In that series of questions, Lipper had testified that he had "explained precisely to Mr. Kephart" how he inferred that Monsanto might take another look at B,D. "Mr. Whitehead doesn't usually call me," he told the B,D attorney.

Q: And you told—

A: That's precisely what I told [Kephart].

Q: You told all this to Mr. Kephart at the time you mentioned the fact that Monsanto might have an interest?

A: Except I didn't use the name Mr. Whitehead nor the name of Monsanto, for reasons of propriety.

Q: I thought a moment ago you said you had told [Mr. Kephart] all of this.

[220]

A: Yes. I told him "a senior official" instead of using Mr. Whitehead's name, and I told him "a major chemical company" instead of using Monsanto's name.

Q: Did you ask Mr. Whitehead whether or not Monsanto had an interest?

A: I didn't think it was exactly the proper question to ask Mr. Whitehead. He would have told me that if that was the message he was telling me.

Q: You understood that [Whitehead's firm] Goldman, Sachs had a policy against participating in hostile takeovers. Didn't you understand that?

A: Goldman, Sachs has participated as an advisor as opposed to the tender agent in hostile takeovers. I understood that.

Q: Did you ask him whether or not there was any change in Goldman, Sachs' policy?

A: There would not need to be any change for them to advise Monsanto. As a matter of fact, they were going to join forces with us in the prior discussions.

Q: The ones that led to nothing?

A: That led initially to their turndown of Becton, Dickinson.

*   *   *

Much of the case went that way, the pendulum of credibility swinging this way and that as each side pushed for its version of the truth. It was hard to say what the impact was on Judge Carter. He'd prodded all of the law-yers with questions, kept them moving through the inevi-table digressions, sometimes took over the job of guiding a witness on his own, and now at the end of the case pro-nounced himself puzzled. What about Sun? Tender offer or private purchase? "When this hearing started I was sev-enty-five percent convinced there was no violation," said Judge Carter. "Twenty-five percent has been eroded. I'm up in the air and I can go either way.

"On the fiduciary question," he added, "it's clear my emotions and sentiments are with Mr. Dickinson. I find it difficult to find that a man treated like this man was treated should be required to stand still and not make an effort to protect himself."

And that was where Judge Carter left things as the transcript closed on the lawyers' final arguments. Carter's decision was months away, but the issues he was trying were a lot more than just a cluster of legalistic abstractions. They had real-life consequences for almost everyone involved, and not all of them were pleasant. One of the first visible signs of the tremendous internal pressures building at Sun came in the story tip the seemingly ubiquitous Richard Cheney was dropping on reporters everywhere. Why had Sun so abruptly postponed an annual meeting that was to have been a corporate happen-ing—a happening to be piped from the cavernous Civic Center in Philadelphia by closed-circuit television to satellite shareholder meetings in Toledo, Dallas, and Tulsa? As it turned out, Sun needed more time so its original proxy material could be amended to include the startling news that the founding Pew family, which controls a third of the company, intended to add two new representatives to the board. That would give the family and/or the Glenmede Trust Company, through which most of the Pew stock is held, a total of four seats on an enlarged sixteen-member board.

Securities analysts and reporters were quick to make the linkage. The conservative Pews, jealous of their good reputation, were reacting to the cannonade of publicity exactly as the B,D strategists had hoped. "The most important thing for the Pews is their name," one oil analyst told the *Wall Street Journal.* "They don't want to be associated with anything that looks like hanky-panky." Was that a vote of no-confidence in CEO Robert Sharbaugh and the policy of aggressive diversification out of the oil business? Not so, insisted Sun's management. Sharbaugh was still firmly in the saddle and a majority of the board was as committed as ever to breaking out of the company's traditional mold.

There was evidence of stress, though, that couldn't be papered over. Robert G. Dunlop, who had been president and chairman of Sun for almost a quarter-century before his retirement in 1974, was on the board of both the oil company and the Glenmede Trust. He was the Pew family's man, a cautious, conscientious Wharton School grad who started with Sun as an auditor and moved upward through the company from the accounting and controller's side of the business.

Dunlop had gone to the corporate development meeting to which Sun directors had been invited on January 5— eleven days before the strike on B,D. Almost all of the two-and-a-half-hour meeting was dedicated to a discussion of B,D and the advisability of buying a beachhead position in it. Questioned by Paul, Weiss associate Jack Hassid, Dunlop remembered being told there was a "one-week time frame" for the decision to go or not with the investment because B,D "was a likely candidate for acquisition by others."

Dunlop had a lot of questions of his own. An unfriendly takeover would carry both business and legal implications. What about price? Was health care "an acceptable industry for Sun to diversify its efforts; and was Becton, Dickinson a company of the stature we would want to acquire?" How was the deal going to be financed? Many of those questions were answered but not entirely to Dunlop's satisfaction.

He was concerned that the full board had not been given a chance "to sit down and dialogue this." Dunlop also wanted to talk things over with his colleagues on the Glenmede Trust board. His personal lawyers, fearful that Dunlop might run afoul of the insider confidentiality rules, advised him not to do so. Dunlop was so uneasy that he abstained from the executive committee vote that gave Sharbaugh the go-ahead on January 13—a Friday. He was the only committee member to do so.

Dunlop's reservations reflected the ambivalence with which one part of his constituency—some members of the Pew family—regarded outside acquisitions generally. Heavy with cash, but short on crude oil, the company had reached out for more reserves in the late sixties with the purchase of Sunray DX. Conversion of the preferred stock issued in that acquisition was one of the reasons why the family's position had been diluted from more than 50 percent to 34 percent. The beachhead strategy promised more of the same and Sharbaugh had ruffled a lot of sensitive feathers in carrying out his mandate to reshape the company into a cluster of independent operating units. Sharbaugh put as good a face on things as he could, but behind the scenes a major reassessment was going on. The lawsuits and the SEC investigation meant that the $290 million Sun had put into B,D might be tied up for years—a trap Sun's takeover strategy had theoretically been designed to prevent. Further, each day seemed to bring a fresh crop of damaging headlines. The shouting did begin to die down after a while, but Robert Sharbaugh, ironically, was in much the same position as Wesley Howe and Marvin Asnes. Fairleigh Dickinson had wanted them to institutionalize the company he had controlled for so long—but he didn't want them to institutionalize it too much. That was the split Sharbaugh had tried to exploit. He himself was the chosen instrument of a controlling family that wanted its company reshaped—but not too quickly. The crucial difference was that Howe and Asnes survived—and Sharbaugh didn't.

The axe dropped a couple of days after the Labor Day weekend. Sharbaugh was out as CEO, replaced by Theodore Burtis, and would resign as chairman the following May when his term as director expired. The Sun statement quoted Sharbaugh as saying it was "an appropriate time"— a month before his fiftieth birthday—to consider another career. Sun insisted he hadn't been fired and so did Sharbaugh. Several careers were preferable to "one long one." "It may seem unusual, but that's where the situation is," Sharbaugh told the *Wall Street Journal*. Would that mean another shift in Sun's diversification efforts? Not so, said Ted Burtis. He had been charged "by the board to continue moving the company in the direction it has been following," and intended to "fulfill the board's expectations."

None of the face-saving press-agentry could quite conceal the fact that the directions in which Sun—and Becton, Dickinson—could move were to some degree circumscribed by what had gone on in court. How would Judge Carter rule? Would Jack Howe and Marvin Asnes have to face the prospect of continuing in yoke with Sun as a major partner—perhaps the only partner—in B,D's business? Would Sun be forced to back away from a vital diversification move, made in a supposedly free market, on narrow, legalistic grounds? And what of the Takeover Game itself? Would Judge Carter validate a novel buying technique that could intensify the level of play? Or would he put a chill on the Game by tightening the strictures of the Williams Act?

The Judge's critique of what he called Sun's "brilliantly designed lightning strike" was delivered almost anticlimactically on a hot, muggy evening in early July. It was clear from the opening that Carter was no strict constructionist. Carter's findings of fact described what he saw as a "complex drama." "Personality conflicts, animosity, distrust, and corporate politics," he wrote, had all combined with "a display of ingenuity and sophistication by brokers, investment bankers and corporate counsel" to create that drama.

The intrigue at Becton, the Judge said, had deepened as Fairleigh Dickinson scotched the National Medical Care merger with the help of the Salomon Brothers' report and Dottie Matonti began tracking his movements in the so-called Spy File. Carter took a rather sympathetic view of

Dickinson. Being deposed as chairman "must have been a terrible personal blow," the Judge said. "Dickinson had been stripped of all power within what he must still have regarded as a family enterprise."

Tracing the development of the purchases that began in Dickinson's hospital room and culminated in the Midnight Raid, Judge Carter described Sun's plan as "well structured, brilliantly conceived, and well executed." He did not see, however, how it could be described as either "privately negotiated" or a "series of separate, independent con-tracts." "It was a single, integrated project, planned and executed to secure Sun some 33⅓ percent of outstanding B,D shares, secretly and quickly so that the acquisition could not be aborted or halted at mid-point by legal action or other countermoves by B,D."

That made the Sun gambit a public offering, carrying all the hallmarks of a tender offer; i.e., a widespread solicita-tion for a substantial proportion of outstanding stock at a premium above the market in a comparatively short time frame under circumstances that put pressure on the sellers. It was not enough for Sun to argue that the sellers were sophisticated investors who did not need the protection of the Williams Act. The sellers were just not given enough information on which to exercise their sophistication. A "swift, masked maneuver," the Midnight Raid was "in-fected with the basic evil which Congress sought to cure by enacting" the Williams Act. The lawyers "simply sought to devise a strategy to meet Sun's needs and those of the investment bankers whose fee was contingent on a success-ful acquisition," the Judge said. "The strategy was purposed to avoid the pitfalls which compliance with the Act mandated." Then came the ruling on what was in legal terms the most complex side of the case. "In acquiring 34 percent of the B,D stock at issue here, Sun made a tender offer without a pre-acquisition filing in violation of Section 14(d) of the Williams Act."

Had Dickinson and others formed a group planning a shift in control of B,D without giving the proper notice? The seventy-five-year-old J. H. Fitzgerald Dunning, pleading poor health, signed a consent decree which neither admitted nor denied that he had been a member of such a group. As a part of the settlement, he agreed to pay $275,000 to B,D shareholders and $100,000 directly to the company. That took him out of the case. Judge Carter noted, though, that Fairleigh Dickinson had kept Dunning "abreast of what was going on," and added that the deposed chairman had "personally engaged" with Eberstadt and Salomon in "the search for a willing buyer." All of the potential buyers, the Judge said, "had been assured of Dickinson's and Dunning's willingness to sell and of the availability of the half-million shares of the Chemical Fund." The fund directors really had no independent say over the disposition of the B,D stock. "It would indeed be substituting shadow for substance and exalting form over substance" to assert that Eberstadt and [its investment company advisory arm] . . . were not the beneficial owners [of the fund holdings] for the purpose of combining them with other shares to effectuate a shift in corporate control." Thus, B,D and the SEC won the group issue, too. Lipper, Salomon, Zeller, and Eberstadt were found to have "aided and abetted" the 14(d) violation, while Lipper, Salomon, and Zeller "were aiders and abettors" of the group violation.

Wrapping up the rest of the case, Judge Carter found the

13(d) statement Sun ultimately filed on B,D to have "sufficiently complied" with the rules on the subject of negative control. B,D and the SEC carried the day on every other major issue but one—the allegation that Fairleigh Dickinson had breached his fiduciary responsibilities by failing to advise B,D management that he was shopping around for a buyer and accepting a premium for his own stock in a deal that was closed to other B,D shareholders. There was "no merit" to either contention. Dickinson had not tipped any inside information to outsiders, "did not feel that management was acting in shareholders' best interests," and was "under no duty to follow management blindly." In fact, said the Judge, Dickinson had been "stripped of all effectiveness within the organization by the time he sold his stock," and his efforts to promote a takeover were "not per se violative of any fiduciary obligations." The Williams Act, noted the Judge, was "not designed to favor management in takeover attempts or to prevent takeovers."

The reaction was predictable. Even as Wesley Howe was pronouncing himself "gratified," Salomon said it planned to appeal and so did Fairleigh Dickinson. Sun, too, said it was exploring the possibility of appeal, but was pretty much left holding the baby. B,D had asked the court for an order that would freeze Sun's voting rights and require the oil company to offer $45 a share to other B,D holders (at a possible cost of about $600 million), all to be followed by divestiture. Judge Carter's ruling established liability, but did not get to the question of remedies. They would have to be threshed out at still another hearing.

For Sun's new management, it looked like a war of attrition. As if to emphasize that Robert Sharbaugh's departure meant an end to the cult of the individual, the company's top brass had been redeployed as a team effort into the newly created office of the Chief Executive. Chairman and president Theodore Burtis would direct overall strategy and company-wide performance from the "Goldfish Bowl"—a reference to the three glass walls of his office—but would share power with three executive vice-presidents. The new look seemed to suggest that Sun was heading back to its old look. The company would salvage as much as it could from the beachhead investment in B,D. If the recently announced acquisition of Elk River Resources and its 200 million tons of coal reserves for $300 million worth of stock meant anything, however, Sun's objective was to get closer to its original roots in mother earth.

That signal was subsequently confirmed when Sun, in a coup that carried all of the panache of the Midnight Raid, beat out Mobil Corporation and at least one other company in a $2.3-billion bid for the assets of Texas Pacific Oil, a subsidiary of the Seagram Co. The purchase, one of the biggest ever in the industry, added substantially to Sun's comparatively thin oil and gas reserves and almost doubled the unexplored acreage on its property sheet. The decontrol in oil prices made it easy for Sun's new management to back away from the chic of conglomerate diversification. The billion dollars or so a year that Sun generates in fresh capital would be going back into energy. It was an ambitious blueprint that left little room for pondering the detritus of past mistakes. The sortie against B,D had tied up a lot of cash that could be used to better advantage in big, front-end, long-term investments of the kind Sun had been managing for almost a century—coal, oil sands, geothermal domes. Appeal of the Carter decision could drag on for years. The impetus was all toward settlement. What was the best way to unscramble the omelette? By the give and take of hard bargaining, of course.

In the end, Sun agreed to settle the clutch of B,D stockholders suits with a payment of $2.6 million. The company would get back its investment in B,D—and then some—by selling $389.1 million worth of debentures convertible in B,D stock at $60 a share. The conversion factor, and other safeguards in the agreement, meant that the big concentration of B,D stock Sun controlled would be broken up and parceled among many smaller holders. The mechanism was designed to ensure that Wesley Howe and company would not on some future snowy Tuesday morning find that some other raider had shut down trading in B,D. The agreement was reinforced by a provision that required Sun to vote its shares with the majority during a conversion period that might last as long as a quarter-century.

How did it all turn out? B,D came away seemingly takeover-proof at a cost of several million dollars in legal fees. The struggle left some psychic scars. "It was among people who had known each other for a long time," said Wesley Howe. At its peak, Howe adds, the battle absorbed "maybe seventy percent" of his time "and somewhat less" of Marvin Asnes'. "Despite it all," continues Howe, "we've been able to produce a very solid series of numbers. We've got good decentralized management. I don't come here every morning and wind the place up." To Howe, it's a happy ending of sorts. Conflict between professional management and a strong-willed major stockholder like

Fairleigh Dickinson, says Howe, "was probably inevitable if you consider the way we've evolved." There was a lot of pain in it, but B,D had at last become institutionalized. The market recognized the transition—and the company's expanding earnings base—by pushing B,D common above 50 for the first time in seven lean years.

Ironically enough, that recognition gave Sun a nice paper profit—and reinforced Howe's arguments that B,D was worth a lot more than $45 a share. In pure money terms, Sun is out of pocket several millions in legal fees and settlement costs, and is paying heavy interest charges on the debenture issue it sold as part of the settlement. Its bottom line depends on how quickly B,D common gets above the conversion price of $60. The quicker that happens, the lower its interest costs will run. Intangibly, of course, Sun suffered some psychic scars, too. No company with its traditions likes to appear inept. On the whole, though, the structure seems to have adapted. Sun may not be a better company than the one that went into the Midnight Raid, but it certainly is a different one; and one with a sharper appreciation of its own special skills. It is an environment in which Robert Sharbaugh might have been very comfortable if the signals had not been changed on him. The deposed CEO went into his second career as a consultant with the customary golden handshake that included close to $200,000 a year in annual retirement benefits.

Fairleigh Dickinson still talks of "humanitarian values" and the need to "deemphasize the bottom line in favor of experimentation and innovation." The imperative is delivered in the customary wry, self-effacing fashion. "People used to hear that and they'd say, 'There goes the chairman, trying to run the company as if he still owned 20 percent of the stock,'" he says. Dickinson is following his own deep bent toward experimentation through the ownership of a small company working in biogenetics. "It's very nice," he says. "There aren't very many people, and I can put a face and a name on every one of them."

Name and Face. In the larger sense of the words, both are extremely important to Dickinson. He was the only defendant to file an appeal from Judge Carter's ruling on the 13(d) group and had high hopes of vindication. As the judicial process inched forward, the community and continuity of the family name were very much on Dickinson's mind. He talked of bequeathing the home he was brought up in to Fairleigh Dickinson University for use as a president's house. He hoped the University could "rationalize" it. "They've got a little house there in Teaneck," said Dickinson, "but it really doesn't do the things a president's house should do." The town of Rutherford might object to the house being taken off the tax rolls, but that can be worked out. Dickinson talked with the calm assurance of a man who has arranged the future as best he can, but there was pain there, too. "When you don't have something to do that you know how to do and have been doing for years," he said, "it is very hard to fill your life up with Mickey Mouse."

Still, there is nothing ephemeral about Becton, Dickinson versus Sun Company, Fairleigh Dickinson, *et al.* Lawyers on both sides think the case has put a definite crimp in "private purchase" takeover strategies. Hope, though, still burns bright in the hearts of the acquisitors. Judge Carter's decision had been down for months and the terms of the B,D–Sun settlement long hammered into place when the indefatigable American Home Products Corporation dropped a surprise announcement—a plan to buy "in excess of $15 million" worth of B,D stock in the open market or "otherwise." William LaPorte was once again knocking on the door. What did that mean? "I don't know," said B,D counsel Roy Weber, "but we're going to chase them away." And they did.

10

What Does It All Mean?

For a man who has walked through the fire, Wesley Howe is remarkably sanguine on the topic of takeovers. Maybe it comes from being flameproof. On the one hand, he sees the Sun bid for B,D as "simply a shuffling of the financial cards." In theory, Sun could have given B,D "access to unlimited capital," but that would not have meant very much. B,D is generating all the cash it needs internally and "an acceleration of growth would probably strain our management systems," said Howe. Frowning over an economic climate in which the billion-dollar takeover has become commonplace, Howe sees larger issues than the fate of B,D at stake. "The simple capacity of one company to absorb another," he says, "doesn't add anything to the national good."

On the other hand, an appreciable amount of B,D's own

growth has come from the outside and Howe is not about to downgrade acquisition merely because Sun happened to mishandle what he regards as a useful management tool. "A lot of mergers start out unfriendly, but people make their peace," said the B,D executive. "I wouldn't want to see takeovers judged by the legislative process. We're free-market people here and some things just have to be left to the judgment of the marketplace." The statement rings with conviction. Howe is the first to admit that if Sun had mounted a straightforward tender offer instead of a raid, the free market would almost certainly have consigned his company to the highest bidder—just one more piece of property on a megabuck Monopoly board.

Becton, though, like every successful business venture, is a lot more than the sum of its assets. It is an ecosystem that creates jobs for more than 20,000; keeps such communities as East Rutherford thriving, buys hundreds of millions of dollars' worth of goods and services a year, and not incidentally helps a lot of sick people to get well. Stockholders, of course, are an important element in the life chain and for stockholders, generally, the brisk market in takeovers has been a good thing. They have been bought out at prices that have not been seen for a long, long time—if ever. Thus, on one level, takeovers are a social good; they create wealth that flows who knows where—into other stocks, venture capital, tax shelters, co-op apartments, new automobiles, orthodontists' bank accounts, tuition bills, and income taxes.

Inevitably, though, the boom in takeovers has created a backlash. Businessmen such as Walter Kissinger, brother of the other Kissinger, and academicians such as Harold M. Williams, former chairman of the SEC, are aghast at the

$100 billion or so that has been pumped into takeovers in the last several years. They are beginning to argue that what is good for stockholders is not necessarily good for the United States. Williams, for one, finds the "legitimacy" with which hostile takeovers have been graced extremely disturbing. He thinks the profits and excitement of The Game have debased business consciousness to the point where corporations are being viewed as trading cards rather than as "a complex of interpersonal and contractural relationships" in which society as a whole has an important stake.

All too often, argues Williams, the stockholders who benefit most from takeovers are not the long-term, deserving Aunt Janes of this world, but such sharp-shooting arbitrageurs as Guy Wyser-Pratte and Carl Icahn "who see profits in betting against the corporation." Further, contends Williams, much of the cash being tamped into takeovers is not being very creatively spent. It is going "to rearranging the ownership of existing corporate assets" rather than into new plants, new products, or new jobs. Is that, he asks, an "appropriate use of corporate resources" at a time when the United States, trying to compete with rising powers such as Japan, is burdened with "the highest percentage of obsolete plant, lowest percentage of capital investment, growth in productivity and in savings of any major industrialized society?" It's a tough indictment, balanced by the concession that the threat of takeover can put pressure on inefficient managers to perform or else; and that there are major efficiencies to be had in acquisitions that work.

The arguments are familiar enough. They've been voiced in one form or another with almost every merger wave that has swept the country since the turn of the century. The cash takeover, though—particularly the hostile takeover—has raised the level of debate. If stockholders do in fact own a company, aren't they entitled to the best return they can get on their money, regardless of whether that return means the disappearance of another independent voice—B,D into Sun, for example? Are the interests of employee-stockholders, anxious about the impact of a takeover on the plant in which they work and the community in which they live, somehow paramount over the interest of stockholders generally? And what about the pros, the arbitrageurs, who often spell the difference between failure and success in a takeover? Are their rights of ownership somehow subordinate to the supposed virtue of the stereotypical long-term investor? What about a management that decides to fight a hostile bid to the last ditch? Is there an irreconcilable conflict between the personal ambitions of the careerists in the executive suite and stockholders whose ambition it is to maximize their own profits?

Nobody buys stock to lose money, and that includes the institutional investors—mutual funds, pension funds, and insurance companies—who are among the biggest beneficiaries of the capital gains the takeover boom has produced. Are there baleful social implications in a rising tide of investment income that enables a pension fund to improve its benefits or allows an insurance company to plow more capital into utility bonds or high-technology start-ups? With rare exceptions like B,D, stockholders have done badly in takeover situations where management has succeeded in driving off an aggressor. A sample of eleven such companies shows eight of the stocks still trading well below the bid price offered for them, anywhere from two to four years after the event. It takes years of hard-won dividend increases to make up for a forfeited premium of 50 percent or more.

What about the economic costs? Would the United States really be a lot more competitive if all that takeover money had gone back into new plant and presumably higher productivity? The fact is that American business over the last several years has been plowing a significantly higher proportion of gross national product back into new plant than it did between 1948 and 1965, when productivity was climbing sharply. It might well be that the United States' aging industrial plant would benefit from still heavier infusions of cash, but rising productivity hinges on more than just money. Labor–management relations, the quality of the labor force, inflation, tight-money policies, and the drift from a manufacturing to a service type economy all have an impact on how efficiently we produce.

Big money is going into takeovers precisely because they can be good investments—and are almost invariably less risky investments than trying to build a major new business from the ground up. That may mean that businessmen are less venturesome than the corporate folklore makes them out to be, but that doesn't mean they are dumb or even particularly predatory. Becton, for example, has been growing at the rate of about 15 percent a year, earns around 14 percent on stockholders' money, and at a price of $45 a share was a perfectly good buy. Takeovers have to be viewed not as isolated phenomena, but as a manifestation of the economic climate in which they have taken root. The tax incentives that nurture new investment are

[239]

still not what they might be, and the stock market is still pricing companies cheap in terms of their real assets. The attraction of buying good values in a period of high inflation and paying for them with depreciating dollars is hard to fight.

Takeovers can be unsettling, but in a way that almost any change is unsettling. They almost invariably mean executive shuffles, and often plant closings or relocations. Some are often no more than hit-and-run operations. Look at Victor Posner, for example, the Miami Beach entrepreneur who through the Sharon Steel Corporation and a fat pyramid of other acquisitive outfits has at one point or other owned minority positions in at least forty companies. Posner has become such a bugaboo to some fretful managements that they willingly pay him to go away. One recent day brought an announcement that Bundy Corporation, a Detroit, Michigan, producer of steel tubing, had bought back about 5.6 percent of its own shares from Posner at a price that gave one of his companies a quick profit of about a half-million dollars on its investment. At the same time Posner indicated he was giving up on a possible tactical threat to double his holdings in Simplicity Pattern Company, and had agreed to sell 1.4 million shares of the company to a more favorably regarded suitor at a comfortable pre-tax profit of $8 million. "Everything I have has a price," Posner told Jim Montgomery of the *Wall Street Journal*. "I buy to sell and make a profit on it." The prospect of quick profits appeals mightily to the boardroom buccaneer in many of the Takeover Game's most aggressive players.

Thomas Mellon Evans, for example, has amassed a sizable personal fortune over the last forty years by a series of more than eighty acquisitions that have boosted the sales of the two companies he controls—H. K. Porter Company, a steel fabricator, and the Crane Company, a building-materials conglomerate—to better than $2 billion. On at least seven occasions in the last several years, Evans' tough-guy reputation has sent threatened managements scurrying for White Knights. Evans was bought out of every one of those situations at pre-tax gains which probably amount to close to $100 million. Evans is white-haired and rubicund, with a wry sense of humor, and could easily pass as the central-casting prototype of the jolly uncle. Put the question to him: Is there an element of macho in the Takeover Game? His pleased grin is the answer. Most of the Street's merger and acquisition people are considerably more explicit. "A lot of takeovers have to be seen as expressions of the CEO's ego," says one specialist, "and that may be one of the reasons why some of these things just don't work. Too much wishful thinking."

The short-term incentives that make management run are part of the equation, too. If the size of an executive's paycheck is keyed to such indications of annual "performance" as pre-tax profits, return on equity, or the market price of the company's stock, there is at least a subliminal bias in the direction of instant gratification. Takeovers are one way to make the numbers and make them now, whereas the returns on a long-term plowback of capital into new fields usually take a long time to materialize. Those who sow are not always those who reap. Thus, growth—or at least the appearance of growth—is part of a reward system that has imbued many managers with what one analyst calls the "ideology of the cancer cell."

That ideology may go a long way to explaining why so

many acquisitions that look good on paper prove to be so painful in practice. The ideal of synergy—two plus two equals five—has a perverse way of becoming a reality where two plus two equals three. Horror stories abound. Mobil Corporation, for example, has had to pump millions into Montgomery Ward & Company just to keep the ailing retailer afloat. No addition to earning power there. Mc-Graw-Edison paid top dollar for Studebaker-Worthington and found the company so hard to digest that the Moody's ratings on its debentures were dropped two notches. Even so canny an operation as the Colgate-Palmolive Company has been purging itself of a number of mistakes, including Helena Rubinstein, once one of the most perfumed brand names in cosmetics. Bought for stock valued at $142.3 million, the company was unloaded at the distress-merchandise price of $20 million. The marketing skills that move Colgate toothpaste and soap in bumper volume just did not rub off on such extraneous items as Helena Rubinstein's medicated makeup.

Many of the atrocity stories evolved out of at least theoretically friendly situations in which the buyer had enough time to check the foundations, rap on the walls, and pose all of the questions that should be raised in a multimillion-dollar proposition. The pace of the Takeover Game, however, has accelerated to the point where decisions have to be made very, very quickly—decisions that in this supercharged atmosphere can affect the fortunes of not just one, but two, three, four, or more companies, and hundreds of thousands of stockholders. UV Industries, for example, is an effort to escape the clutches of Victor Posner's Sharon Steel Corporation, elected to go into liquidation. Death before Dishonor. One of UV's major assets, Federal Pacific Electric Company, a producer of electric circuit-breakers, was snapped up for $345 million by the Reliance Electric Company. Reliance, in turn, after presumably diligent study, was snapped up by Exxon Corporation for $1.24 billion. Subsequently, to everyone's deep embarrassment, it developed that there were serious problems with the design of Federal Pacific's circuit-breakers. A spate of product recalls heavily penalized Reliance's profits. Reliance alleged there were misrepresentations in the way Federal Pacific got its product line approved by Underwriters' Laboratories and sued to have the purchase rescinded. The charges were denied. Exxon, at least for the moment, is earning a fraction of 1 percent on its investment in Reliance, and a flurry of litigation blocked the payment of more than $500 million from the liquidating trust to the former UV Industries shareholders.

There is one other rub. The announced objective in buying Reliance was to get the specialized aid of a major electrical-equipment producer to market an alternating current synthesizer Exxon had developed. The controls system promised to make electric motors more efficient, reduce their energy consumption by as much as 50 percent, and save the United States up to a million barrels of oil a day. Almost two years went by, and then Boom! Exxon announced the synthesizer, as originally designed, just couldn't cut the mustard. Back to the drawing board, as competitors with designs that did work crowded into the market and critics contended (and Exxon denied) that the synthesizer publicity was a smokescreen to enable the big oil company to diversify into electric motors with a minimum of outcry.

The saga of Kennecott Copper Corporation is yet another example of how destabilizing the Takeover Game can be. In an effort to diversify out of the traditionally volatile copper markets, Kennecott bought the Peabody Coal Company, despite objections from the Federal Trade Commission. The FTC sued and won. Kennecott was forced to divest, and sold Peabody for about $1.2 billion— a huge chunk of cash that was bound to excite the interest of the takeover crowd. Kennecott tried to dilute that interest by putting almost half the proceeds—about $570 million—into the acquisition of the Carborundum Company. It paid about fourteen times earnings for the company in a market where similar stocks are trading at around eight times earnings.

Then came T. Roland Berner, CEO of the Curtiss-Wright Co., which almost overnight acquired just under 10 percent of Kennecott. Berner contended that Kennecott had grossly overpaid for Carborundum. He opened a proxy fight, campaigning on the promises to sell off the abrasives producer and distribute the proceeds to Kennecott stockholders. The proxy fight ended in a draw.

The uneasy peace was broken when Curtiss added to its holdings. Kennecott launched a preemptive strike in the form of a tender offer. The offer was well over the market, but failed to bring control of Curtiss-Wright. There was a settlement. Kennecott bought back its shares from Curtiss-Wright, and swapped the C-W stock it owned for Curtiss-Wright's Dorr Oliver division, a producer of industrial-process equipment. The total cost to Kennecott was estimated at around $290 million. The long war of attrition, the difficulties of ingesting Carborundum, erratic copper prices, and the highest mining costs in the industry all cut deeply into Kennecott's earning power. The Curtiss-Wright buyout pushed Kennecott's debt load to a burdensome $840 million, some 58 percent of equity.

Then came Standard Oil Company (Ohio), with an offer of $1.77 billion for all of Kennecott's common stock. The bid was accepted with lightning speed. The rationale: that the cash-heavy crude producer could compensate for the capital that Kennecott dissipated in the takeover wars, and provide the company with the money it needed to upgrade its sorely neglected plant. At a bid of $62 a share, a premium of 130 percent over the market, Kennecott stockholders were well rewarded. Management, free for the first time in years of the need to fight the barbarians at the gates, could actually settle down to running Kennecott.

Like all such atrocity stories, the Kennecott saga raises serious questions about some of the excesses that have crept into the Takeover Game. What the excesses boil down to are mainly questions about judgment and the quality of management. It begins to look as though Kennecott actually did pay too much for Carborundum, and that the acquisition just didn't fit in the way the management then in command hoped it would. But there are success stories, too—United Technologies Corporation, for example.

When Harry J. Gray was named president of what was then United Aircraft in 1971 he was the number-three man, senior executive vice-president, at Litton Industries. In his rise through one of the first and most heavily publicized of the big conglomerates, Gray made his mark as a generalist. He did public relations for a while, moved into operations as head of a subsidiary that produced printed circuits, ran the defense products group, and was

[245]

for a time senior vice-president for finance and administration. Acquisition was the name of the game at Litton and with seventeen years of seasoning behind him, Gray was a logical choice for the top spot at United.

The company was deep in the red and Gray's mandate was deceptively simple: to wean United Aircraft from its dependence on the roller-coaster vicissitudes of the aerospace and other government contracts that accounted for half the company's sales. The quick way to do that was by acquisition. Beginning in 1974, in swift succession, United bought up seven companies—Essex International, a producer of wire and cable; Otis Elevator; Ambac Industries, which makes fuel-injection equipment; Dynell Electronics, a producer of marine radar gear; Terminal Communications, an electronics company; Carrier Corporation; and Mostek Corporation, a semiconductor producer.

There were some misfires—withdrawal from the overheated battle with J. Ray McDermott for control of Babcock & Wilcox, and the pullback from a similar bidding match for ESB Ray-O-Vac Corporation. Neither of those companies has yet turned out to be great buys and Gray is not unhappy about having lucked out of losing situations. He seized on them, in fact, to buttress the argument that there is none of the Napoleonic growth-for-growth's sake about his strategy. "If that were true," he said, "I would have gone ahead and bid the price up on ESB and Babcock & Wilcox. We had enough money to stay in there and outbid them, but it got to the point of crossover where there was no contribution to income and a dilution of net worth. If you're just going for macho and empire building," continued Gray, "you totally disregard your own stockholders, whether you're diluting their

[246]

equity, whether you're diluting their earnings per share."

True to his Southern heritage, the Georgia-born Gray can be a charmer, but there is plenty of iron behind the soft talk. He won both a Bronze Star and a Silver Star as an infantry officer during World War II and toughed out eight months of painful rehabilitation after a nearly fatal motorcycle accident in 1963 before he was able to do what the doctors said he would never do again—walk normally.

Gray brings the same determination to his acquisition program. Both the Otis and Carrier takeovers were unfriendly, and UTC moved into Mostek in the highly unusual posture of a White Knight. Gray now dismisses the Otis fight as one of those ballets in which management resisted just enough to get the price up. The Carrier fight was something else again. Its management had set out on a diversification tack of its own and wanted no part of UTC. "They did not want to join us. There is no secret about that," said Gray. United Tech got hit with a lot of negative research, including what Gray calls a "carefully orchestrated program" alleging that the huge Carrier plant in Syracuse would be moved out of town. Gray personally did a lot of fence-mending and insists there is now "a very pleasant relationship with the community—a big change."

Many managements, as Fairleigh Dickinson learned, will simply not do an unfriendly deal. Gray thinks "it is easier" to do friendly takeovers but argues that "if the acquisition makes sense, it is the responsibility of the interested corporation to pursue it." So long as you've done enough homework to know that you're not breaking the law, and the deal makes "economic sense," Gray "really doesn't see a lot of difference between friendly and unfriendly."

The distinction does not appear to have affected UTC's

operating results, which show an unbroken string of rising sales, rising earnings, and rising stock prices. Gray likes his goals big. When he took over United, sales were running at $2 billion a year. Gray promised they would double in seven years and pulled the trick in four. He then set another objective—revenues of $11 billion by the end of 1985, when he intends to retire at age sixty-five. With UTC's sales running at close to $10 billion, Gray again upgraded his target—$20 billion by the end of 1985, adjusted for an annual inflation factor of 8 percent.

The Takeover Game has clearly done a lot for UTC. Acquisitions account for about half the company's sales volume. Government billings, true to the original mandate, have been cut to about 22 percent of total sales and Gray thinks that UTC's expanding ability to master technological change will continue to generate a lot of internal growth. He argued that every one of the acquisitions has benefitted from being brought in under the UTC Big Top. Mostek, for example, he said, now has access to the capital it needs to penetrate new markets, while the maturing elevator and air-conditioning businesses will take on new dimensions because of the work UTC has done in such energy-conserving technology as digital controls.

There are negatives. Like everyone else in The Game, Harry Gray has taken quite legitimate advantage of the accounting rules to make his numbers look as good as they possibly can. That hasn't escaped the attention of that hawk-eyed scourge of the accounting profession, Abraham J. Briloff, Emanuel Saxe Distinguished Professor of Accountancy at the City University of New York's Baruch College. In general, UTC has typically paid well over book value for its acquisitions, allocated sizable chunks of the difference to "goodwill," and stretched out the writeoff on it to a quarter-century. The effect is to ease the impact of the amortization on earnings. All of that disturbs the conservative in Brilloff, who in his book, *The Truth About Corporate Accounting*, raises a waspish rhetorical question about UTC: "How much water can a balance sheet hold before it sinks?"

Gray insists he is not playing with accounting mirrors. "It's not a large amount of goodwill for the sales volume, the profitability and the net worth," he responds, "and had we spent the money to go into a number of these areas on a *de novo* basis, we'd have spent a lot more than that on an after-tax basis to get it." Ticking off the numbers on the rise in stockholders' equity and dividends with his customary machine-gun rapidity, Gray says, "You can't do that with mirrors." Briloff, he adds, has picked a "specific line to criticize us on. You can criticize anyone, including a saint, on one thing in the course of his life."

One other criticism of the Takeover Game is that it gives aggressive entrepreneurs such as Gray too much to say over people's lives—where the plants are going to be located, and where the jobs are. Gray concedes that some communities are at risk. "Every major acquisition that we've made," he said, "has had some element in it that really didn't necessarily fit." In most aggressor companies, including UTC, anything that doesn't fit gets sold. If an asset can't be sold as a going business, it is liquidated—in effect, junked, as was one of Essex International's appendages, a motor freight company. "It did not belong in our business," said Gray. "We tried to sell it; we couldn't; so we liquidated."

All takeovers almost invariably mean some dislocation

for some people, but total employment at UTC, thanks to Harry Gray's expansionist gospel, has jumped from 133,400 to 200,000 in the last five years; and it is probably fair to say that those jobs are a lot more secure now than before Gray came aboard. Gray argues that the takeover is here to stay. Everything in the business climate—and a *laissez-faire* regulating climate—seems to suggest that he is right. Even Salomon Brothers, the artificer of so many consolidations, ultimately took the plunge. Its 550 million dollar merger into Phibro Corporation, a big international commodities trader, freed large amounts of personal capital Salomon's older partners were pledged to leave on tap with the firm for years, and generated sizable capital gains for them as well. The consolidation ensured that Salomon would continue to be able to compete on equal terms in a Wall Street environment whose balance had been changed radically by such big ticket mergers as Shearson Loeb Rhoades into American Express and the Bache Group into Prudential Insurance. The sale came, though, only after months of sharp debate among Salomon's top partners as to the direction the firm should take. The Salomon name continues, but as employees of a publicly owned company, the erstwhile Salomon partners are no longer absolute masters of a house that had been one of the most independent on Wall Street for more than seven decades. Like capitalism itself, the takeover is an imprecise tool; but in competent hands, it works. The most important thing about The Game, in fact, may not be its demonstrable excesses, but its demonstration that the entrepreneurial spirit still roves the land.

Index

AB Electrolux, 139
Accounting practices, 66, 78–79, 248–49
Acquisitions
    accounting practices and, 66, 78–79,
        249
    to avoid being bought out, 67–68, 70
    cash, 67, 134–35, 238
    climate suitable to, 76–77, 239–40
    concept, 111–14
    dislocation and, 240, 249–50
    diversification and, 21, 22, 73–74, 78
    economic costs of, 239–42, 249–50
    entrepreneurial spirit demonstrated by,
        250
    foreign, 39–40, 77–78, 173
    machismo attached to, 70–71, 241
    and national economy, 235–37
    1920s and 1960s, 66
    1970s, 67
    pace of, and destabilizing effect of,
        242–45
    stock, 67, 132–33
    sums spent on, 236–37
    synergism as purpose of, 66, 242

    warlike strategies of, 71
    wealth derived from, 72, 73
        See also Profit, takeover
    See also Saturday Night Special; Sun
        Company-Becton, Dickinson Com-
        pany takeover; specific companies and
        specific aspects of acquisitions, for
        example: Arbitrageurs; Competing
        bids
AHP, see American Home Products Cor-
    poration
Air New England, 20, 40
Air Products & Chemicals, 196
Alinsky, Saul, 194
Allegheny Corporation, 168
Allen, Dave, 156
Ambac Industries, 246
American Bar Association, 132
American Express Company, 80, 94, 131,
    137, 138, 174–75, 193, 250
American Hardware, 168
American Home Products Corporation
    (AHP), 24, 61, 89, 99–105, 213,
    234

Howe (cont.)
  NMC negotiations and, 50–55
  SEC suit and, 226, 229
  Sun-B,D takeover and
    defense strategies of, 158, 191
    informed of buying attempt, 153
    reactions expected from, 87
    Sharbaugh communication with, 157
    testimony in Congress on, 187
    trying to obtain information on,
      154–56
    White Knight option offered to,
      160–61
Huber, John, 186
Hudson's Bay Oil & Gas Company, 68
Huyck Corporation, 69–70

IBM (International Business Machines), 73
Icahn, Carl, 138–39, 237
I.D.S. (mutual fund), 16, 29
Imperial Group, 77–78
Individual investors, 238
  and Sun-B,D takeover
    collection strategies for, 88, 89
    deal gotten by, 188–89, 191
    NMC negotiations and, 56
    SEC suit and, 228–30
Inside information, 143–51
  McGraw-Hill–American Express take-
    over attempt and, 174
  trading on, as fraud, 144, 145
  use of, by arbitrageurs, 147–50
Institute for Securities Regulation, 93
Institutional Investor (magazine), 148, 150
Institutional investors
  with big holdings in target companies,
    need to identify, 14–15
  effects of, on acquisition climate, 79
  profits derived from takeovers by, 238
  Sun-B,D takeover and, 23, 25
    agree to sell, 29–32
    balance of power held by, 16
    collecting from, 81, 87–88
    and Midnight Raid, 23, 25, 179
    the press and, 188
    strategies for approaching, 27–29
  See also specific institutional investors
Internal Revenue Service (IRS), 95

International Business Machines (IBM), 73
International Telephone & Telegraph
  (ITT), 115
Investment bankers
  concept deals and, 111–14
  profits made by, 114, 115
  See also specific investment firms
Investment Company Act, 201
Investors, see Individual investors; Institu-
  tional investors
Ira Haupt & Company, 14, 126
IRS (Internal Revenue Service), 95
"Issues for Consideration Concerning the
    Proposed Acquisition of National
    Medical Care" (report), 53–55
ITT (International Telephone & Tele-
    graph), 115
Ivan F. Boesky & Company, 130

Johns-Manville Corporation, 147, 149,
  150
Jollay, James F., 28–30
Justice, Department of, 133, 179

Kane, David, 59
Kekst, Gershon, 192–93
Kekst & Company, 192
Kennecott Copper Corporation, 148, 149,
  244–45
Kennedy, Edward M., 181
Kennedy, John F., 180
Kephart, Horace, 111, 191, 216
  SEC suit and, 202
    in Lipper's testimony, 218–20
  Sun-B,D takeover and, 116
    collection efforts of, 81–83, 86, 87
    institutional investors' responses to,
      84
    in Midnight Raid, 22–23, 25–27, 31,
      32
    prospect of fight and, 89
Kerr, Mr., 215
Kidder, Peabody & Company, 80, 114
Kinney Shoe (firm), 77
Kissinger, Henry, 236
Kissinger, Walter, 236
Klein, Frederick, 142, 143
Koppers Company, 93